# The Oak Island Affair

OTHER WORKS BY JANE BOW

FICTION: *Dead And Living*
NON-FICTION: *At The Foot Of The Rapids*
PLAYS: *Through The Fire*
*Soul Skin*

# The Oak Island Affair

## Jane Bow

EPIGRAPH
RHINEBECK, NEW YORK

THE OAK ISLAND AFFAIR © 2007 by Jane Bow. All rights reserved. No part of this book may be used or reproduced in any manner without written permission from the author except in critical articles and reviews.
   Contact the publisher for information:
   Epigraph
   27 Lamoree Road
   Rhinebeck, N.Y. 12572

Printed in The United States of America.

Library of Congress Control Number: 2007925249

ISBN 978-0-9789427-6-2

Pertaining to the epigraph:
Lines from "Notes Toward a Supreme Fiction," from THE COLLECTED POEMS OF WALLACE STEVENS by Wallace Stevens, copyright 1954 by Wallace Stevens and renewed 1982 by Holly Stevens. Used by permission of Alfred A. Knopf, a division of Random House, Inc.

Line from THE ALCHEMIST by Paulo Coelho, translated by Alan R. Clarke. Copyright (c) 1988 by Paulo Coelho. English translation copyright (c) 1993 by Paulo Coelho and Alan R. Clarke. Reprinted by permission of Harper Collins Publishers.

Bulk purchase discounts for educational or promotional purposes are available.

First Edition

10 9 8 7 6 5 4 3 2 1

Epigraph
A Division of Monkfish Book Publishing Company
27 Lamoree Road
Rhinebeck, N.Y. 12572
www.epigraphps.com

*For Sarah and Christopher*
*&*
*in memory of Malcolm Bow*

*... It is a brave affair...*
*But to impose is not*
*To discover. To discover an order... to find*
*Not to impose, not to have reasoned at all*
*Out of nothing to have come on major weather.*
*It is possible, possible, possible. It must*
*Be possible.*

*- Wallace Stevens, "Notes Toward A Supreme Fiction."*



*"You've got to find the treasure," (said the alchemist) "so that everything you have learned along the way makes sense."*

*- Paulo Coelho, T*HE *A*LCHEMIST

## Preface

During the last 212 years Canadian-American treasure hunting consortia have sunk several million dollars into the search for gold on Nova Scotia's Oak Island but still, at the time of writing, the little island continues to guard her treasure secret. Facts about the real Oak Island treasure hunt presented in The Oak Island Affair come from the many books and articles on the subject. All characters past and present, their writings and their actions, are the product of my imagination.

Jane Bow

Peterborough, Ontario
February, 2007

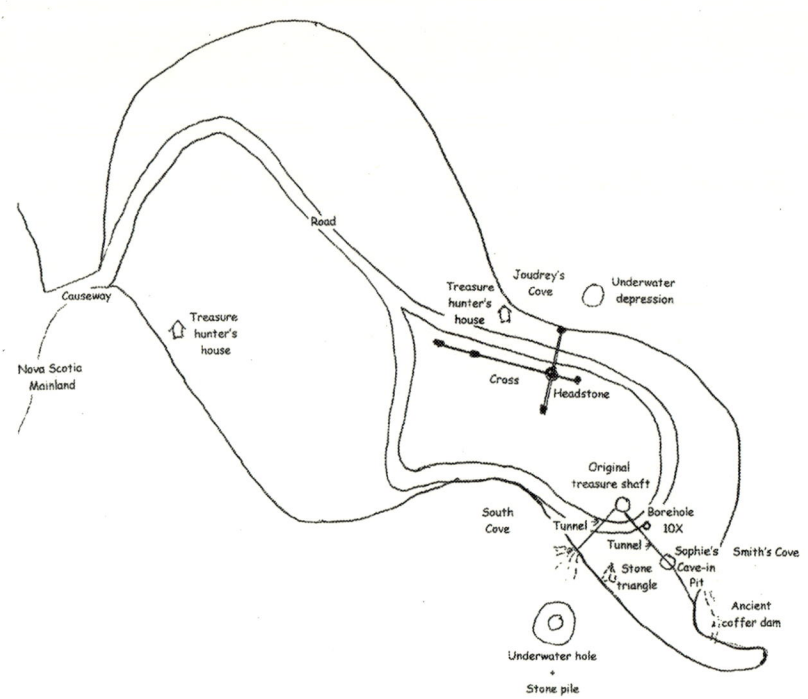

Vanessa's Map of Recorded Oak Island Discoveries

# I

THE WALLS OF GRAN'S WHITE shingled house shuddered in the wind of a spring storm off the Atlantic. Gran had died six months ago and the For Sale sign Uncle Vilhelm had hammered into the front lawn was squealing in the rain when Vanessa climbed the drop-down ladder to the attic. The air up here smelled of must. She would rather be running or lifting weights, pushing and pulling into the grunting repetitions that would shut out everything, everybody... Charlie; but the wind was too high, the sheets of rain too harsh to run through, and there was no health club in Chester, Nova Scotia. So she would clear out the attic.

Her hand found the overhead bulb's hanging string just as the storm reached a new crescendo. Nails squeaked in the roof as she pulled the light on but not until she had worked her way past the steamer trunks, between broken bed frames and legless chairs, a wicker pram full of baleful china-headed dolls, did Vanessa glimpse a glint of metal in one of the farthest crannies, where the attic's dust-coated floor met the roof beams.

The box she pulled out was no bigger than a jewelry case and maybe it was the smell of its cedar lining, of trapped heat, leather and ancient paper that quickened something, as if her nerve endings were divining a message her brain could not yet fathom.

Inside the box a package was wrapped first in silk embroidered with strange designs, then in oil cloth tied up with rotting twine that fell apart as she slid it off. When she tried to open the oil cloth, it broke into pieces. It had, however, done its job. The black leather book inside, its cover tooled with a simple cross, had been well protected.

The spine cracked as she opened it. The pages were thick, rudely made, speckled with inlaid hair and thread and the trails of tiny bugs that had crawled between them to die. The writing was faded, reddish brown under the attic's bare bulb, the downstrokes wide, upstrokes light, done with a quill pen, the letters angular, loosely jointed, austere, ancient... Spanish.

Skin oils, sweat, human breath should not touch this artifact. Carefully Vanessa laid it back in its box, came to her feet, her nerve endings tapping a tattoo now as, gathering the metal box, she snapped off the light, forgot the sorting job.

Dogeared dictionaries — Spanish to English, archaic to modern Spanish — and Spanish word derivation books had been sitting in the bookshelf downstairs since Vanessa's family had had to leave Spain eighteen years earlier. After that her father, who had grown up in this house, had liked to spend his summer holidays here translating Cervantes, Lope de Vega, and later, when Vanessa had returned to Spain to study history at the University of Madrid, research documents she had found and copied for him. Occasionally Vanessa would lean over his shoulder to offer variations of interpretation — not that he ever took her suggestions seriously:

"Finish your PhD and then I'll be inclined to listen." Knowledge, to Carl Holdt, had been the Earth's greatest treasure. "You can find knowledge anywhere — under rocks, inside churches, at the bottom of the sea — all you need to know is how and where to look." Vanessa could still see him standing in the Spanish sun, arms raised like a preacher, extolling the perfect symmetry of the Roman aqueduct at Merida, not far from their home in Altamira on Spain's south coast, or standing centre stage in the ancient amphitheatre he had helped unearth down the coast at Cadiz, where Roman wisdoms had played out a thousand years before the Spanish treasure fleets had sailed in from South America: "The Romans gave us our irrigation, transportation, parliamentary systems..." But in those days Vanessa had been too busy — poking her older brother Adrian, or practicing with the spinning plate and stick set she had just used all her savings to buy, or waiting to ask permission to run down to the fishing wharves where once the great treasure galleons had been unloaded — to pay attention. Now her father was dead, struck suddenly with a heart attack one morning last year on his way to teach at the University of Ottawa.

She needed gloves. A pair of elbow-length white cotton evening gloves in the cedar chest at the back of Gran's bedroom closet looked as if they had never been worn. In the bottom drawer of her desk Vanessa found a supply of the exercise books Gran had used for accounting. Outside, rain slapped at the living room's picture window, wind whipped Gran's lilac bush at the bottom of the garden, roiled the grey sea but, bringing a desk lamp to the long pine dining table, wriggling her fingers into the gloves, opening the diary, Vanessa did not notice.

The spellings were strange, the *s*'s shaped like *f*'s, but how many times had she teased the meanings out of the ancient records stored in the archives at Cadiz? And though that was six years ago now, language skills, once imprinted on the cortex, are never far from reach. Within a few minutes Vanessa had the title page:

> *The last living testament of Bartolomeo, Brother in Christ*
> *of the Holy Order of Santo Domingo in Altamira, Espana*

Altamira? Where the flat blue sea reached out to meet Spain's southern sky? Where the wavelets had rolled her child's body over and back, over and back in the sun warmed sand; where the old Dominican monastery had housed Vanessa's own convent school; where stout women dressed in black called *'Uno para hoy!'* (Buy one for today!) at the *Plaza Mayor* market, their calloused hands moving among the onions, garlic, peppers, olives, oranges laid out on stalls, their eyes sharp as crows'; where the butcher hacked the legs off a lamb carcass, blood dripping onto the cobblestones, and the town potter guarded his terra cotta wine jugs from the gaggle of darting children; where storms were sudden, hot, full of the smell of lightning, then gone.

> *Written at Santa Alicia de la Estrella, Cuba*
> *June, MDLXXXIX*
>     M: 1000

D: 500
L: 50
XXX: 3 x 10
IX: 9

1589: this little diary was more than four hundred years old! Vanessa stared at it. Four hundred years ago Philip II was king of Spain, his Inquisition rooting out, torturing and killing infidels while overseas his *conquistadores* filled the king's treasure fleets with South American gold and silver. Across the English Channel Queen Elizabeth I was searching out and hanging Catholics, forcing her people to pray to the Protestant God. An evil ruler according to Sister Maria Teresa of Avila, Vanessa's history teacher who would not hesitate to rap you over the knuckles with a ruler on God's behalf or make you stand in the garbage pail if you accidentally got out of your chair, Queen Elizabeth was also sending out seafaring plunderers, including the Devil's own Sir Frances Drake — *El Draque,* the Dragon — to steal Spain's God-given treasures.

1589: in London, William Shakespeare's plays had not yet reached the stage; Spain's Cervantes, creator of Don Quixote, had just published his first novel; while in Cuba a feverish Dominican monk was penning this little book:

*Dear Father in Heaven,*

*As I lie here in the summer heat, the fever sweeping through me, racking my limbs, soaking my bed sheets, leaving me weak as a lamb and quaking with fear, I know that the horses are bridled, the chariot is waiting. But You and I know also that as it stands now this poor monk's last journey will take him straight into the fires of Hell.*

*Please though, I do beseech You Father, grant a few last moments of attention to a poor brother who has tried since the innocent age of nine to devote his life to You — not that I had any choice. My father having died at sea, my mother had too many mouths to feed; there was no choice but to give me to the monks. Now, forty years later, my kind host has placed a pen, ink and this little book on the stand beside my cot, and in these lucid dawn hours while the cocks crow and the cat stretches in a patch of sunlight on the windowsill, I can use what little courage You have bestowed upon me to try to show You, before it is too late, that whatever evidence there is to the contrary, this wandering and very faulty soul does have Faith. For although I was the first white man to behold the gold—*

Gold? Here? Vanessa looked at the metal box, the broken the oil cloth, rotting twine, the embroidered silk. Why hadn't her father ever found this book? He had been an expert in antiquities, head of the Altamira Institute for the Study of Roman Ruins and then a classics professor in Ottawa. He would have recognized its value. And he had spent his boyhood here.

*— and although this gold was a most glorious sight, and I weep to think that I might have been the reason it was won at such high cost, I can promise in the best of faith that never once on this God-forsaken journey have I coveted it for its own sake—*

This gold, a most glorious sight! You must have gone into the attic, Dad? And what about you, Gran?

Beyond the lamplight only grey silence and the lashing rain responded.

Deciphering the letters of the ancient script, looking up every other word, rooting through derivations, guessing at the meanings of phrases that were not in the dictionaries, was slow going but soon Vanessa found herself slipping into the method she had worked out during her first post-graduate year in Spain. Studying the history of the treasures that, gathered by Spain, had made their way into so many conundrums across the world had required a vocabulary beyond Vanessa's adolescent Spanish, so she had developed the habit of translating the archival texts into English first. A much more voluminous language thanks to its roots in Latin and Greek and bastardizations of Anglo, Saxon, medieval French, German, Gaelic and Norse words, English gave her the analytical tools she needed and a breadth of nuance she then learned, painstakingly, to transfer into her modern Spanish treatises. Now, gradually unraveling Brother Bartolomeo's narrative, she climbed with him and a retinue of Spanish soldiers into the high mountains of South America's Nueva Granada:

*Spain has been taking gold, silver and emeralds out of the lush Nueva Granada mountains for years, engaging the labour of "savages" in our mines while teaching them the ways of our Lord. But still there are pockets of pagans in the remote regions. We Dominicans are sent to teach simplicity, devotion to God, but now I find myself agreeing with my esteemed namesake and Brother-in-Christ Bartolomeo de las Casas who has warned both King and Church again and again that enslaving the native people, bringing them disease, hopelessness, death, could not have been Your intention. So let us be honest, Father. The truth is that You are only the excuse. The real prize is not the souls. It is the gold. That is why in the spring of 1588 I traveled, with twelve soldiers, into the interior.*

*The mountaintops were shrouded in clouds one minute, bathed in sunlight the next, the path so steep the natives had carved steps into the rock but these were so shallow that only the balls of the great paddles I call feet fit onto them, and so slippery. A thousand feet below the Rio Oro foamed down through the cleft between the green mountainsides. I prayed aloud as I climbed. Jose laughed at me. He too came from Altamira. A burly brute, the first to fight in the street, always the wrestling champion at school, Jose was the kind for whom the soldier's uniform was a second skin. Now he was a sergeant and the leader of our little expedition.*

*On the twelfth day the path began to angle down, the landscape opening into a bowl surrounded by snow-capped peaks. A little cluster of dwellings stood at the edge of the most beautiful, emerald green lake. New spring growth had turned the ground and trees into a panorama of greens. On catching sight of our little band the women, dressed in cotton skirts and skins against the mountain cold, stopped sweeping their doorways, planting a freshly tilled patch of ground, bending to fill their water jugs at the lake. Their children hid behind their skirts. There were no men. The natives were not the only ones frightened. We had the eerie feeling that we were being watched. Our soldiers kept reaching for their swords.*

*It was noon, the sun high overhead. I sat on a rock down by the water, took out a chunk of bread. Jose put some men to patrol the village perimeter. Soon the children were edging close to me, their jet black eyes fixed upon my lunch, my white whiskery face. I smiled. They pointed at the silver crucifix that hung from my monk's robe, whispering to each other, giggling while the women glanced around at the woods. I was eating my bread and ruminating on the incredible beauty of these people, their sun-darkened skins so smooth, when a light emerged from the woods by the shore, suddenly blinding me. I squeezed my eyes shut. When I dared to open them I saw that it was a man's chest plate made of solid polished gold that was shooting rays of sunlight into my eyes.*

*Jose had unsheathed his sword. Two of his soldiers closed on the man.*

*"No," I stood. "Deja le. He comes in peace."*

*The chest plate must have weighed half as much as the man yet his bearing was straight. And now I could see the designs worked into the gold — a sun, human and animal figures, snakes intertwined. Inlaid emeralds caught the sunlight. His headband was decorated with gold encrusted with jewels. Coloured feathers waved above his eyebrows. He must be the chief. Behind him his warriors now appeared, two score of them wearing short cotton skirts and cotton capelike tops painted with red and black designs, knotted at the shoulder, leaving their arms free.*

*I offered the chief a piece of bread and we ate together in silence, each of us probing the moment. He watched me, his onyx eyes sharp with intelligence. After some moments of silence he motioned to me to follow him.*

*Just outside the village an elaborate thatched temple had been constructed out of wood. Inside, sunlight angling in through openings set high in the walls lit solid gold paneling into which designs of sun and moon, people, animals, birds, plants and snakes had been worked. I stood transfixed. The day's warmth, stored in the floor, came up through my sandals and I knew without thought or prayer that though these mountain people were heathens, standing inside their golden temple I was in Your presence.*

*By the time we returned to the village, the warriors had relieved my soldiers of their weapons.*

Moving her pen word by word across the pages of the exercise book, Vanessa did not notice as, beyond the orb cast by her table lamp, shadows crept across the Indian carpet on Gran's living room floor, edging towards darkness.

Δ Δ Δ

A tear dropped onto the diary, blurring the ancient ink. Vanessa jumped up in horror. Students, researchers, guardians of antiquities and the treasures that are all we have left of past worlds do not cry all over them. How could she have been so careless, foolish, so selfish? This book should be locked inside the safety of its box, away from her, the moisture of her breath, her sweat, her greed to know, to be there with Brother Bart, to find out what had happened. She tried to dab the tiny puddle with a tissue. The blotch seeped into the ancient parchment. Vanessa backed away, knocking over her chair. The living room's pearly gloom seemed to murmur of death.

Her eyes ached. She switched on all the lights, sank into Gran's wingback chair. It still smelled of her lavender water. How, Vanessa wondered again, could Gran and her Dad not have known what was in their own attic?

Her Dad had been bright, so after his mother had died of polio when he was thirteen, Grandad Holdt, who was a sea captain, had sent him to a boarding school in Montreal. After that there had been summer camps, trips to meet his father in foreign seaports and then at eighteen Carl Holdt had left Chester, first for the University of Toronto, then on a scholarship to Cambridge. He had not returned to live here until the summer Vanessa was fifteen. Grandad had died by then. Gran had been Grandma Holdt's friend. She had moved in to nurse her, then had stayed on to housekeep and finally to marry the sea captain. She did not speak Spanish. Maybe she had never known what the diary was.

Or had she known and never told? Outside, beyond the seafield of whitecaps running for shore, Mahone Bay's scattering of islands was a smudged line of ragged, darkened green: a perfect, inhospitably wild and nondescript hiding place for gold. Stories about Captain Kidd, John Morgan, Sir Frances Drake, of found sea chests, stray bags of doubloons, had been circulating Mahone Bay taverns for several hundred years. Then there were the 18th century pirates who had lain in wait here for British and French army payroll and tax ships, and American privateers loaded to the gunwales with gold and silver ransomed from towns up and down this coast. Even the name of this bay, Mahone, came from the Turkish word for the low, fast ships pirates favoured. And always there were the Oak Island tales of strange sightings, and of the two young men who, having spotted fires burning on the little offshore island, had rowed out to investigate. And never returned.

But Gran's eyes had always flashed anger at the mention of the Oak Island treasure: "Two hundred years men have been turning that poor little island into Swiss cheese, dying even, not to mention pointing guns, taking each other to court, and for what? A few doubloons, bits and pieces of old wood. You stay away from there, Vanessa. The Holdt family is not interested in Oak Island."

As if a fifteen-year old recently bereft of the only world she had ever known, of the Altamira sun and beach and harbour and *La Montaña* lying like an ancient bone behind it, of her best friend Carlita, and Paco and Santi and the others, of a world full of stories about ancient ships and castles and treasures; as if she were not going to talk her brother Adrian, who was two years older, into borrowing two rickety bikes from Gran's shed, riding down the coast road, hiding the bikes in the weed-choked ditch to jump the chain across the Oak Island causeway, to sneak around the dilapidated museum building and then the water-logged pits that pocked the denuded east end of the island where treasure hunters had spent millions of dollars and more than two hundred years digging. But then seventeen-year old Adrian had found a holiday girlfriend and at the end of the summer their parents had moved the family to Ottawa.

Her father had always dismissed the idea of treasure on Oak Island. Where, he wanted to know, was any hard evidence?

Vanessa looked at Brother Bartolomeo's diary nestled among the dictionaries on the table. Maybe right here, Dad.

She had to tell someone — Gran's old black telephone was still hooked up — but whom?

She dialed Brigit, her closest friend. She had called Brigit's cell phone in British Columbia three nights ago after she had fled her life in Toronto, had cried into the receiver, but then Brigit's phone had started to crackle: "Hang in, Van," Brigit had shouted: "I'm up in the mainland mountains, but am on my way home now. I'll call you when I get there." A jewelry designer, Brigit left her Vancouver Island studio regularly to augment her income by gathering mountain flora for a research biologist at the University of Victoria.

There was no answer.

Vanessa's mother was in England on a pilgrimage back to Cambridge University where she and Vanessa's father had met, and then home to Cornwall. Anyway, though her mother had a thin intensity that could have come out of an El Greco painting, her English tongue had never adapted easily to Spanish. Vanessa meanwhile had lived in the language from birth, chattering in it even with Adrian at home, her body and soul grounded in its sounds, rhythms, contexts. Inevitably a gap had opened. Now Adrian was traveling in Australia.

She would not call Charlie.

Vanessa made a sandwich, opened a bottle of Gran's favourite Chablis and flicked on the television, sat back as a ballerina twirled to a piano riff, beautiful; the music was reaching into her tired mind, the camera closing on the dancer's supple grace, when a word crossed the screen: the name of a menstrual tampon.

"Oh for God's sake." Vanessa jabbed the remote's "off" button, got up to open the French doors to the deck overlooking the sea.

The storm had blown itself away, leaving a sky studded with stars. To Vanessa's left rags of cloud were flying across the face of a three-quarter moon. Vanessa leaned against the deck's railing, letting the breeze and the play of the heavens cool her. North American native people believed that when you died your soul went up to join the stars. Now a single point of light detached itself from the canopy, shot across the blue-black night.

Dad? Gran? Brother Bartolomeo? The girl he had loved?

The star's light went out soundlessly, as if it had never existed, as if it had had no part in the shaping of this universe.

Stars were random explosions of gas, nothing more. There was no divine plan, no ascension out of the nameless blameless pain of day-to-day existence. The elements, like the sea breaking against the rocks at the bottom of Gran's backyard, had no care for the paltry existence of humans.

The deck was equipped with a hot tub. Vanessa turned it on, lit the candles in the glass globes of a wrought iron floor candelabra, brought her boom box out onto the deck and slipped Paul Simon's Graceland into the CD tray. The house shielded her from the road. Unless someone pulled right up to the dock at the bottom of the garden, nobody could see her strip off her old York University track suit and underwear, tie up her mess of gold blond hair to lie in the water's womb-like warmth. Above her the moon sailed higher, laying a path of silver across the sea. A chorus of candle flames danced inside their globes.

This fickle light, wavering on every passing breath of air, was the kind by which Brother Bart would have written. Vanessa's painstaking delivery of the ancient words into modern English had imprinted his story on her heart:

*The chief found a hut for me and the women laid out fruits and fish and drink. Then the chief returned the soldiers' muskets as a gesture of trust and they began to relax a little, even Jose.*

*During the next few days I kept noticing the women, their wrists, ears, necks decorated with jeweled gold. When the sun rose they shook off their skins. Under them their cotton tops were pinned up to leave their breasts exposed. There was one particular young woman who, every time I needed food or a drink, brought it to me and I could not help admiring the grace in her long legs and her breasts so high and firm and virginal. When I thanked her the smile she returned was full of sunlight, warming the very marrow of my monk's bones. Her name was Mia. One day she packed a basket and led me away, up a path through the woods into a small mountain pasture. I thought she had been detailed to show me something, a sacred shrine perhaps. Small* birds twittered amongst the surrounding trees. Yellow, blue, orange butterflies flitted among the stalks of the many coloured wildflowers while high overhead an eagle circled.

She spread a beautifully woven cotton rug and then proceeded to disrobe, her bracelets jingling, as if this were the most natural state, and the sun glowed on the roundness of her buttocks and breasts, the long slope of her back, the tautness of her thighs. She must, Heavenly Father, have been amongst Your most perfect creations.

She did not appear to know that monks must remain celibate, and I know that I am supposed to believe that this was my test: temptation proffered as surely as Satan offered it to Blessed Jesus in the desert. But as she helped me off with my monk's robe, so that for the first time in forty-odd years of memory I too could glory in the sun's warmth, the breeze on my skin, I thought that one could also, with the genuine sincerity of honest contemplation, take the view that it was You leading me, that if she was offering herself to me, I should give thanks for the opportunity to join myself to the perfection of Your creation. For You must know, dear Father, that there was, in the miraculous hours that followed, something much more precious in that mountain meadow than simple carnal gratification. It is a moment I hold sacred.

Mia told me, through hand sketches and sign language, that she was a half-breed, a baby born of a native to this village who had been impregnated by a Spanish prospector. Her mother had died in childbirth. The tribe had raised Mia, but now it was time for her to begin a life of her own. Because of her racial impurity, none of the tribe's sons had chosen her. She thought I had a kind face and a mighty heart.

I listened and knew, in spite of a lifetime devoted to You, that here in the arms of this innocence was where a man's truest communion was to be found. Never, even in church, had I felt this sense of total acceptance, of wholeness. Could there be a greater sweetness? Mia felt it too and I could not bring myself to believe that such gentle loving, the touch of her fingers light as a butterfly's wings on my body, and such towering, shuddering, monumental joy could be any kind of sin against You. Hours of prayer, listening for Your voice, have not touched this, Father, in spite of what happened next...

High above the hot tub the three-quarter moon had a face. Her eyes were full of compassion, her nose long and straight, her mouth declining judgment though she had been there four hundred years ago, had witnessed the whole story.

The jangle of Gran's phone brought Vanessa up out of the water, a tidal wave sloshing over the lip of the tub as, before she knew what she was doing, she was standing naked and dripping on the living room's hardwood floor.

Uncle Vilhelm's real estate agent was sorry to call so late, but thought he'd seen a light. And since she was there, would she please have the house looking presentable for a showing tomorrow morning?

Politeness, acquiescence. Why? 'Before anyone comes to view the place,' Brigit had advised on that first night, before the phone had died. 'Burn something really vile smelling, rubber preferably.'

Gran's house had been in the family for six generations. Vanessa had been coming here every summer since the age of fifteen. Her father's and now Gran's deaths had settled a clammy emptiness into the house, but if it sold Vanessa would lose the only place she had left to call home. Uncle William — Vilhelm, according to Adrian, as in the Kaiser who had worn one of those metal hats with a spike — had put it up for sale the day after Gran's funeral. There was no choice, he had said. His share of the taxes and upkeep was too costly and the value of a heritage home on Chester's waterfront meant that Vanessa, her mother and brother could not afford to buy him out.

Vanessa wrapped herself in Gran's towel robe, made tea, sat back down at the dining room table and picked up her pen.

## II

Yesterday's storm had given the lilac bush, in full bloom at the bottom of the garden, and the blue spruce beyond the deck a shiny, freshly scrubbed look as they danced on the wind. Whitecaps raced on a sea coloured blue by the morning sky.

Vanessa had found Gran's ancient rubber bathing cap with nobbles on it stuck to the back of one of her dresser drawers. She pictured herself laying a fire, saw the bathing cap curl into the flames, begin to melt. But any vile smell would go straight up the chimney. She would have to close the damper, but then the smoke would billow out into the room, set off the fire alarm—

And now here came her father's voice:

"Are you sure this is the Right Choice—?"

Vanessa dropped the bathing cap onto the coffee table, wrapped the diary into its embroidered cloth, packed it and her translation into the metal box and left the house.

Up at the top of the hill beside Chester's white clapboard library, Mademoiselle Durocher's ancient white 'float mobile' (Adrian's word) sat in the librarian's parking space.

"Vanessa, oh my dear!" The old lady came out from behind her desk. She must be over seventy by now but she looked exactly as she had for the last eighteen years: the collar of her fake silk blouse a size too large, with a filigree silver dragonfly at the neck. Vanessa would have liked to hug her but theirs had never been a touching friendship. Mlle. Durocher took in the smudges under Vanessa's eyes, the metal box she was carrying and, tipping her head towards the wood paneled reading room across the hall, brushed a finger across her lips. A man in his late forties was sitting with his back to them at a table beside the tiled fireplace. Document scrolls curled on the tabletop as he made notes. His styled salt and pepper hair, pink golf shirt and freshly pressed khaki slacks made the library's threadbare little collection of reference books look shabby. Mlle. Durocher motioned Vanessa towards the kitchen where a sign on the door read: Employees Only.

"You sit, *chérie*, while I make us a nice cup of tea. It is early yet, the library will take care of itself."

"Who is that man, Mademoiselle?"

"Phttt, an American," The old librarian was not impressed. "He says he is interested in Oak Island."

A red and white checked cloth still covered the kitchen's small table; a spider plant still sunned itself on the window ledge.

"Milk, no sugar. You see how I remember?" The old lady brought two chipped mugs full of tea and sat across from Vanessa. "Now tell me, you are in Chester because your Gran's house has sold?"

"No, I..." Vanessa looked into her lap. Sympathy would undo her, release the ricocheting pain of losses she had not come here to cry about. "I just need some time to think." A new diamond as large as a pebble hung from Mlle. Durocher's ring finger as she pushed Vanessa's mug across the table. Vanessa reached out to touch it.

"What's this, Mademoiselle?"

"Oh," The old lady drew her hand back, "I have a friend. The ring is too big but it was his mother's—"

"Really!"

"What?" Mlle. Durocher's blue eyes snapped. "You think that because I am old, because I have spent my life dusting library shelves and stamping other people's books and reading, reading, that *enfin* I should not get a life?"

Vanessa sipped her tea. "What's his name? Does he come to the library? Can I meet him?"

Mlle. Durocher fingered her dragonfly, flicked her eyes over Vanessa's face looking for mockery, found none.

"He is Robert. He lives in Halifax and yes, you will meet him. Now, would you like to tell me what is in your box?"

Vanessa found a smile. How snug, safe, cozy was this sunny kitchen, how fine to be sitting here again.

After the Oak Island bicycle trip that first summer, Mademoiselle Durocher had steered Vanessa towards a shelf full of books about Nova Scotia's history, pirates, treasure. Vanessa had begun to take refuge there as it turned out the librarian was an expert on Oak Island's two hundred-year old, multi-million dollar treasure hunt.

"Gran and my Dad say the whole treasure hunt is a hoax," Vanessa had told her.

"Do they?" The old lady's faded blue eyes had sparked behind her glasses. "And do they also explain why pirates ships were sneaking about, hiding throughout Mahone Bay's three hundred islands during those years? And what the wooden cribwork for an ancient coffer dam under the sea in Smith's Cove was for? And what about the stones with a G cut into them, the antique iron scissors, dagger, boatswain's whistle, the copper coin, the brass buckle? Are they aware that some of these finds have been radio-carbon dated at sometime between 1490 and 1660?"

"Dad says everything they've found could have been left by early settlers or explorers."

"Ah, that Carl Holdt has been away too long. He needs to read the records," Mlle Durocher's hand swept towards the books. "There is no question that the young colonist Daniel McGinnis decided to explore the little island at the back of the bay one spring day in 1795. He could easily row the two hundred yards from the mainland. What he found — the depression in the ground at the base of an oak tree on the east end of the island, cut stumps and new, young oak trees growing between them — is a matter of record, as are the layer of flagstones he and his friends dug up two feet under the depression, then the flooring of oak logs ten feet under that, more dirt then a second oak floor at twenty feet." Mlle. Durocher smiled. "But then the work got too hard. They filled in the shaft, covered it with brush, and eight years passed before anyone came back."

"Eight years!"

The old lady's shoulders lifted.

"Think: who was here then? Natives and immigrants: British, Scottish, Irish, Dutch, French, Germans who would rather swear allegiance to the British Crown than live in revolutionary America. These people were much too busy fishing and clearing the land to take any interest in digging for treasure."

Word of McGinnis' find had kept circulating however, until in 1803 a Nova Scotia colonel, a surveyor, a town clerk and Justice of the Peace, a sheriff and some businessmen started the first Oak Island treasure hunting company. At thirty feet they found a third log platform, covered with charcoal. The logs at forty feet were covered with blue clay. At fifty feet smooth beach stones covered in strange symbols lay across the logs. At sixty feet they found manila grass and coconut fibre. At ninety feet a large flat stone was cut with strange symbols — circles, squares, dots. Decoders said the message read: 'two million pounds are buried here,' but when the treasure hunters dislodged the stone the sea oozed up from underneath. By the next morning the shaft was under sixty feet of water.

"Their money soon ran out, and another forty years went by," said Mlle. Durocher.

The next consortium sank a hand turned drill down through the water to one hundred and five feet. It bored through five inches of spruce then, a foot below that, four inches of oak, then twenty inches of metal in small pieces, then eight more inches of oak, twenty more inches of metal, four more inches of oak, then hard clay. Three tiny gold chain links that came up with the drill convinced them they had found treasure chests cleverly buried below the water level. The shaft's originator had hidden shallow intake shafts lined with coconut fibre under the beach stones at Smith's Cove, then angled a five hundred-foot tunnel down to meet the vertical shaft one hundred and ten feet below the surface. Directional markers such as stones laid in the shape of a triangle with a plumb line running through it were later found.

The treasure hunters dammed the Smith's Cove tunnel and dug shafts all around the original one, trying to pump out the sea water, but then whole bottom of the treasure shaft caved in.

"Once again money ran out. Daniel McGinnis died. A farmer called Anthony Graves bought most of Oak Island and built his house at

Joudrey's Cove, on the seaward side. He appeared to take no interest in treasure but," Mlle. Durocher winked, "the legend is that he paid for his groceries with gold coins. There were no more finds recorded though until 1878, when Anthony Grave's daughter, Sophie Sellars, was plowing the strip of land between the original shaft and Smith's Cove. Suddenly the ground under her two oxen caved in. Sophie and her husband pulled the oxen out and backfilled the hole. There was nothing in it, they said, but soon after that, they leased their land to a new set of treasure hunters for $30,000. Later investigators found a man-made shaft connecting Sophie's Cave-In Pit to the Smith's Cove tunnel."

The next find was with another drill. At just over 150 feet treasure hunters found cement, wood, loose metal, a tiny piece of ancient parchment, more wood, more cement, eleven feet of blue clay, then a metal obstruction: the treasure at last, they thought. But when they dug down to retrieve it, once again the sea rushed in. A second intake tunnel from South Cove, on the other side of the island, intersected with the shaft just below 150 feet. The finds brought new investors, however, including Franklin D. Roosevelt, just after the turn of the last century.

At least six people had died from accidents on Oak Island by the time a California geologist arrived in the 1960's. He built a causeway from the mainland to Oak Island, brought in a digger and bulldozers, and shoveled tons of clay into Smith's and South Coves. Then he excavated a hole nearly 100 feet wide where the original shaft had been, tearing out most of the earlier tunnels, cribbing and markers. But his machinery kept breaking down.

"Then it started to rain."

Vanessa laughed.

The old lady restrained a smile.

"It rained and rained: one of the worst summer storms on record. The Californian refilled the hole, then dug out Sophie Sellars' Cave-In Pit, turning it into a huge water filled-crater, and still it rained. Finally he ran out of money and left."

The Oak Island treasure hunters who lived there now took over. And every summer when she arrived, Vanessa and Mlle. Durocher discussed the latest Oak Island developments. One of the treasure hunters, who had built a bungalow at the island end of the causeway, drilled a hole he called Borehole 10X near the original treasure shaft. He lined it with steel cylinders. When he couldn't go any deeper, he hung concrete retaining walls in the shaft until, at 220 feet, he struck bedrock. Drilling showed that the rock formed the roof of an underwater cavern at 230 feet. A camera he lowered into it revealed what might be a treasure chest with a key in the lock, and the head, forearm and hand of a man lying on his side inside the cavern. But then the walls of Borehole 10X collapsed.

The other treasure hunter, who reached his bungalow at Joudrey's Cove by boat, discovered rocks with markings on them, a line of wooden stakes sunk into the ground, and five large cone-shaped granite boulders laid out in the shape of a cross. A skull-shaped headstone marked the point where the arms of the cross met its body. . .

Now Vanessa unwrapped the embroidered cloth around Brother Bartolomeo's book.

"It's 16th century, Spanish."

Mlle. Durocher put out a finger to touch the black leather, as if in recognition.

"You know this book?" asked Vanessa.

The old librarian had a way of blinking rapidly when she was thinking.

"I do. Though it must be what, sixty years? You know your Grandad Holdt's youngest sister, Celia, was my friend at school."

Vanessa nodded, though she had never known much about Grandad Holdt, only that he had dropped dead of heart disease.

"I had forgotten all about this book," Mlle. Durocher was saying. "It was so long ago. We were only about twelve. The day Celia found it in this same box in the attic she swore me to secrecy, but," Mlle. Durocher looked towards the ceiling and crossed herself. "Now she's gone, bless her soul, I don't think she will mind. Did you see the note from Seamus Holdt, your ancestor?"

"No!"

"It was tucked into the ribbon, dated 1803, if I remember. Cee must have lost it. Or destroyed it. Seamus was a fisherman but then he heard that a group of Nova Scotia business men, including a colonel and a judge and the sheriff, was starting a treasure hunting company... His note was an apology for losing the family savings on Oak Island." Mlle. Durocher smiled at Vanessa. "A stranded Spanish sailor had taken room and board in return for helping Seamus repair his boat and nets. This sailor also helped with the Oak Island digging, but when the money ran out, he caught a ship for home. This book was his present to Seamus by way of thanks. He said it was very valuable, Seamus wrote, but because it was in Spanish no one could read it. The minister wanted to burn it, thinking it must be Papist propaganda, but Seamus hid it in the attic."

"Thank God! And Celia? Why didn't she take it to Halifax, find a translator?"

"This was sixty years ago, *chérie*. The second World War was over, the boys were coming home and we were very young." The old lady smiled at her memories, then lifted the cover of the diary with her finger to peek at the handwriting inside.

"Here," Vanessa took the exercise book out of the box. "I've started a rough translation." She told Mlle. Durocher about Brother Bartolomeo and the golden temple and Mia's taking him up into the hills, and then read:

*"We came down into the village in the afternoon and the women immediately led Mia away. One of the tribesmen took me to a hut off to one side of the village. When he pulled back the door flap steam poured out. The hut was full of naked men. The chief invited the soldiers too, but they shook their heads.*

*"'Damned if I'm going to be boiled alive,' said Jose.*

*"The chief sniffed the air near him, then wrinkled his nose. His men laughed. Jose took a step towards him, but I moved in front of him.*

*"'God is with us here.' The chief gestured to me to remove my robe and I entered the hut. One of the men transferred red hot stones from a fire outside to a pit in the centre of the hut. The chief poured water on the stones and now the whole room became stifling hot. It was hard to breathe. I prayed, wondering if I was about to become a heathen sacrifice. But then my muscles relaxed, became fluid. My mind let go, drifting into a place where words do not live, where after awhile, as*

the water hissed on the rocks, my whole self began to float, unconstrained, free.

"A long time later we came out, ran down the path and jumped into the lake. The water closed over my skin, expelled my breath. New, clean breath poured in and, coming out, drying off, my body tingled with life. The chief gave me a cotton skirt and a tunic embroidered across the upper chest, and a deerskin cape. I put them on and the cloth felt so soft against my skin. As soon as I was dressed the men led me to the temple.

"How could I not know what I was doing? I did know and, praying to You all the while, I did it anyway because now I began to wonder, in the final analysis, beyond the credos and rules designed by the Church, what human can say or even truly know what is right for another?

"The temple's golden interior glowed with torchlight tonight. And there, by what must be the altar, Mia stood waiting. Her jet black hair shone under a gold circlet studded with emeralds. The chief chanted something and then took off two of his rings, made of heavy yellow gold. He gave one to Mia and, smiling shyly, she slipped it onto the third finger of my left hand. On it the jeweled face of the sun radiated light. Now the chief handed the second ring to me: a golden butterfly, its wings glittering red, green, blue in the torch light, so beautiful on my Mia's long slim finger. The chief raised one of two silver goblets on which jewels every colour winked in the torchlight. He shouted something and then drank. The other goblet, or chalice, was passed first to me and then to Mia. My Mia, my wife.

"But happiness makes a man blind and deaf.

"'Be ready,' Jose kept warning me. I did not hear anything other than the words.

"Late on the night of my wedding Mia and I lay in my bed, sated, her body curled up in my arms, her heart beating against the inside of my wrist when Jose shook me awake. And now my ears began to take in thumping, grunting sounds outside, a scream cut short, running feet, a strangled shout. Another soldier appeared in the doorway, wrestled Mia out of my arms:

"'No!' Father, You must have heard my cry.

"But still the soldier slit my Mia's throat."

Vanessa had to stop. Tears were coursing down her cheeks.

"'Come on, Brother.' Jose tried to pull me to my feet. But the sound of Mia's last breath gurgling out, the sweet smell of her blood, the new screaming — I did not know it then as my own — shut out everything else.

"Jose tried to use his strength to drag me out but I pleaded piteously for one more moment with my Mia, crawled back to kneel beside her, to cradle her body, so limp, so light in death, and I would have rather died there than move, but now here was Jose again, slapping and cursing, dodging the flailing fists with which I tried to kill him.

"Yes Father, forgive me that in that moment I would have killed.

"The only thing I managed to save of Mia was her butterfly ring.

"Outside there was silence now. The only light came from the waning crescent moon and the soldiers' torches leaping, dodging, flickering across the corpses flung down, necks askew in doorways, on the paths—"

Vanessa could not go on. Mlle. Durocher slid a box of tissues across the table.

"The soldiers ripped down the temple's gold paneling, stuffed the jeweled chalices and everything else they could find into sacks and turned Brother Bart, the sinner, into a packhorse."

Mlle. Durocher shook her head sadly:

"Brutality: it changes its dress, its religion, but always it stays rooted, it seems, in the nature of the human."

Vanessa was blowing her nose when the kitchen door opened.

"Excuse me, ladies." It was the man from the reading room.

"Yes, Mr. Sanger?" Mlle. Durocher jumped up, trying surreptitiously to shield the table with her body. Behind her Vanessa put the journal and the exercise book back into the box and closed the lid. The man came into the kitchen, saw Vanessa as she stood up.

"Well hello there." His hand was large, dry, warm. "Edward Sanger, from Philadelphia." His accent was flat, American. Vanessa watched him take in her box, the embroidered cloth lying beside it. "Say, is that a Mason's apron?"

22

"Why, yes." Mlle. Durocher snatched the apron off the table, shook it out. "I was just showing Vanessa here: see the radiant eye, the compass and square, the Star of David. You know the Freemasons, Monsieur, the ancient society devoted to Goodness, Truth and Brotherhood?"

"I guess I do, Ma'am." Sanger extended his left hand. The face of a gold signet ring on his baby finger was engraved with a mathematics compass pointing down over a set square that faced up. The Star of David in the centre was made of tiny diamonds. "Masons have been in Philadelphia since before the Revolution." His smile held the relaxed easyness that comes with success. "Ben Franklin was a Mason."

"Ah yes, Benjamin Franklin." Mlle. Durocher turned to Vanessa, saw that the journal was out of sight: "History: always there is so much more than what is written. Did you know that when Benjamin Franklin first applied to become a member, in 1731, the Philadelphia Freemasons would not have him?"

"No!" Vanessa tried to hide her interest. Where did the old lady get all this stuff?

"Yes, he had left his fiancee to go off to England in 1724, where he had lived a dissipated existence. It was not until he returned to Philadelphia and became so ill that he thought he would die, that his thinking changed. When he recovered he started a printing plant, married, and decided to be a Freemason."

Sanger's smile had become polite:
"Like George Washington and Paul Revere."

"But the club members black-balled him." Mlle. Durocher held Sanger with her eyes. "So Franklin used his press to publish a venomous attack on the society, and announced that he would go on doing so. Needless to say, they soon taught him their secret handshake." The old lady glanced at Vanessa, then raised her shoulders. "He had power, so he used it. Is that not right, *Monsieur* Sanger?"

"To get into a society devoted to Goodness, Truth and Brotherhood?" Vanessa looked at Sanger.

"Ben Franklin went on to become one of its leading members." Sanger held a book out to Mlle. Durocher. "I was wondering if I could borrow this? I'm not a resident but they'll vouch for me up at Stewart Hall." Built on top of the hill behind Chester as a 19th Century lumber baron's summer retreat, Stewart Hall was now a guest mansion geared to the privacy needs of the wealthy and famous.

"But of course, *Monsieur* Sanger." Mlle. Durocher took Sanger's elbow, propelled him towards the door.

Sanger looked back at Vanessa and the metal box, and smiled.

"I do hope we'll meet again."

As soon as the door closed Vanessa picked up the apron with its embroidered Star of David, its radiant eye.

So Great Uncle Seamus was a Freemason. She was wrapping the diary in his apron when Mlle. Durocher returned.

"He has gone, at last."

"You don't think he heard me reading?"

Mlle. Durocher pursed her lips. "How would he have known to listen? But," She shook out her birdlike shoulders, "This man, he has the eyes of the hawk."

Vanessa laughed.

"He belongs to a society devoted to Truth, Goodness and Brotherhood, Mademoiselle."

"Ah, those are words Vanessa. Did you not see the way his eyes fastened on Seamus' Freemason's apron? And now he has just told me he is thinking of buying Oak Island." Mlle. Durocher looked around the kitchen, as if the spider plant might be taking notes. "I think not. But *écoute chérie*, you must take this journal straight to the museum in Halifax so that it may be stored under lock and key at the right temperature, with no humidity. Then tomorrow after lunch you come back to me. I will have some books to help us explore..." Delight, excitement written into its wrinkles made her elderly face beautiful.

"I will," said Vanessa, "as soon as I finish working with it."

# III

S HE COULD GO NO FURTHER. Close translating, fitting the words together syllable by syllable, required mental acuity and Vanessa's eyes could barely focus now on the ancient script. She took tonight's glass of Chablis out onto the deck, turned on Paul Simon. The June light was fading, leaching the colour out of the sea, the trees, Gran's flowers, leaving only the starkness of shadowed outlines jittering in a freshening wind as the three-quarter moon cleared the eastern horizon. Vanessa thought of Brother Bartolomeo. His diary was here because love and the treasure had brought him north into *a wilderness bay full of islands.* This bay?

Oak Island was only twenty minutes away by sailboat.

You could go there. There is still an hour of daylight left and you are an excellent sailor. The thought seemed to come from the moon: Go down to the boathouse and get Dancer out.

No. Oak Island was closed to the public.

So, who will expect a visitor to come from the sea at this hour?

No, ridiculous. Never sail alone, you know that, Moon.

Was that how suicides happened? Sane, normally cautious people made just one incredibly stupid move from which there was no turning back? Because who in their right mind would take a sixteen-foot sailboat out at this time of day in this wind? Anyway, Oak Island would be deep in shadow by now, desolate in twilight. And Dancer had not been put in the water this year—

Winching her down is not hard and her sails are all there.

So? Say I do all that and manage to sail safely across, and then trespass. To do what?

To look around. To get out of yourself, to walk where Brother Bartolomeo of Altamira might have been, to feel what he had had with Mia, the *towering, shuddering, monumental joy of what must surely be the truest communion.*

She was crying again, a thirty three-year old student of history standing on a Nova Scotia deck weeping in the twilight about a four hundred-year old brutality: crazy.

No. The loss of love, its sights, sounds, joys, the tastes and scents of it stripped away — how could you not weep? Vanessa had never told a soul about the wake of her first loss. In the Spain of her childhood Carlita's grandma had called Vanessa *un beecho raro*, a strange creature, but running, exploring, laughing with her friends, sharing all her secrets with Carlita over *churros*, the sugary strings of deep fried dough bought from the vendor across the street from the convent school, Vanessa's difference had never accounted for anything more than a license to freedom from catechism lessons, confirmation, confession. Until the day her Spanish world had been taken from her. Freshly arrived in Canada, to whom could she confide about lying in bed in the Ottawa house terrified of the urge that came every night, ordering her to get up, go into the kitchen, pick out the longest sharpest knife, walk into her sleeping parents' bedroom and plunge it first into her mother, then into her father? She could hardly bear, still, to remember the imagined blood as the knife blade cut through the flesh of those she most loved, and struck bone. Alone, she had tried to defeat the urge by imagining herself getting out of bed and leaving the house, walking away into the darkness, huddling under a hedge against the November sleet, the blizzards in February. As the months passed, her primped blonde fifteen-year old Canadian classmates began to whisper about the strange, exhausted new girl from Spain. Not until the spring track and field season, when she had discovered that she was good at running — the nuns' grudging concession to physical fitness had been once-a-week access to a climber in the town park — had Vanessa's world begun slowly to rotate properly on its axis.

Eighteen years later here she was lost again—

Old telephones have a jarring, clamorous ring.

Vanessa sipped her wine. Let it ring. Because what if it was Charlie? What if he was lying in their bed in Toronto, missing her? His thick black hair would be standing in spikes, and if he wanted her back he would paint word pictures she was powerless to resist, would erect logical structures she could not refute. She would catch the next plane back to Toronto. His arms would close around her...

The rhythm of one of Paul Simon's love songs filled the evening air. Vanessa lit the candles on the deck, turned on the hot tub, poured herself another glass of wine, the wind whipping her hair as she stood watching the darkening sea.

Six years ago at another seaside, in the Canary Islands where she and Brigit were camping on a deserted beach, she had been standing in the morning surf brushing her teeth, wearing only bikini bottoms and a t-shirt, when Charlie had come out of the shoulder-high tomato plants behind the beach. She had moved up to the bamboo and palm leaf shelter the tomato pickers had left behind, had watched him come across the sand. Brigit was in the village learning to solder silver from a German expatriate jeweler. Vanessa was alone.

He was five foot ten, two inches taller than she was, madras shirt and jeans, a backpack with a Canadian flag on it, and he had a lovely fluid erectness, nothing to do with rigidity or convictions, more like the easy grace of a plant stalk. His eyes were green. He was looking for a place to sleep and some guys in the village had told him about two Canadian girls who were camping on the beach behind the deserted tomato plantation.

She had picked up a tomato, offered him a bite. He took it, smiling, then handed it back, watching as she bit into it. A lump of tomato squirted onto the front of her t-shirt. Its juice spread, sticking the cotton to her breast. And standing there by the azure sea, the beach long and empty in the sun, suddenly she had whipped the stained t-shirt over her head, had run, laughing, into the warm Canary Island surf. He had dropped his knapsack, ripped off his jeans and shirt and something in him was so beautiful, so unaffected. Inside her a river of heat and light erased caution. How could there be any reason, out there among the breakers, not to play?

Later they had lain together on her sleeping bag under the palm leaf shelter, marveling at what had happened. He told her about growing up in Red Deer, Alberta, trading in his skates for computer gaming with his friend Pete, saving to get to Europe. From there it had been a short hop to Morocco and some of the finest weed in the world, and then into Paulo Coelho's alchemist's desert. But camels were hideously uncomfortable and sandstorms had threatened to skin him alive, so now he was on his way home.

She had told him about growing up in Altamira, about Carlita and Paco and going out in their grandfather's red fishing dory, looking through his glass-bottomed box at the many coloured fish around which he would drop his net, and Charlie had listened, stroking her, exploring her curves and hills and crevices until once again the tide had risen.

Love: the perfect joyful confluence of two separate and distinct people, miraculous. After Brigit had left to continue studying jewelry with the Navajos in the western United States, Vanessa had abandoned her studies in Madrid to return with Charlie to Toronto. Her PhD ambitions, she realized, had been founded on the need to recapture the Spain she had lost. What she really wanted was to write, to breathe life into the fantastic confluences of human history with its treasures. While Charlie and Pete designed revolutionary new computer games, Vanessa would learn to write for newspapers and magazines, maybe television. She had been sending out proposals and eking out a preliminary living writing pamphlets on Raising A Pet With Personality, How To Establish A Healthy Relationship With Your Houseplants, and 'articles' for fact factories that peddled company press releases as news, when Charlie and Pete launched their first game, 'Sky!' Rated 'the game all the business execs are playing,' 'Sky!' had brought dollars, first a trickle then a cascade, into Charlie's bank account. They had popped champagne corks, made love on the living room rug, bought a condominium overlooking Lake Ontario...

The Paul Simon CD was over. Vanessa sank into the hot tub, let the water's warmth rise over her chin, her mouth, her nose, let it close over her head, tugging at her hair as it began to float. Failed to hear the door bell, or the knocking, did not register the sound of footsteps.

"Hello! Van?"

Vanessa sat up. Brigit was climbing the steps at the side of the deck. Her black hair, cut in a pixie style, gleamed blue in the spill of light from the living room.

"You sounded so low when the phone cut out the other night, so instead of going home I drove to Calgary and then flew—"

Vanessa gaped.

"Well why not? My professor's away, and I've sold everything I've made." Business men visiting Vancouver paid hundreds of dollars for Brigit's intricately designed gold and silver bracelets, rings, pendants. "So, I thought, how long is it since I've taken a holiday?" The sides of a brown paper bag she had put down on one of the chaises began to crackle in and out. "Lobsters. I picked them up at a place up the highway. I called..."

As if dropping everything to fly four thousand kilometres across the country to comfort a friend was natural, ordinary behaviour.

"Am I dreaming?" Vanessa stood up, reached for her robe, and then they were hugging, laughing, crying in an evening full of the scents of lilac and spruce and the sea.

## IV

Brigit and Vanessa had met at the beginning of their first year at York University's Glendon College, one night when Brigit had knocked on Vanessa's door in residence, looking for a cigarette. Vanessa had tossed her the package, also an old pasteboard photograph. The assignment was to explore their roots by examining family photographs, talking to aged relatives, meshing these with recorded history. The woman in the picture had light coloured hair — probably honey gold like Vanessa's — but done up in braids pinned around the top of her head. The high cheek bones and grey eyes could have been Vanessa's too but their look was austere. Her tight-lipped mouth was tucked at each side.

Brigit tilted the picture towards the desk light.

"Hmm, I see a woman who met this guy who told her he was a preacher and took her off into the fields to show her God's marvels..." She flicked a glance at Vanessa, who took the picture back.

"And then whispering, 'The Lord is my shepherd...' he unlaced her corsets—"

"And suddenly she was on fire—!"

"But when she had his baby she turned into the most pious, self-righteous prude. God," Vanessa tossed the photograph back onto the stack on the floor. "How am I ever going to have a life with ancestors like that?"

There was nothing unique about the macrame necklaces Brigit wore or the multi-coloured Indian bangles jangling on her wrists, or her earrings, exotic dangling designs one day, garnet studs to match an antique garnet necklace the next. But there was an authenticity to Brigit, her choices inspired by the energy governing her daily relationship to the world: army fatigues today, a slinky skirt and boots tomorrow. Brigit had studied meditation during three high school years in India, where her parents had run an irrigation project, so now she and Vanessa could trade stories about their shock on finding, here in Canada, classrooms where girls and boys were allowed to wear whatever they imagined would attract the opposite sex; where teachers did not seem to mind interruptions from the public address system or the telephone and nobody did anything about the spitballs that punctuated the social studies lessons; where green playing fields lay empty and unused for most of the day. One afternoon Brigit had simply got up and left the classroom, had taken her grade twelve English poetry book out across the high school's empty football field to read William Wordsworth under an old oak tree on the far side and then to sit, eyes closed, until the chipmunks, mice, ants, beetles returned to the grasses beside her, until all that faded too so that only the damp chlorophyll earthiness of Wordsworth's sorrow remained.

After graduation Brigit had returned to India and Vanessa thought she had lost her best friend to a closed community of contemplation until one rainy winter evening four years later when, answering the door of her cubbyhole apartment in Madrid, she had found a smiling Brigit. Huddled by Vanessa's gas heater, they had cracked open a bottle of *vino tinto* and talked into the small hours. Brigit was on her way home.

"Hermithood doesn't work for me. I need to live the teachings, I'm not sure how yet. But, oh Van, the symbols are so perfect. So beautiful, their geometry flawless! And the same geometric designs have been popping up all over the globe forever. Why? Because everything, nature, the winds, the storms, heat, chemistry, everything inside and outside us is the same thing: energy! Is that not cool?"

Vanessa was blinking at the concept, wondering if coffee was a good idea at 3 am, when Brigit had bounced to her feet:

"What you need, girl, is a break. Why don't we go south like the birds, out of this cold. You can show me Altamira—"

"No." Vanessa had already taken the train down over the mountains to the south coast, had rehearsed the hugs she would give Carlita and Paco; and had found that both were gone, Carlita to Valencia where she was married and already raising three children, and Paco to join the military. She had tried to see past the new Altamira hotels, neon nightclubs, buses belching tourists onto the headland above the ancient harbour while down on the beach a large lobster-pink family of British bathers in straw hats were calling to each other: "Cooooee—!"

"All right then," Brigit had said, "let's take a ferry from Algeciras to the Canary Islands. . ."

Now Vanessa took Brigit's assortment of embroidered tote bags inside the French doors, then poured her a glass of wine.

"You must be tired. I'll get you a robe and then why don't you join me in the tub?"

And lying in the hot water under the June moon there was such joy in sharing her find and Brother Bart's story of love and treasure.

"So let me get this straight," said Brigit when finally Vanessa came to the end. "You, who grew up in Altamira, who are the only person within hundreds of miles who can read ancient Spanish, who has been coming down here for years and knows all about the Oak Island treasure hunt, you arrive here feeling lost and alone and discover a diary about lost love and hidden treasure written by a monk—"

"A failed monk."

"—from Altamira. Who may have been here." Brigit's face, all that was visible of her, looked as if it was floating, an oracle on the water's candlelit surface: "You know what they say, Van: 'coincidence' is a word used by people who don't know any better."

Vanessa stood up, shrugged into her robe. "Why don't I put the lobster water on to boil? Then, while we're waiting, you can start your holiday with a massage." Before Charlie had turned up on the Canary Island beach, a Austrian masseur in the village had taught Vanessa his skills.

∆ ∆ ∆

Franz Schubert's "Ave Maria" swelled into Gran's living room. Brigit lay on a beach towel spread across the long pine dining table, a glass of white wine within reach by her head as Vanessa kneaded the soles of her feet.

"Oh God, Van, I've died and gone to Heaven." Brigit raised her head to sip her wine. "You won't believe what I did on the way here. Remember the old wooden minehead we found that time, after I went west and you came out to visit?"

"Right. It was sticking up out of the trees beside a rushing creek where there was a gold mine—"

"Where I met Daniel."

There had been a little log museum below the mine tower. It was closed but there were photographs in the window: a man in a rumpled wool jacket standing beside a sluice box, holding a gold nugget the size of a fist. He had turned out to be Daniel's ancestor.

Vanessa finished massaging Brigit's calves, dribbled more lotion onto her hands, and started to work on her thigh muscles.

"I remember we decided to walk a little way up the path to the gorge the creek had cut, just far enough to peek into some of the original mine shafts, and you could practically hear the little rail cars loaded with ore that once rattled down through the gorge to the minehead—"

Three years later it was good, Vanessa thought, that they could talk about it.

"Yes. Well, I went back there this week. Remember how the path turned right at the edge of the gorge—?"

"And became a ledge about a foot wide, with little pole bridges in places, thirty feet above the rushing water. How could I forget? I was terrified, remember? I turned back."

A piano began to pound out Schubert's "The Erlkonig."

"A woman died there last year, an anthropology professor from Vancouver. Apparently she stepped onto one of those bridges and the support snapped—"

"But still you went out there all alone—?" Vanessa had to raise her voice.

"I was taking a walk, and anyway that part's fixed now. So what was there to be afraid of?"

"Bears! Men! Crumbling rock—!"

A mezzo-soprano burst into song.

"Ouch!" Brigit pulled away from the knot Vanessa's fingers were digging out of her buttock.

"—A broken ankle miles from anywhere and nobody on the face of the earth knowing where you were!"

"So what would you have me do? Stay in the car?" Brigit had to shout over the soprano. "Not go anywhere, do anything ever because maybe a bear or the wind or God-only-knows-what-else might get me?" She drank some wine, waited while the soprano finished scaling the heights, then twisted around. "Life happens wherever we are Van, and I'd rather not live caged up—"

Vanessa pushed her back down.

"I need to feel the air on my skin, to hear the trees — Ouch! Take it easy, will you?"

"Sorry. But there is so much tension built up." Vanessa worked upwards, kneading the small of Brigit's back. Three years ago, after Vanessa had gone back down to the car, Brigit had turned a corner in the cliffside path to see the opening of a new mine tunnel on the other side of the creek. Above it a huge orange pipe, a metre in diameter, with an accordion elbow bending it upstream, hung out over the creek, suspended from a wire attached to a steel cable strung across the gorge. Upstream the creek dropped, laughing, over a waterfall. It would not laugh for long. At the top of the falls a new three-sided concrete dam extended out from this side of the creek. A second cable and wire holding this end of the orange pipe crossed the gorge right above Brigit's head. When the pipe was joined to the dam it would suck the life out of the creek, send it down into the tunnel to wash chiseled rock out of the mountain's vein into a sluice box somewhere further down. As she stood under those ugly pipes and cables, everything that Brigit was had revolted.

Someone had left an aluminum ladder leaning against the side of the gorge. She had climbed it. The cable was wrapped around the trunk of a thick-waisted Douglas fir in a clearing at the top, and there was a heavy woodsman's axe. The shock as the axe struck the cable had nearly knocked Brigit off her feet, but she had hit it again and again, her back arching, then bucking forward, her feet nearly coming off the ground, the clang of metal on metal ringing out over the gorge as the orange pipe screeched and danced. Finally her grip on the wooden axe handle must have loosened. When Brigit brought the axe down the next time the impact sent a shock back up the handle into her palms. They let go. The axe flew up, out over the falls. Brigit was shaking, sweating, her tank top sticking to her breasts. There were four tiny shiny dents in the cable. And still no one came.

The glacial water pooling behind the dam was emerald green so she had peeled off her clothes, the water pricking her skin as she waded in, sending a sweet ache up through her bones into her skull. She had come up gasping, had splashed out onto the riverbank, but still there was no sound beyond the occasional creaking hemlock, the pines soughing, the chucking of a whisky jack. She was lying in the sun on top of the dam when Daniel arrived, the sun highlighting the scraggly ends of auburn hair sticking out from under a ridiculous bucket hat. Big square hands were clenched by his sides: "What the hell do you think you're doing?" he had said, "This is private property." "Private?" Brigit had pulled on her tank top, covered herself with her shorts. "You think this creek and all the fish and birds and plants whose lives you are so busy destroying, you think they're your property?" "Oh great," he had replied, "A hippy-dippy granola-head."

He had followed Brigit back down the path, had met Vanessa at the road. They had thought he was seeing them off the property, but, "Come down to Joe's for steaks." He had wanted to explain that the cables and tubing were portable, extractable, here today gone tomorrow. After Vanessa had flown back to the east, Brigit had returned to the minehead. A week later she was sharing Daniel's tent. "I know it's sudden," she had emailed, "But oh Van, it's as if a closed casing, a bud curled tightly in sleep, unconscious, that's all I've ever been. Now I wake up every morning smiling, my every cell open, my colours unfurling, pistils quivering..."

During the following year Brigit had learned about how molten minerals deposit themselves under the earth, how nuggets found in creeks are distinct from the veins of gold lacing through rock, had broken boulders to discover the hidden beauty of crystallized amethyst, had watched the sun shine through rose quartz and garnets, reflect off polished jade: "And the symbols, oh Van, the geometry, the symmetry they came from is all right here, resonating everywhere, so beautiful!"

But symbols and their meanings had no part in the plan Daniel devised of using ropes to explore the mineral veins in the cliff above another of Daniel's great-great-great grandfather's mining claims north of Hope. Brigit had watched him reach up past where his foot could safely sustain its hold. Below him, at the low end of the rope, she had seen the danger and called to him. But, intent upon gaining the next ledge, Daniel had refused to listen. He had known she was tethered to him but still he had reached. And so, as she clung to the rock below, she had been unable to do anything but watch him shift his weight onto the shaky foothold. The rock under him, crumbling, had sent his body sliding back down towards her, faster, faster, bouncing down past her until the rope that bound them had ripped her off the cliff face too, bashed her again and again against the rock, breaking bones, shredding skin, until the safety spike Daniel had sunk into the cliff above held. She had dangled there, waves of pain washing through her, calling down to Daniel whose skull, split open, was dripping blood. By the time a passing hiker heard her, just before nightfall, he was dead.

"The dam, the cables, the tubes are all still there," Brigit was saying now, "I was so angry, I couldn't stand it. And I had this eerie feeling that Daniel was nearby. I started to yell at him and then I was crying..."

Vanessa went on rubbing Brigit's back, did not trust herself to speak.

"But up at the dam the glacial pool was still emerald green. The sun was hot and I was tired, so I stripped—"

"What, again!"

"Well why not? The place was deserted and I was so hot. Anyway, what had I got to lose? And it felt so good."

Vanessa trickled more cold lotion onto Brigit's upper back, spread it with the palm of her hand, working out from the spine, pressing hard, around and down then up to work her shoulders. Disconnected, that's what Brigit was. What she could not imagine did not exist.

"And then cold, wet, all alone, there you were on that path—"

"Right, but first, here was the same aluminum ladder, as if Daniel were still just around the corner, as if none of it had ever happened—"

"Oh great."

"So I threw it down over the falls!"

"And then, don't tell me, you ran back over the same rotting little bridges where the woman was killed! Because you have to feel the wind up your ass." The Schubert CD was over. So was the massage. "And God forbid you should ever be caged in by any kind of rational thought." Vanessa was wiping the leftover lotion off her hands with the edge of the beach towel when cold liquid trickled through the piled up mass of her hair, tickled her scalp, slid down her neck, dripped off her nose, filled the air with the white wine's bouquet.

Holding the empty wine glass, Brigit looked as surprised as Vanessa did. Then a giggle broke free—

Dripping wine, Vanessa ran into the kitchen. Brigit slithered off the table, was putting on the towel robe Vanessa had laid out for her when Vanessa's cry, sharp with alarm, came through to her.

"What?" Brigit hurried through the doorway. Straight into a wall of warm, salty, freshly launched lobster water. Vanessa's timing had been perfect. Eight litres of water sent Brigit staggering, slipping backwards to land, incredulous, on her bottom.

Laughter, great peals of it, gobbled Vanessa's breath, doubled her over, the empty lobster pot still dangling from her fingers. Her feet slid out from under her. She landed in a puddle of warm water as the laughter switched, the way laughter loaded with too rich a mix of emotion sometimes does, into tears, sobs. And then waves of pain—

"Easy, Van." Brigit slithered across the floor, put an arm around her. Vanessa dug a piece of damp tissue out of the pocket of her robe, blew her nose. Brigit found the wine bottle and passed it to her. Vanessa took a swallow, another, then leaned her head back against the kitchen cupboards. Above them in the sink, the lobsters' legs tapped against the stainless steel.

"I'm sorry." Vanessa waited for her breathing to steady itself. "It's just that you and Daniel, Brother Bart and Mia, Charlie and me: what is it that keeps destroying love? You saw what Charlie and I had, even when we came back to Canada... But now—" Another squall of tears.

How to explain what exactly had been wrong with the quickening pace of their lives: wake-up, black coffee, one eye on the time, then research, meetings, proposals designed on computer, then phone calls, emails, research on line; sunset aerobics or a quick game of squash, then a Noodle Box dinner, anything to quash the need to cook, to think. To look. Charlie loved it, fed on the lightning-paced thrust and parry, the thrill of the race, the wins and the grace of Gucci shoes, gowns from Farouche. And so did she... Except that sometimes when she came home from a meeting and kicked off her shoes, and Charlie brought her a Scotch and started to move a hand to her breast, his voice a caress, as if kiss fuck 'I love you,' as if that were enough, sometimes when she stood at the picture window, looking down at the sailboats flitting like water bugs back and forth to Toronto Island, even if he was right there with her...

"Life seemed so barren. That's crazy, I know. Our life was so neat, ordered, like one of those neighbourhoods where all the pretty houses are lined up along the streets, lawns neatly trimmed, stop signs at the corners, trees planted where they will give shade, people out raking away the winter's debris, pruning their hedges, toddlers riding tricycles. But then... then suddenly last week it was as if this hole opened right in the middle of this perfect neighbourhood and before I could do anything these flames were leaping up!" Vanessa wiped her nose again.

"Flames? Why?" Brigit stroked her arm until Vanessa was calm enough to tell her about the National Magazine Awards banquet three days ago, how she had been nominated for Best New Writer on the basis of her first full length magazine article, "Treasure Island North," how she had waited in the hotel mezzanine, writers in rented tuxedos and backless spring gowns streaming past her into a banquet room. Any minute now, she kept thinking, Charlie would come leaping up the mezzanine's spiral staircase, or the elevator door would open and he would stop to whistle at her new royal blue gown. Her hair was up in a chignon. Her earrings, lapis lazuli and silver, had been his present last Christmas. But twenty minutes later the elevator had released a last dribble of guests. The waiter removing the doorstops had looked at her with sympathy.

'Vanessa Holdt and Guest' had been placed at a round table for eight. She tried to stay calm, to chat as if the empty seat beside her did not exist. Three courses later, when the master of ceremonies called for quiet, Charlie's chair was still empty. Vanessa's body inside the blue gown began to shake, sweat trickled down her sides—

"This year's choice of the Best New Writer was difficult..."

Vanessa hung onto her hands. The microphoned words dissolved into cacophony, but she thought she heard "Treasure Island." Air stopped somewhere inside her windpipe. Then people around her table started smiling at her, clapping.

It was raining, but she walked the twelve blocks home. Let the June rain join her tears. Let it soak her hair, the new dress, her gold medal. Let him see what his absence had made of this, her most special night in which the only certainty had been the fact, irrefutable, unalterable no matter what the explanation, that the sea of applauding people had contained no friend.

Her dress was a puddle of blue silk on the bedroom floor when Charlie's key turned in the front door lock.

'Tunnel Warrior,' the new computer game he and Pete were designing, was in its final phase and timing was crucial, she knew that, so when a last minute glitch had arisen she would understand— "And if you would carry the cell phone I bought you, I could have—"

"What?" She hated cell phones, the jingled summons from the depths of her handbag. She put the imaginary receiver to her ear. "Sorry babe, when it comes to choosing between supporting you at probably the most important night of your life and—"

"No! I was just trying to explain—"

"That your game matters more." There it was: the truth, naked as a charged nerve.

"Anyway, I won!" Vanessa tried to push past Charlie into the living room, but he must have thought she was coming to him, that the flush spreading up her neck was glee, because now he took hold of her arm, pulled her to him, kissed her.

"That's so great!" He ran his hand down her back. "And I really am so sorry, sweetheart. So let's not argue?"

Vanessa stared. He thought a kiss was all it took? Problem solved? The charge ignited, flame leaping, sucking the air. She did not know she had pulled away until she found herself beside the little table by the front door. They kept their keys there, in a shallow brass bowl. Her hand picked up the bowl, spilled out the keys. She watched from somewhere outside herself, fascinated, as the enameled Chinese garden painted in the bowl spun frisbee style through the air.

Charlie ducked, thought again, put out a hand to stop the bowl before it struck the living room's picture window. It glanced off the side of his palm, hit the wall, clattered to the floor.

Vanessa's father had given her a china flamenco dancer — ruffled crimson skirt swirling, feet stamping to the sound of an unheard beat, black eyes flashing — the night before they had left Spain, and Vanessa never tired of the dancer's china grace, the long proud line of her back, the sleekness of her hair. The figurine stood on the table at the end of their white leather sofa. ("White leather!" her mother had yelped, "Is that practical? What will dirty diapers and throw up and crayons do—?") Vanessa snatched up the dancer.

Charlie was staring at the blood welling up out of the split skin on the side of his hand.

Vanessa's arm went back.

Charlie shook his head. "No, Vanessa, don't!"

But Flamenco Dancer was already flying head first straight at Charlie. She began to wobble, probably because of the lack of symmetry in her skirts. The flame died. Vanessa's hand reached out. Too late.

Charlie dodged. Flamenco Dancer crashed into the window. Her head snapped off. A crack spread across the glass. Charlie looked down at the broken figurine. On his face was a terrible blankness. He walked past Vanessa, out the door.

She had knelt, her fingers gathering up the china pieces, trying, in the charred silence, to fit them together...

"And now I've been thinking that maybe I lose everything on purpose, maybe I make it happen because all I know is how to be different, how to lose—"

"Stop." Brigit tipped up the wine bottle. "Because how does that explain what happened to Brother Bart and Mia, or to Daniel and me?" She took a last swig. "Love." The word thunked, dull as the empty bottle hitting the floor.

Vanessa looked up in surprise. Brigit had always maintained that love was divine, the energy that pushes up the grass. DaVinci was in its thrall when he conceived the Mona Lisa, Mozart when he heard the Magic Flute, Shakespeare when he dreamed up King Lear. Love, she said, could show in an instant the essence of a complete stranger. But now—

"Daniel loved me and look what he did."

"Not on purpose!"

"Still, he killed himself. He could have listened to me. He could have stopped." Brigit started drawing lines through the water on the kitchen linoleum. "But he was determined to take control of the landscape—"

"He was crazy about you, Brig."

"And he's dead." Brigit looked at her. "And Charlie's not there for you. And you know what else? In order to make a perfect neighbourhood somebody has to bring in a steam shovel, rip out all the trees, bulldoze the wildflowers, pave over the rabbit warrens, fox holes, snake holes. What could be more barren than that?"

Above them the lobsters' claws scratched at the sink. Brigit tucked her feet under her, got up.

"Wise people are hermits for a reason, Van. Give me the woods, rocks, trees, birds, bears, the sea over people any day." Brigit reached down to help Vanessa up. "Still, look on the bright side. Everything that's happened has brought us here now, just a few minutes away from one of the world's great unsolved treasure hunts with a diary nobody else alive has ever read. And didn't your Cornish Grampa, the one who used to visit you in Spain, say something once about gold and love?"

Vanessa's mind cartwheeled back through the years, into the Altamira evenings, sitting on the porch, watching the fishing boats' lights move across the black night sea, eating the sun-sweet muscatel grapes they had picked in the afternoon, and listening as Grampa's gravelly voice, lilting on an accent older than time, took her and Adrian into the stories of the Celtic Great Cauldron, of the Holy Grail and King

Arthur's knights who had ridden through dark forests, cut their way through undergrowth, had slain so many dragons in search of the Grail. The Green Knight finally won the golden Grail cup, according to Grampa. Then he lost it again. "And do you know why?" Vanessa and Adrian had had to wait forever while he lit and sucked, lit and sucked on his pipe, clouding the air over their heads with the fragrance of his smoke... Twenty years later the old man was confined to a nursing home according to Vanessa's mother, lost inside his memories, but now his voice came to Vanessa in the flooded kitchen:

"Because gold stands for love."

## V

GOLDEN LOVE AND BARREN GROUND, breaking waves, a jeweled crown, as she tossed in the netherland between sleep and wakefulness Vanessa's mind swirled, melting time, images eddying, carrying her down, down into the hole at the top of the Altamira headland—

She woke to find herself covered in sweat, her heart beating out loud. She must have forgotten to draw the curtains last night because the first light of dawn was picking out the quince bush outside the window — a splash of crimson during the day — now an abstract in grey shadows on the bedroom ceiling, shivering to the pulse of her memory: Altamira, treasure, love—

Vanessa rolled out of bed, padded into the kitchen for tea. It was 6:01 am, but her recall was clear of the day she and Carlita, Paco, Adrian and his friend Santi had lain down on the stony headland above Altamira's harbour.

"There's treasure down there." At seventeen, Santi knew everything so she and Carlita had followed the boys down into the chimney of rock, down and down, feeling their way into the darkness until there were no more footholds, no choice but to let go, to fall blindly—

The floor of the sea cavern was sandy. Outside, the tide was low but still Vanessa could hear it whispering. In some places little trickles of wet made the walls look shiny in the leftover light from above, in others the black was absolute: tunnel openings. Santi built a fire in a circle of stones on the sand and now, as the cave walls twitched in the firelight, Adrian handed around the Canadian marshmallows their father imported and they toasted them on the tip of Santi's fishing knife while he told about the heathens hundreds of years ago in South America, who had had so much gold and silver that they threw piles of it into lakes to honour their gods.

"No!" Paco turned to Adrian. "Have you met any of these Americanos?"

Vanessa's family were the only North Americans living in Altamira. Adrian shook his head:

"Those *Indios* were the Incas. They're extinct now."

"Extinct?"

"Wiped out, murdered, skewered, shot—"

"Anyway, it's true about the gold," Santi continued, "the great treasure ships lay right here, offshore, waiting to unload down at Cadiz. What people don't know is that not all of the treasure made it to the king." His teeth flashed in the firelight, "Some nights my six-times great grandfather — maybe yours too, Paco — rowed out—"

"They stole treasure from right under the king's nose and nobody talked?" Vanessa couldn't imagine it.

"Bars of gold, jeweled crowns. If anyone had talked, *hija*," Santi sliced the tip of his knife across the air in front of his throat: "But my grandfather said no one in Altamira ever saw a single piece of that gold—"

"Why not?" Carlita asked.

Paco snorted:

"Probably they all killed each other."

"No. Listen!" Now the light dancing across Santi's face painted shadows under his cheekbones. "One night they were rowing out when a man swam towards them in the moonlight: 'Go back,' he told them, 'The ship has already been looted.' They dragged him into the boat. He was half drowned but later my grandfather said he told them about a much greater cache of gold hidden up the coast of *Norte America*—"

Treasure in North America?

"—so our people decided to use the gold they had stolen to finance a ship."

"Because what else could they do with it anyway?" Paco's mind was always the quickest. "If they had tried to spend it, the king would have known. They would have been hanged."

"Our six-times great grandfathers went across the ocean?" Nobody Carlita knew had ever been anywhere further away than Madrid.

"No," Santi sighed, "they kept trying to get ready, to get a ship. But then they started to fight... and don't you see? It means they never used the money—"

The next afternoon at low tide Vanessa, Carlita and Paco had borrowed Vanessa's father's flashlight, and a rope which they tied to a bush above the hole. Carlita was left to keep watch.

Vanessa had not noticed the dripping in the cavern when the others had been there, or the hundreds of tiny eyes, pinpricks of light, staring. Now the only warmth came from Paco's hand. Vanessa held onto it, flashed the light along one of the cavern walls, found two of the tunnels, leading where? A third, wider tunnel opened in the direction of the sea.

"Sshh!" Paco had no sooner spoken than Vanessa felt a movement of air. Then came the sounds: footsteps in the sand, something being dragged, a voice muttering. "Switch out the light!"

The muttering grew louder. It was coming from the sea tunnel. They flattened themselves against the cavern wall; edged towards the closest, smaller tunnel. Reached it just as a figure came out of the darkness into the circle of light from the chimney. It was stooped, female, dressed in a black hooded cloak.

*La Vieja!* Paco's hand tightened around Vanessa's. No one had ever met the Old Woman. No one knew where she lived, whose family she belonged to, but everybody had a story about how she waited behind a barn, sprang out of the shadows to take a chicken, a goat, a cow, maybe even a child from those who did not *ten cuidado* — be careful. "She's a folk tale, a nonsense," said Vanessa's father. Now the folk tale was dragging the carcass of a goat into the cavern by one of its legs. Its neck was broken. The head, nearly torn off, bounced along behind it, leaving a path of something dark in the sand. Vanessa and Paco watched as *La Vieja* stopped, dropped the goat's foot, sniffed the air. Then, grunting, she squatted beside Santi's fire pit. The cloying stink of her reached in through Vanessa's nose, lodged in her throat. There was a scraping sound: knife against goat hide.

Paco and Vanessa moved further into the tunnel. Maybe it led out of the cavern. They tried to keep their sandals from crunching in the sand, stopped after every step to listen because to see around corners was nothing to *La Vieja*.

The tunnel turned, the blackness grew thick.

"*Dame la luz,*" said Paco, "give me the light."

The walls snaked away ahead of them, smooth and wet as the insides of a worm. The occasional plink echoed: water leaking in through the roof and there was no sense of time down here, no sense of direction, just the crunch of their footsteps and the warmth of their hands joined in the darkness this side of the flashlight beam.

Paco stopped, shone the beam up. The tunnel roof opened into a high ceiling. Twisted, ropy things hung down: roots of the bushes and trees in the world above.

"*Madre de Dios.*" He let go of Vanessa's hand, moved forward and then stumbled. The flashlight flew out of his hand, clattered across the stones, and dropped out of sight.

Vanessa inched forward in the darkness. Three feet ahead of where Paco had tripped the floor of the tunnel turned into a water filled hole. They watched the flashlight beam drown in rocky depths no living creature had ever disturbed.

A shiver went through Paco. Vanessa received it: a sweet, surprising, body-electric feeling. Turning to him, she found him already close in the darkness, smelling of warmth and salt. His lips brushed across her nose, searching clumsily. Her own lips went to meet him, just for a moment, before confusion crowded in.

At the bottom of the chimney *La Vieja* was feeding by the fire. Paco squeezed Vanessa's hand: ready?

He stepped into the light:

"*Oye, Vieja!*" The Old Woman turned towards Paco, her face smeared with goat's blood, her eyes gleaming. A strange guttural squeal issued from her mouth. Vanessa ran to the rope, began to climb as Paco taunted *La Vieja* from the opening of the sea tunnel.

"Help, Carlita! Pull!"

*La Vieja's* squealing had followed Vanessa up through the rock chimney, into the sunlight, and then down through the years into her dreams: wild, high pitched, insistent.

Vanessa jiggled the teabag in her mug.

Gran's exercise book was open and waiting on the dining room table:

*You could say that Jose saved my life. Handing me my monk's robe, he told me that if I would repent my giving in to the Devil's temptation so that my prayers for their safety would have some validity, he would see to it that the men said nothing about my conduct when we arrived in Cartagena. I hid the golden butterfly, symbol in the midst of darkness of life's great beauty, and also my own ring on a string under my robe. You will call this heresy. So would the soldiers and the priests, but had they got their hands on those rings, they would most certainly have sold them for profit.*

*What, exactly, was I to repent, Father? Mia in that mountain pasture, the joy we had shared, this came from someplace beyond earthly sin. You must have wanted me to know it. Why?*

*We are taught that that which happens is Your will, but I don't accept that any more than I accept that what we are doing to the natives in America is Your will.*

An hour later Brigit appeared at the bottom of the stairs, disappeared into the kitchen, came back with coffee. Vanessa told her about the memory, then:

"Brother Bart and the sergeant, Jose, were sent home with the treasure *flota* the following spring. Brother Bart started this diary in Cuba, where they put in for repairs."

"Was Havana a safe harbour?"

"The safest in the Caribbean, but in the summer there was swamp fever in Cuba. Dozens of seamen died and finally, after administering the last rites to who knows how many of them, Brother Bart came down with it. He was sent out into the country, and that's where he started writing to God."

"Because he thought he was going to die?"

"Right, but instead he recovered. One day several weeks later he was walking in the garden when a man appeared. He made a hand signal, some sort of secret code. Brother Bart didn't understand it but he told the man to approach. Vanessa turned back to the exercise book:

"Listen:

*"He insisted I go with him down the coast, to a hut hidden in the dunes behind an isolated beach. Inside, a man was lying on a straw pallet, his body wasted, stinking of the horrors with which disease signals the approach of death. One of his hands moved slightly as I knelt beside him. I took hold of it. He looked at me, and only then did I recognize Jose:*

*"'My sins are great, Brother,' His voice came on tiny puffs of breath. I took my prayer book out of my pocket, for myself as much as for him, for how could I ever forgive what he had done to my Mia and her people? How could I forgive You either, for that matter?*

*"'But listen, Bartito,' He closed his eyes, reached for breath: 'I have joined a secret society. It is very old, very dangerous...' In his last hour, sure that the doors of Hell were gaping below him, Jose began to cry, 'Because the Pope is against it.' He looked into my eyes, whispered, 'But I thought that you of all people might understand. This society is devoted to God and to the truth that lies beyond the church. Many people, some in very high places, belong to it. And we have heard that the Englishman, El Draque, is in these waters so we have been removing the King's treasure, secretly, from the fort in Habana, Mia's people's treasure, Bartito.'*

Vanessa looked up:

"This secret society's plan was to smuggle the riches over to the Isla de Pinos, an island just off the Cuban coast, to hide the chests there until they could arrange for ships that were smaller and faster than the galleons to slip in, pick up the treasure, and take it safely home to the King of Spain."

"And Brother Bart went along with this?"

Vanessa turned the page:

"Jose summoned a few rags of strength: 'All I wanted was to serve my King with honour, for Maria and my chicitos to have something by way of reward. So now I am begging you, brother, to forgive my sins and work for our King. To look after my family for me.' A wave of something putrid wafted up out of him. I prayed not to gag. He mustered another breath, spoke quickly, before it ran out: 'You can trust Jesus here. He is a trader who knows every cove and kink in this coastline. You must go with him to the place where we load the boats, tonight. Go with the treasure to the Isla de Pinos, and make sure—'

"Bartolomeo, the man, wanted to spit upon him, to turn away, let him rot in Hell. Heaven had come to me in the form of Mia in the Nueva Granada mountains, Father. Miraculously it had come inside the life, the skin, the very heart and soul of a homely, lonely old monk. So then, must not this man who had torn my Heaven asunder be Satan? Consigned to Hell? Should I not turn my back...? But Bartolomeo, Jose's last confessor, clung to his Bible, knowing from a lifetime of training that he had been put into this moment to pray for this man as he died. And may I report that in spite of Jose's great crime and the bully he had always been, I do find myself glad that I did Your bidding, though I had barely begun the last rites when his breathing stopped. I would have gone on praying then for guidance in what to do next, but now Jose's man Jesus took it for granted that I would uphold Jose's dying request."

"They crossed to Cuba's *Isla de Pinos* at night and were hauling the crates full of treasure across a deserted beach when two longboats glided in past the point." Vanessa read on:

"We were only half a dozen men. We held our torches high. Those who had them drew their knives, cocked their pistols. But, miraculously, the leader of the boatmen executed the same strange hand signal that the man had made to me back in the garden. So Jesus and the others hailed them, thinking they were with us."

"But a few hours later every chest and crate Jose and his group had tried to save had been loaded into a little frigate called L'Amitié which was one of two ships lying just round the end of the point. One flag had *an hourglass and a man holding a sword on it, the other the dreaded skull and crossbones."*

"Pirates!"

"They were French—"

Out in the hall the door bell was chiming.

"Who the hell—?" The ringing continued.

Fake brown hair, grey suit shiny in the early sunlight, a hand extended:

"Vanessa Holdt? Frank DeCarlo, Coldwake Real Estate. I've been trying to reach you."

Vanessa held her robe together with one hand, gave him the other.

"Sorry about the early call," he said, "But yesterday's buyers would like to view the house again. First thing this morning, before they catch their plane." His smile was as fake as his hair colour: "Can you have the place looking good in, say an hour?"

"An hour?" said Brigit after the door closed. "How 'bout right now." She took a mouthful of coffee, looked sorrowfully into the mug and then overturned it. The steaming coffee splashed onto the hardwood floor.

Vanessa started, then as the milky brown puddle slid along a urethaned crack between the floorboards she felt a tickle of laughter—

But right on its heels came censure: get a cloth, clean it up before it spreads further—

"Why don't we sail over to Oak Island?" Brigit was looking out at the morning. The sun, just clear of the eastern horizon, was marbling the rippling sea with peach-pink and silver. "You said that the treasure hunters were old." She looked at her watch. "If we leave right away we can be back before they finish breakfast."

Vanessa was still watching the coffee puddle. She shook her head.

"The island's not open—"

"And we're not tourists. And who will ever know?"

Vanessa looked at the early squalls chasing each other across the bay.

"Come on, Van. What if the 'the treasure in America' was Brother Bart's? You have the diary and who's done more Oak Island research? And I have ways of perceiving— Together how can we fail?"

The brisk north-easterly would carry them quickly. And it was Friday; the Joudry's Cove treasure hunter who spent his weekends on the island would not be there yet.

Treasure in America. Half her lifetime later Vanessa glimpsed again, through the memory, the delicious dance of fear with freedom.

# VI

Skimming across the waves in Dancer, feeling the wind tugging at the mainsail sheet, the sea pulling the tiller, herself a tiny human link between the powers of Earth's great elements, thrilled Vanessa every summer. She had been nine the first time her father had let her take command of the little eighteen-footer they had sailed in the same Altamira waters through which the great treasure galleons had moved on their way down the coast to Cadiz: "Coming about!" She remembered her glee as her mother, father and older brother jumped to the tasks of unclamping the jib sheet, shifting sides, ducking out of the way of the mainsail's boom.

"Van, look!" Now Brigit was sitting opposite her, one hand holding onto Dancer's jib stay, a multi-coloured cotton sunhat pulled down low against the sun. She was gazing behind Vanessa at the eastern horizon.

Vanessa took a quick look over her shoulder. A wooden sailing ship, the sails on its two yardarms furled, looked as if it had been painted on the white early morning sky.

"That's one of those 'tall ships', Brig. They sail up from Boston." Vanessa's grin was a little wicked. "Who did you think it was, Brother Bart?" Vanessa laughed. Brigit still insisted that all life was nothing more than clusters of energy. It was the human's eyes/brains/senses that turned these concentrations into visions, sounds. Fairies, angels, daimons, the old man, the white light, the dog that people had seen on Oak Island, Vanessa's own *La Vieja*, they were all energies living here with us. It was a matter of tuning into the way to perceive them.

"Don't mock what you don't know how to see, Van," she said now.

Vanessa had anchored her ponytail with an old Blue Jays baseball cap she had once given her father. She adjusted the peak to take another look.

"I'll give you this much: that is exactly what Brother Bart's pirates' ship would have looked like."

"And in the hold—"

Face to the wind, using the outline of a tree that was taller than the rest on the far side of the bay as her landmark, Vanessa recited from memory:

*"I was ordered to pry open the chests, the idea being, I suppose, that only those who had already seen the treasure should cast eyes upon it. And so it was that in the torchlit hold of L'Amitié, I beheld again the beauty of my marriage chalice, the patterns worked into the silver, the green, red, blue of emeralds, rubies, sapphires glittering in the light—"*

"Oh Van, imagine if we could find that!"

*"—Tears poured down my cheeks. The captain put the chalice back in the chest.*

*"'Fear not, brother,' He put a hand on my shoulder, 'Your beautiful treasure is in the safest hands now.'"*

Wind, waves, the past, the present stitched together a moment for which there were no words.

When the Mahone Bay coastline opened into Chester Basin on their starboard side, Vanessa pointed at a line of trees.

"You can't see the way the shoreline works from here, but Brother Bart speaks of a bluff, and the only bluff around here is in Chester Basin."

A flashing channel marker mounted on a rocky outcropping came up on their port side:

"That's Warren's Ledge," said Vanessa. "Some people think the treasure was buried there, underwater on a shoal that disappears at high tide, that the Oak Island treasure shaft is nothing more than a decoy."

And now here, to starboard was Oak Island. Its pebble beach, strewn with tangled seaweed, driftwood and boulders, widened at Joudrey's Cove where the windows of the treasure hunter's bungalow reflected the newly risen sun. Nobody would see them land at Joudrey's Cove. Both treasure hunters were elderly now. The one who lived beside the causeway on the other side of the island would not be out walking this early, and there was no aluminum boat on the Joudrey's Cove beach. The owner of the bungalow was not there.

The bungalow receded, a jumble of jackpines separating it from the chaos at the island's denuded eastern end where, at the top of the little rise above Smith's Cove, a white metal shed protected the shaft called Borehole 10X. A backhoe sitting in the midst of a mess of rusted metal cylinders, an antiquated drill rig, holes full of stagnant green water, looked like a giant mechanical insect. The Smith's Cove beach, where treasure hunters long ago had discovered an ingeniously engineered tunnel to the treasure shaft, was a tumble of bulldozed rocks.

"Coming about!" Vanessa cruised back, sailing parallel to the Oak Island shore. There was no sign of life but: "I don't know about this, Brig."

The Oak Island treasure hunters had sunk their lives and every penny they could raise into the little island. They had pointed shotguns, taken each other to court. The Right Choice was to sail away.

Right Choices. Suddenly Vanessa was seventeen, landing on this same beach with a member of a Lunenburg motorcycle club, just the two of them with a six-pack of beer and a couple of joints. So romantic, she had thought — what better place to explore the treasures that came from being touched, to finally shed her childhood, to end the summer by sealing a pact? — until the last minute when, lying naked, beach pebbles digging into her back, his breath had come too heavily so that it no longer felt romantic or even fun. When he stopped to put on a condom, she had slithered out from under... And had never seen the boy again. She had left him telephone messages, had made up excuses for him, waited back in Ottawa for a reply to her emails. The glow of Christmas — skating on the Rideau Canal, learning to ski in the Gatineau Hills — had given way to March storms, Saturdays at the mall, canned television laughter and Vanessa had begun to wonder, what was the purpose of living? Not that she planned to jump off the Parliament buildings. They were too high, the wait too long before you crunched into the pavement in front of some poor politician on his way to lunch. Not that she was even suicidal. There was, however, a park on the way to school where the Rideau River tumbled over tables of limestone. One Monday morning Vanessa turned in. Spent the morning on a bench, not thinking. Not doing anything at all. The next day she brought bread crumbs for a family of Canada geese that had not flown south. At the end of the week the principal telephoned her parents. Her father called Vanessa into his study.

"Listen to me, Vanessa. Confusion, displacement, disappointment, we all go through these things. But if you want any kind of future, you have to face reality, have a plan, make the Right Choices. If you don't, life will make your choices for you."

She had tried not to listen but the words, echoing through the emptiness that was her life, blowing closed one door, had opened another. Her choice would be to find a way to return to Spain. . .

"Think of it, Van: emeralds, rubies, sapphires!" The wind had touched Brigit's cheeks with pink. "Come on, land!"

"I'm just not sure what we're going to achieve, and what if—?"

Brigit turned towards the Oak Island shoreline, cupped her hands around her mouth: "Hello! Anybody home?"

"Sssh!"

"Why?" Brigit laughed. "We're allowed to be in the ocean." She shouted again: "If we're disturbing anyone, please tell us and we'll go away!"

They listened. On shore nothing moved. Brigit looked at her.

"Okay, okay. Bring down the jib, and check the water for deadheads." Vanessa pointed Dancer's bow at the beach, uncleated the mainsail halyard. Dancer rocked gently forward on the tide, the leftover wind nibbling at the edge of the mainsail, rattling the rigging, and now Oak Island's sounds came across the water: waves shuffling, sucking at the pebble beach, the flap of wings as a cormorant took flight. Out in the bay, a loon's call could have been the cry of a lost soul. And then the beach was less than six feet away, the early sunlight angling into the trees, casting shadows. Vanessa pulled up the centerboard.

"Hello-o-o-o," Brigit laughed. "I said is anyone there?"

Vanessa winced. Aspen leaves on shore whispered in the sea wind.

"This is your last chance!"

Waves lapping, rigging chattering, human silence.

"There," said Brigit, "if anyone was going to shoot us, don't you think they would have done so by now?"

"Shot you maybe."

∆ ∆ ∆

PRIVATE PROPERTY
TRESPASSERS WILL BE PROSECUTED

A white limousine stopped at the chain across the Oak Island causeway. Inside it Edward 'Teach' Sanger, founder and chief executive officer of Philadelphia's Alpha Corporation, sat for a moment listening to the final strains of a Bizet concert as the rising sun tinted the horizon a peach pink.

Edward Sanger was a morning man. Thinking, planning, where Sanger came from you did it after a five mile run and a shower, before the dew left the roses. Timing, precision, those were the keys. Add the right research, a few dollars and some balls: that was all it took to make a profit.

The driver opened his door and Sanger stepped out, shook his legs to straighten the creases in his slacks, looked around at the ditch choked with grass and purple lupins, at the drooping Solomon's seal and the mosquito-infested march behind him, the endless wall of scrubby trees. Ahead of him the causeway, a line of piled boulders and gravel, crossed the shallows between him and Oak Island. At the other end, beyond the treasure hunter's bungalow, weeds were growing knee high around the doorway of a barn with a dilapidated 'Oak Island Museum' sign. Once there had been tours of the island, but money for the insurance premiums had long since run out.

Sanger had meetings with the treasure hunters set for later this morning. He would get the video one of them had shot inside the cavern under Borehole 10X. Then later today he would get the old lady at the library to give him a copy of the government's report on its underwater exploration around Oak Island. This bay full of islands, beautiful in summer, cruel, they said, as a witch's fingernails in winter, was ripe for the plucking. And after thirteen years of research and analysis, Sanger's theory about where the treasure lay was as nearly formed as a bird's egg just before it hatches. He was here to buy Oak Island, the approach, the causeway, all of it. He would pay the treasure hunters who owned it whatever it took because he had all the information now, and all the tools to match wits, in this flea-bitten Canadian backwash, with the genius who had conceived the Oak Island mystery. There was treasure here, of that he had no doubt, and an important one. But the priceless booty, its value and its beauty, would be his alone to appreciate. Because it was in the treasure riddle, not its solution, that the richest vein of profit lay.

A year from now the economy of this whole bay would turn around. Lights, music, characters in costume would advertise the world's most exciting new entertainment mall: the world's scariest roller coaster, bungie jumps, water slides, a labyrinth of tunnels and secret caves complete with clues, seawater lagoons, strategically placed 'pieces of eight'— all of it under cover against the elements. Submersibles would cruise an undersea zoo stocked with real Titanic relics and fake treasure chests, robot sharks and whatever else millions of Americans from Boston, New York City and the whole eastern seaboard as well as Canadians from Toronto, Montreal, and all points west required. The world was so small now, some strategic advertising could bring tourists, business conferences, from Japan, the new China, Europe to see the Spanish galleon replica that would shoot multi-colored rockets through the mall's removable roof into the empty Canadian night. A theme hotel, swimming pools, Imax theatres, restaurants would provide employment for people across this downtrodden province by catering to two timeless truths:

1. Give any ten-year old a choice between a real and a virtual game, and he will choose the real one every time; and
2. No matter what their debts, people will always buy what they have been told they want. How many times have McDonald's, Disneyworld proven that?

Across on the other side of the causeway the treasure hunter's bungalow was still in darkness. Well into his seventies, the man must still be asleep. Thirty years he'd been here, according to Sanger's research. He must be tired. Good. Sanger would seal the deal and be home by the end of the week.

His mind drifted to the walk-up apartment he kept in downtown Philly and the girl presently occupying it, the daughter of one of his golf partners: so young, green, supple as a sapling, puppy eager. He liked to take his time with her, feeling her swell under his touch, lush as the passion fruit he had eaten for breakfast. His wife Molly did not mind, she had her own arrangements. As long as she was the woman on his arm at the galas, the openings, the $1000-a-plate fund-raising dinners, she chose not to know about his dalliances. He had been thinking he would bring the girl something from Canada. A red plastic Mountie? A wooden totem pole? God this was a boring country... Except for the young woman with the golden hair, the one at the library with the Freemasons' apron and the metal box.

Sanger stepped over the chain across the causeway. Before he invested in a new project, or executed plans, he liked to spend some private, early morning time observing, getting the lay of the land.

Δ Δ Δ

The surf was only as deep as their knees, and Dancer was easy enough to haul up onto the beach.

Jagged-edged sandstone, limestone pebbles, shells tossed up, boulders half buried by tides over the millennia: she should be taking notes, Vanessa thought, for the sequel to "Treasure Island North." Because this frisson of electricity running up her spine was more than fear even though this island shore, in the wash of the day's first light, did not speak of anything out of the ordinary. Dancer's rigging chattered in the wind squalling through the grasses. Brigit was peering into the shadows around the bungalow, at the mob of jackpines crowding the shore at the far end of the beach, listening past the wind.

"The whole eastern end of the island is limestone and that's where the treasure shaft and tunnels have been found." Vanessa pulled a book out of her jacket pocket.

"That's the end that's been dug up and bulldozed?"

"Right. But the Joudrey's Cove treasure hunter discovered a giant cross marked out on the island with cone-shaped granite boulders. One of the boulders is right here on this beach." A photograph in the book showed a rock with a chunk in the shape of a piece of cake sliced out of it. "There!" Vanessa jogged down the beach.

Squatting at the water's edge, the tide nibbling its base, the rock looked as insignificant as any other glacial detritus. The granite felt cold under Vanessa's hand.

Brigit ran the palm of her hand over the rock, then closed her eyes:

"Come on Van, let's try to empty our minds."

Vanessa looked around, checking the chaos of jackpines at the end of the beach, the bungalow's empty windows. Birds flittered through grasses swaying in the early morning wind.

"Just close your eyes. Let the energy of the place flow into you."

Vanessa tried. The pines sighed, grasses whispered, waves replied. Pebbles crunched: a footstep? Someone watching them, wondering why two women were standing stock still...? No second crunch came. Was it memory then, because wasn't it right near here, under the little bluff where the grasses met the beach that she and the motorcyclist had spread their blanket? Where—

Brigit's voice interrupted her:

"The practice requires discipline, Van. You have to keep your mind clear. If images come you don't get involved, you just observe them. Jung called that 'active imagining.' The natives call it 'entering dreamtime.'"

Brigit was so good at it. She might be holding an interesting knot of wood or a shell patterned with whorls in a west coast forest and when she closed her eyes, reached into the still centre of the moment, tuned into the prevailing energy, the shape or design of the piece of jewelry she would make with it sometimes arrived as clearly as if she were looking at it with her eyes. Now, sneaking a peek, Vanessa saw that Brigit was trembling. She put out a hand to steady her.

Brigit took the hand and put it back on the stone.

"No," Vanessa pulled away. "I can't do it—"

"Think of Brother Bart's jeweled chalice, Van! What if it's right here?"

Vanessa looked around at the scrubby island.

"Look," said Brigit, "we have a choice. We can go the route of all the others, get out our shovels or bulldozers or backhoes, show the God damned island who's boss, and get flooded out. Or we can pay attention, open up our minds. Stop thinking."

"I'm too nervous, Brig. Let's find the rest of the cross." It was marked out in the book. Vanessa began to pace up the beach, counting. Brigit followed her past the bungalow, an outbuilding, rusted pieces of machinery, over a dirt road, three hundred and sixty feet through diamond-dew grass, and in here among the mounds of disturbed earth on which new shoots of grass were sprouting, where the spring daisies nodded among the rotting logs of trees that had been sawed down, the air whispered of obsession and greed and secrecy, of the owners of the ancient Spanish coins, the piece of an old ship, the hinge of what might have been a chest, the branding iron that had been dug out of what was once a swamp.

The headstone, at the confluence of the cross's arms with its body, was lying on its side in the grass, as if it were just any rock, its edges shaped by Earth's shifting tempers over the millennia. Brigit tilted her head to see the overhanging brow, the eye holes, the nose and mouth of a Caucasian male.

"It's sandstone," Vanessa read, "the stuff of bedrock. So what's it doing here in the swampy lowland at the centre of Oak Island?"

Brigit knelt in the wet weeds, trying not to squash two nearby daisies. She stared into the face.

Somewhere off to the left a twig snapped.

A mouse? A rabbit? Not a treasure hunter at this hour. Because why would they be stealthy? Vanessa checked the shrubbery but there was no one.

"Did you know the cross symbol was around way before Christianity?" said Brigit. "The Navajo, the Chinese, the Maya, the Tibetans all drew crosses as the symbol of life, the four points symbolizing the four directions. Some of them believed the cross's axis from east to west represented the mind. North to south stood for action. The centre, where the two lines intersected was the doorway to the Otherworld, to universal mind and energy... But," Brigit looked up at her: "didn't the treasure hunter who found this headstone dig under it and find nothing?"

"Right. And when you think about it, hiding anything here would have been a little obvious."

"Still, there's something..." Brigit gestured for Vanessa to kneel, to feel the roughness of the stone under her hand. "So let's try again. Maybe with the two of us... Let your mind go. Focus only on breathing, and every time your thoughts distract you, say 'thinking.' So your mind stays open but focused. It's a bit like walking a tightrope."

"How would you know that?"

Brigit grinned. "I was at a Vancouver Island fall fair. This tightrope walker set up a wire about three feet high beside my jewelry stall, so of course I had to try it. 'Think, even for a fraction of a second that you could fall, think anything at all, and you will lose your balance,' he told me, 'But empty your mind, focus a couple of feet above the wire...' This is the same thing, a matter of reaching the still point: perfect balance. So come on, close your eyes."

Off in the trees to the right a squirrel scolded them but there was no movement, no sound beyond the cawing of a crow somewhere further inland. Still, balance for Vanessa would remain out of reach as long as the morning wind failed to penetrate the scrub bush. Mosquitoes danced, dived, buzzed in under her Blue Jays cap. And black/white, real/imagined, success/failure, Vanessa could not help it: these were the definitions of the world she lived in... Maybe there would be something about this headstone in Brother Bart's diary. She should have finished it before they came here. Vanessa slapped her neck.

"You really are hopeless, you know."

"I'm sorry."

Brigit got up.

"How far to the boulder marking the end of the other arm of the cross?"

Vanessa consulted the book:

"Three hundred and sixty feet, that way." She pointed inland. Pant legs dew-soaked, sleeves catching on sun-dappled branches that seemed to reach out, they paced the distance, tried to avoid treading on the tiny violets growing underfoot and now Vanessa recalled her father asking Brigit once why she did not set herself up in a fulltime jewelry business: "You'd make a lot more than you do tramping through the woods collecting specimens." Brigit had agreed, but the prospect of the requisite government forms, taxes, phone calls to return, rent and license and health and safety regulations kept stalling her. She would rather spend her days collecting specimens for the biology professor, taking an hour to watch a black widow spider spin her perfect web in a shaft of sunlight between some spiky branches poking up through a jumble of boulders. And, hiking with her sometimes, Vanessa had to admit to the miracles. At first, when you stopped, knelt, unsheathed your magnifying glass, everything intensified: the blackflies, mosquitoes, no-seeums buzzing around your head, lowering their legs, preparing to land, the hermit thrush singing, the red squirrel leaning out of a Douglas fir, scolding, birth and death playing one upon the other in the sunlit mountain woods. The spider, twice the size of a fingernail, was round and shiny, and there on her belly was the black widow's trademark red hourglass. One of her rear legs shot out then folded in, out in, out in, efficient as a sewing machine needle, her other seven legs guiding as she reached across empty space, joined the gossamer strand issuing out of her rump to the lacework she had made. What would she snare before the storm forecast for tonight ripped through this rocky clearing? A drop of dew fell from one of the new green hawthorn leaves above, bounced on the web, broke a sudden stray shaft of sunlight into red orange yellow green blue purple. The spider's leg stopped.

"Polished ebony for the body," Brigit had whispered. Her legs were black, but Brigit would use silver: "For the hourglass, a ruby? No, too expensive. A garnet? Too dark. Maybe cut crystal—"

"Symbolizing what?" Vanessa had cried, "Crimson Passion in the Face of Death? What man in his right mind is going to buy his lover a black widow spider brooch, Brig…"

The lichen covered rock at the end of the cross's other arm sat among the chokecherry, alder, baby firs, unremarkable, unspectacular. Vanessa read from the book:

"The treasure hunter dug up the remains of an iron stove and a pair of scissors, a broken plate, knives and forks. The stove was in pieces."

"Was it Brother Bart's, I wonder? Was his bare back welted red from the mosquito bites as he pushed down with all the others on the tree trunk they would have used to lever the rock up while they dug a hole under it—?"

"So no one would know they had been here." Vanessa swiped at the bugs. "Maybe they used this rock because it's inland and away from the treasure shaft. No one would have any reason to find it."

"Where is the treasure shaft from here?" Brigit looked around. "Could we just look?"

There was no sign of activity there either. Craters full of dirty water were open wounds on a terrain strewn with the rusted drill rig and backhoe they had seen from the water, and a pile of huge metal cylinders. The white metal shack was padlocked.

"Borehole 10X," said Vanessa, "apparently there are caverns and tunnels deep under this ground." Vanessa squinted down the road that circled the area, and at the ragged pines on the other side. There was no sound beyond the wind.

Brigit shivered.

"What?" Vanessa asked.

"Greed, there are layers upon layers of it here. Can't you feel it?"

Vanessa pointed south.

"Rocks with strange markings carved into them and stones laid in a triangle with a plumb line through it were found."

"A triangle, really?" Brigit sounded excited. "Where?"

"It was over there, pointing just off north, towards the treasure shaft, but it's gone now, like everything else: bulldozed, ruined."

"Too bad! People all over the world have been revering the triangle for four thousand years. Think pyramids, for instance. The ancients thought the top of the triangle signified the Deity..." Brigit wandered over to look at a large crater filled with green water just above the beach at Smith's Cove.

"That's Sophie Sellers' Cave-In Pit," said Vanessa. "Sophie, whose father, Anthony Graves, owned the island then, was ploughing here one day when the ground under the oxen suddenly caved in. It was a sinkhole."

"Sinkhole?"

"Where the tides eddy up from underneath, wearing away the stone."

"And? Did they find anything in it?"

"Not according to the Sellers. They got the oxen out and filled in the hole. Which turned out to lie directly above the tunnel linking Smith's Cove to the treasure shaft—"

"So the tunnellers could have dug up into the roof of the tunnel to hide something close to the surface that they would then mark with above ground symbols. Ingenious!"

Vanessa shook her head.

"Mademoiselle D. says if treasure had been hidden in the Cave-In Pit, it would not have escaped notice. And it wasn't long after that that Sophie's husband Henry leased the land to the next group of treasure hunters."

"You mean the whole Sophie's Cave-In thing could have been a ruse, to reawaken interest in the treasure hunt?"

"That's what my father would say."

"What about the triangle then? How do we know that was ever really here?"

"All we have are the records, but there are too many disparate records about too many finds for it all to be a hoax."

Down the slope at Smith's Cove the early sun lit up a mess of bulldozed stones and trapped, stagnant sea water. Brigit stood in the wind.

"The greed here has sharp teeth, mean piggy eyes."

Vanessa hugged her arms, glanced over her shoulder back up the rise, then pointed to the cove's chaos of water and rocks in a grey-green lagoon. It smelled of salt, seaweed, decay. "This is where the underwater tunnel started. Its splayed, finger-like intake shafts were lined with coconut fibres."

"From the Caribbean?"

"Probably. They were hidden under the stones."

"So," Brigit looked around at the devastation: "Here we are at the limestone end of the island, where there are sinkholes, caverns, tunnels..."

"Someone chopped down trees and waded out, right here, into the receding tide with the huge logs and stones, trying to build a coffer dam to keep the sea from flooding in. The remains are still there, under the water. Like the treasure, probably." Vanessa told Brigit about the drill that had brought up pieces of oak, then metal, a piece of parchment, then more oak from more than a hundred and fifty feet down, before the bottom of the original treasure shaft and all those that followed it had collapsed.

On the way back to Joudrey's Cove Brigit suddenly veered off the road to the left: another cone-shaped boulder was wearing the green yellow rust of lichen. Grasses kissed its base, daisies nodded. Vanessa opened her book.

"This must be the top of the cross."

Brigit pointed inland, away from the treasure shaft site, in the direction of the headstone.

"So the stem of the cross goes down there?"

"Right. Below the headstone there are two stones marking it."

"Two?"

"One partway down the lower stem, the other at the bottom." Vanessa looked at her watch. "Do you want to see them too?"

"No, but give me another minute at the headstone, Van. I'll meet you at the boat."

In Joudrey's Cove a man was standing beside Dancer.

"Hello!" He waved, smiling: the American from the library.

*Jane Bow*

Vanessa crossed the beach toward him. The treasure hunter's bungalow was still closed up. So what was he doing here? He seemed to be alone.

Before Sanger could say anything, something on the ground by Vanessa's foot distracted his gaze. He bent down:

"Well I'll be damned." Sitting in the palm of his hand as he straightened was a coin.

Vanessa took it, turned it over. It was heavy, the edges rough cut, a head stamped on one side, the Spanish coat of arms on the other.

"This is a gold doubloon!" She looked back towards the road where Brigit had just appeared. "Brigit, come and look!" Vanessa handed it back, started scraping at the pebbles with the edge of her running shoe. "I wonder if there are more."

"It must have been dropped a long time ago." Accent on the 'la-ong', 'time' spoken as 'ta-am.' "You know how stones push up from under the ground." He held the coin out to Vanessa. "It was your foot found it."

Before Vanessa could take it, Brigit arrived. Vanessa smiled at Sanger.

"Brigit, this is Edward Sanger."

Sanger held out his hand.

"My friends call me 'Teach.'"

Brigit stared at the hand.

"Brigit!" Vanessa laughed, embarrassed. "You'll have to excuse her, she's still a little jet-lagged. She just arrived from the west coast."

Sanger's smile did not waver but his interest was in Vanessa. He continued to hold out the doubloon.

"It's yours."

But maybe Brigit's warning was right. Trespassing, taking treasure off someone else's private property would be a Wrong Choice. Vanessa smiled.

"No thanks. You're the one who saw it."

Δ Δ Δ

"'Edward Teach', wasn't that Blackbeard's name?" Brigit yanked the jib sheet free of its clamp. "What kind of man would choose the name of a pirate who stuck lit candles into his beard and went around raping and murdering?"

"Why didn't you ask him instead of just standing there pouting?" Vanessa set the long tack back across the bay.

"As for that doubloon, you don't really think he happened to find it right then?"

Vanessa's annoyance turned into mischief.

"I think he's hot."

"Hot? He's ancient—!"

"Late forties. Distinguished looking."

"Middle-aged cannot equal hot, Van. It's an oxymoron."

"An oxy-what? Did I hear the word 'moron'?"

## VII

"I WONDER IF THERE'S A CONNECTION between Santi's story and the diary." Brigit was sitting in the sunshine on Gran's deck, feet up on the railing as they breakfasted on lobster sandwiches. "Do you think his 'I-don't-know-how-many-times-great' grandfather really did steal gold from the king of Spain?"

"I know that people kept trying. They probably figured that if the king could steal from South America, why not? There was a blacksmith on one of the galleons who made a whole ship's anchor out of bars of gold the men kept slipping to him during the voyage. Painted black the anchor looked just like a normal wrought-iron ship's anchor. Perfect, they thought, because who would ever think to look for contraband gold on the sea bottom? But what they forgot was that when you raise and lower a ship's anchor it scrapes against the bow."

"Oh no."

"And they had to anchor off Altamira, then sail into Cadiz harbour, then—"

"Don't tell me—"

Vanessa nodded ruefully.

"They were all hanged from the yardarms." Vanessa got up. "I'm going to work on the translation."

"How much do you have left?"

"Another few hours."

"And then we have to go back to Oak Island," said Brigit, "I need some uninterrupted time there. I saw these hands, Van, at the headstone."

What Vanessa needed was more facts. "Logic is the route to the past," her father used to say, "In Cadiz we knew it was an important city seventeen hundred years ago, and that the Romans had imported the Greeks' idea of wisdom plays. It was an easy step from there to mapping the way they would have used their city space and then making an educated guess about where the amphitheatre would be." Finding it had been the achievement of his life. When the gold company that had financed his archeological Institute had shut it down, a light at the centre of her father's life had been extinguished. If only he were here with her now.

Gran's telephone rang as Brigit was gathering up their dishes.

"It's probably that stupid agent."

"Vanessa?" The voice was deep, slightly flat, American: Edward Sanger inviting her to dinner at Stewart Hall. "I'll pick you up at eight."

"No, I'm sorry," How had he got her number? Not from Mlle. Durocher. "I couldn't possibly. My friend—"

"I thought maybe she'd want to sleep off her jet lag."

"I can't, I'm sorry."

But he went right on talking. From the moment he had first glimpsed her on the beach in the early sunlight he had thought he was seeing the golden-haired goddess Athena...

Silently, Vanessa began to listen. What was the harm?

By the time she hung up Brigit was hovering.

"You're not really going to go?"

"Sure," Vanessa shrugged, "why not?"

"He's a predator, Van. His name is Blackbeard for God's sake!"

"Well, maybe I need a little wind on my ass too. You don't want me to live my life caged up, do you?" She dodged out of the reach of the Brigit's tea towel.

# VIII

"You remember Brigit, Mademoiselle? She used to come down in the summers sometimes."

"But of course," Mlle. Durocher took Brigit's hand in both of her own. "How could I forget these brown eyes, so whimsical?" She turned to Vanessa. "You have finished translating, *chérie?*"

"Not quite, but he did come up here, Mademoiselle—!"

"No Timmy, not that one." A young mother searching the stacks across the hall with a little boy had a sleeping baby strapped into a chest pouch. "Here, what about Edward Bear?"

"Edward Bear's a wuss."

"Oh Tim..."

Whining commenced in the stacks. They watched Timothy's mother drag him towards the door.

"Sorry Mademoiselle, it's nap time. We'll be back tomorrow, when we're feeling a little more co-operative." Outside clouds were gathering.

Vanessa checked the stacks, the reading room across the hall. They had the library to themselves.

"You must have read everything anyone's ever written about Oak Island," Brigit was saying, "so you must have some ideas about the natures of whoever buried the treasure?"

"Baaf, I think the books about Oak Island have not been written by people who have lived our history." She came out from behind her desk. "They say, for example, that the engineering knowledge that would have been necessary to build this complex treasure shaft and the flood tunnels limits the number of people who could have done it. I say balls to that, if you will pardon my French. Come," They followed her into the reading room. "You modern Anglais think that no one crossed the Atlantic before Columbus. Nothing in this world existed before you invented it! But how do you think my people, the Acadians, constructed their drainage systems? Hundreds of years they'd used engineering to reclaim the sea marshes before the British kicked them all out — 8000 men, women, little children — and took everything they had. Talk about pirates! Or what about the Cornish tin miners, who had been excavating underground for a millennium? Or the medieval builders of those great European cathedrals, do you not think they could have dug a little treasure shaft and a few tunnels?" There was a low shelf on the far side of the room. Mlle. Durocher began to pull out books. "Anyone — pirate, soldier, renegade — could have dug the treasure shaft."

"Wouldn't someone have talked though?"

"Not if they were dead." She passed the books back to Vanessa and Brigit.

"Or couldn't get back here, didn't know the right co-ordinates," said Vanessa. "Navigating at sea is nearly impossible without a chart."

"What about the date?" Brigit looked at Vanessa. "Didn't you tell me once that the new oaks growing in the clearing when Daniel McGinnis discovered the treasure shaft put the time frame in the late 1700's?"

Mlle. Durocher snorted.

"The writers of books that say that, they forgot to read their weather records. If they had, they'd know that in 1759 a huge storm swept across Nova Scotia. Trees all down the coast fell. The ones that grew up again are all the same age." She glanced at the title on the red cloth spine of another book, handed it to Vanessa.

"Could the Acadians have stashed their family fortunes in the treasure shaft while the British and the French were fighting?" Brigit asked.

"Poof," Mlle. Durocher straightened her back. "What fortunes?"

"What about the Acadian pirates who sailed out of Le Have, just down the coast?" Vanessa hazarded. Her arms were full of books now. "They liked to harass the British ships trading in and out of Boston and New York, and they might have been in league with French pirates."

*Jane Bow*

"All that was much later, in the 1700's. But think, Vanessa," The old lady lowered herself into one of the chairs at the reading room table where Edward Sanger had sat. "Remember sergeant Jose's man and the French pirates had a hand signal and there was—"

"Uncle Seamus' apron! They were all Freemasons, like so many of the Oak Island treasure hunters."

Mlle. Durocher smiled.

"Why do you think you are holding all those books?" Vanessa dumped them on the table and settled into one of the other chairs. Behind her the tiled fireplace in the corner stood as a reminder of the days when this had been someone's living room. The ceiling was ten feet high, plaster moulded into a circle of intertwined leaves at the centre. Where once an imported crystal chandelier would have hung, now there was a round frosted glass light cover. How many happy afternoons had she spent here batting ideas back and forth with Mlle. Durocher?

"But first, what more can we know about Brother Bartolomeo's pirates?" asked the old lady.

Vanessa had brought Gran's exercise book.

"Why don't I let Brother Bart tell it himself. You remember, there were two ships:

*"They were French. A few hours later every chest and crate Jose and his group had tried to save had been loaded into the longboats and taken to a little sailing ship called L'Amitié which was lying with another similar ship just round the end of the point. The ship's captain was a slim Frenchman with lush brown hair tied back and a crisp white lace neck ruff: Captain Du Moulin. Perhaps, he smiled, we would like to join him? They needed extra hands.*

*"Some stepped forward. Jesus gestured for me to do the same, but I hesitated. Would they argue if I pleaded my vocation to You? I could find my way back to Habana... To do what? No, I had made a promise to Jose. And all I had left of my Mia was her people's treasure. So I too stepped forward, You will say forsaking my Church and my order. Two men declined the offer. The captain shot them in the head."* Vanessa looked up. "Brother Bart was tall, clumsy, middle-aged, no use in the

rigging, but he had a few words of French so the captain put him to work in the ship's galley.

*"The captain of L'Amitié's sister ship, L'Espérance, was the expedition's leader. His name was Martin St. Clere. His family was one of the oldest in France, but the men told me that he hated the French king. When we anchored for the night Captain St. Clere and his advisor came aboard L'Amitié. The captain was a well-built man, about my height, in his mid-thirties. He wore his red-blond hair short. His eyes were quick, intelligent. In spite of the weeks at sea his doublet and stockings, which were green, looked as if they had been freshly laundered. His advisor was older, steeped apparently in mathematics and science and sorcery.* But listen to this, one of the two ships' flags showed an hourglass and a man holding a sword against a black background, the other was the skull and crossbones."

Mlle. Durocher smiled, started sorting through the pile of books on the table and came up with a slim volume. Inside was a picture of the Jolly Roger flown by a French pirate ship: it was the flag Brother Bart had described.

"Now look at that one." She pointed to a small red book with a frayed binding.

Vanessa opened it, stopped at a photograph of a hammer, chisel, compass, set square, knife, a sextant shaped like a 60-degree triangle with a rounded bottom and a plumb line hanging from the apex. The tools were used by the French Freemasons to symbolize their moral rules.

"Look," Vanessa pushed the open book across the table to Brigit. "This is the exact shape of the sextant they found laid out in pebbles near the treasure shaft."

"And see the sextant and compass set one on the other," Mlle Durocher added, "just like the ones on the ring of that man, the American."

"Blackbeard." said Brigit, "Vanessa's having dinner with him tonight."

Mlle. Durocher looked over her spectacles.

"You will not show him the diary?"

"Of course not! It's a friendly dinner, that's all." Vanessa turned back to the book, where another plate showed the four pillars of the Temple of Solomon, a dagger crossed with a bone, a hammer and chisel crossed, crossed swords, and a Star of David — made of two triangles laid on top of each other, one pointing up, the other down — like the one Vanessa had seen on the embroidered Freemason's apron in which her ancestor Seamus Holdt had wrapped Brother Bart's diary. She turned the page.

"Look!" A third plate showed a coffin with a skull and crossbones on it. "'The coffin, skull and crossbones are emblems of mortality, and cry out with a voice almost more than mortal, prepare to meet thy God...' And listen to this: 'The hourglass is an emblem of human life, the scythe an emblem of time, 'which cuts the brittle thread of life and launches us into eternity.'"

"The pirates' flag!" said Brigit. Mlle. Durocher looked proud as a mother hen.

Vanessa returned to the book:

"'Darkness and death formed an essential part of ancient worships across the world. It was thought that man, once he had been besmirched by lust and greed and evil, must descend into darkness, chaos, must die a symbolic death before he could be reborn and initiated into the higher secrets... In Scottish and French Freemasonry this is reflected by the coffin which symbolizes the Chamber of Reflection, where an aspirant has to spend time before he is initiated.'" Vanessa looked at Mlle. Durocher.

"They buried Brother Bart! — I just finished translating that part — Here, listen. They had sailed up the coast of America looking for something." Vanessa found the place:

"We kept having to heave to while Captain St. Clere put in to shore in a longboat. Finally he came back jubilant. They had found what they were seeking: the outline, carved into a cliff, of a knight. Very ancient, Jesus said."

Mlle. Durocher frowned.
"A knight?"

"A landmark maybe? Because: *We turned west soon after that, running before a south east wind towards what looked at first like a solid land mass. As we came closer, however, the forest broke up into islands, hundreds of them, in what turned out to be a bay, a most beautiful panorama of blue sea and green islands and nowhere, in any direction, a sign of human habitation. Orders were given to furl the mainsails as we had no chart of these waters.*"

Vanessa looked up.

"Wouldn't that have to be Mahone Bay? Where else?" She returned to her notebook. "They anchored near a bluff. And:

"*I noticed, as we began to cut out a clearing on the bluff, that I was feeling weak. I was stripped to the waist, trying to summon enough strength to hack branches off the trees the men were felling for shelters, when two seamen came to take me to the tent where Captains St. Clere and Du Moulin and the old advisor were sitting behind a table that had been brought from one of the ships. The seamen stood on either side of me as if I were a prisoner. The advisor spoke Spanish.*

"'*You are a Dominican.*' *Beside him St. Clere looked peaceful but ruthlessly so, as if he could order my death with no more concern than if he were ordering his dinner. Du Moulin's face was also without expression.*

"'*Si, Señor.*'

"*The advisor had the eyes of a raven.*

"'*Why?*'

"'*Why am I a monk?*' *In forty-some years no one had ever asked me that. I tried shrugging, 'It was the will of God perhaps? I was only a boy...' I looked into the raven's eyes and saw only a reflection of my own ragged self. The air in the tent was close. I was afraid I might faint. Sweat was running down my cheeks, my neck.*

"'*He has the fever. Take him out.*'

"*They built me a lean-to, leafy branches to keep out the sun and rain, and left me. The cook brought a mug of fresh water each morning and evening and my mind became a jumble of faces, whispering voices, swirling colour while You performed what I can only believe was an internal cleansing that had naught to do with creeds and litanies and the Dominican doctrine. When I awoke some days later, in* the wee hours, I felt a blissful coolness. I was too weak to move more than my head, but to the east I could see the first white rays of morning. I thought I would cry at the beauty of it. The cook appeared and, seeing me smile, brought me some soup. By the end of the week I was back in the tent.

"'So you did not die.' St. Clere looked at me the way you might look at a bull you were thinking of buying. The advisor was also looking me over.

"'You recall, of course, the teachings of our own Lord Jesus Christ, Bartolomeo.'

"'Of course.' Was this a trick? Was one of these men an inquisitor who somehow knew of my love and was watching, listening, waiting to pull out my fingernails, burn off my genitals—?

"'And do you also remember that those wisdoms defied politics, the powers of both temple and emperor?'

"'The teachings of Christ come from God.'

"'But if Christ were here now, brother, what state would he support, what church?' The old advisor smiled, 'He would be here with us.'

"And now I thought of Jose, may he rest in peace: 'The Pope is against us,' he had said. The advisor signaled for the men to take me away:

"'You, however, still have to die.'

"A grave had been dug, lined with sail cloth, roofed with logs too heavy for me to shift. Resting on the top of it was a human skull, below it two crossed bones. They fed me salt meat, biscuit, filled me with a double ration of Cuban rum, then they stripped me.

"'But look,' said the cook. 'Qu'est-ce que c'est que ça?' He had found my rings: my own sun and Mia's butterfly, all that I had left of her, except of course for this journal which I kept buried under my cot.

"I tried to take back the rings.

"'Non, non, mon fou.' He spoke quickly to the other men, who held onto me while he put my rings into his pocket. And Father it was then that finally I lost my spirit. Because, divested of this last connection with my beloved, my only moment of love in this world — no thanks to You dear Father, forgive me but I may as well utter the words — now my body, my life, the very centre of myself became nothing to me.

*"They laid me in the pit and shut out the daylight, and how I sobbed. Naked in the dirt, in the dark, I cried until I thought my innards would heave up through my mouth. Had I had the means, I would have put an end right there to my life. For take, take, take, that's what this earthy existence is about, Father. You know it as well as I do. All my life I have been taught about the sacredness of prayer and trial and denial in preparation for Heaven but now I had to wonder: if life on earth is nothing but pain inflicted one upon the other, what is the purpose in that? Where will it end? Will we simply take, kill, destroy until there is nothing left on this blessed Earth?*

*"I must have slept. When I awoke no light came in through the cracks between the logs. There was only darkness, damp earth, salt stained sail, my own breathing, too close. I tried to sit up, banged my head.*

*"So, they had buried me alive. I saw St. Clere's eyes, ruthless, and the advisor's raven eyes, and Du Moulin who had shot two men. I closed my eyes, tried to make ready for my death. But now everything I had been taught, the catechism, the vows, all of it was gone. Even You, Father.*

*"Was this the way to Hell? I lay very still, listening to my breathing. Pictures came: Mia in the meadow. I felt her body, her love, and how I cried. I watched again as the pictures rose, then faded. A life lived. My breathing slowed. I listened to it, completely empty now of thought or prayer or plans or hope. Peaceful at last in my grave."*

Dust motes lit by a stream of sunlight coming in through the reading room window pirouetted through the silence.

"Brother Bart carried his diary out of Cuba, kept it hidden on the ship and wrote in it all the way up the coast, while Captain St. Clere was off searching for the rock knight, and then by candlelight at night in his tent up here," said Vanessa. "He writes that it was risky but once started, he could not give up expressing his thoughts openly, honestly, and *'who better to hear them than You, dear Lord?'*"

"It is a miracle that he was not caught," said Mlle. Durocher. "He would have been executed."

"Someone must have found it eventually," Brigit was doodling crosses.

"A Freemason maybe," said Vanessa, "another pirate devoted to Truth, Goodness, Brotherhood?"

Mlle. Durocher nodded.

"Do I not keep telling you, *chérie*, to understand history you must think it through, put yourself into the skin of the people you are researching. If Freemasons met in secret for the purpose of developing new ideas at a time when power was held in the hands of tightly knit cliques, some of these men were bound to be revolutionaries. Some were intelligent men, privy to education, knowledge, but not to privilege. Younger sons maybe, or cast out for political reasons. We know only, from Brother Bartolomeo, that these pirates hated their king." The corners of her lips twitched up. "They knew each other by the secret handshake. Did you know, by the way, that a stone with a Masonic compass and square, dated at the turn of the 17$^{th}$ Century just a few years after Brother Bartolomeo's pirates were here, was found near Champlain's original settlement at Port Royal in Nova Scotia?"

"Wow." Brigit began to doodle skulls. Now she looked up: "The headstone they found on the Oak Island cross, could it have been a skull?" She looked from Vanessa to Mademoiselle Durocher. "I did see something, an image, just for a fraction of a second, when I was kneeling at the headstone. I was running my hands across the face, and behind the twitter of the birds and the rustle of leaves there was this sense of peace, and then hands: short strong fingers, tiny golden hairs glinting on the backs of them. They didn't belong to Brother Bart. They were holding an iron-topped hammer and a sculptor's chisel, tapping, then feeling the surface of the stone, checking the contour. And one of the fingers had a heavy gold ring on it. Flat topped, very ancient I think. There was an animal — a horse maybe? — with two men on its back."

"An insignia," said Mlle. Durocher, "but I do not know it."

Vanessa picked up the pen and pad of paper.

"Let's make some sense of all this. We'll start with the journal, the new facts according to Brother Bart. First, Brother Bart was on a French pirate ship carrying Spanish treasure."

"And the pirates had a secret hand signal and flags with an hourglass, a scythe, a skull and crossbones on them."

"And they came north to a bay that must be this one. But," Brigit looked confused, "if they were looking for something why would they bury the treasure here?"

Mlle. Durocher smiled.

"If they found what they came here looking for — and remember the carving of the knight, how happy the captain was? — they would have had to leave something behind before loading up to cross the Atlantic."

"So what could they have found?" Vanessa stopped writing.

"The group Jose and then Brother Bart joined in Cuba was a renegade pro-king, anti-Pope group."

"Anti-Pope, but not necessarily anti-Christian," said Mlle. Durocher. "Look at the Knights Templar, for example. They were Christian crusaders but still Pope Clement V excommunicated them. Life was so dangerous then. Torturing, burning, beheading people, this was routine."

"And look how many researchers have linked the Oak Island mystery to the Freemasons and Templars," Vanessa turned to Brigit. "The Knights Templar were wiped out at the beginning of the 1300's but some of them survived because there's a story that one of them, called Henry Sinclair, came over here and built a castle up the Gold River at New Ross. The river empties into Chester Basin, and they say he planted the oak trees on Oak Island as a landmark for refugees."

"But why, I have always wondered, would a Templar build his castle inland at New Ross?" Mlle. Durocher chuckled. "History is so funny, the story so complete when you read it. Then along comes a new discovery — like the ancient ruins that have just been found up in Cape Breton, that might be Chinese. The Chinese here! — and poof, there goes your established 'history.'" The librarian got to her feet, picked up a feather duster she had left on one of the book cases. "And the whole idea of priceless Templar treasure being brought all the way over here in those days, secretly, then removed and taken all the way back with no record of its subsequent storage..." The old lady shook her head.

Brigit had started doodling triangles. Mlle. Durocher came to look over her shoulder.

*Jane Bow*

"Ah yes, the mighty triangle. Look," she took the pen from Brigit, drew four dots in a straight horizontal line then, above it, another three, above them two, a final dot at the top. The result was a pyramid, shaped like an equilateral triangle, made of dots. Brigit grinned.

"The Greek Pythagoras' tetraktys, symbolizing ascension towards the Divine." She showed it to Vanessa. "See, the first four dots stand for the elements: earth, water, wind and fire, and so on up the pyramid to total consciousness at the top."

"The Knights Templar were not the only ones to study alternative routes to the Divine," Mlle. Durocher looked pensive. "There were the Cathars, and the Arabs in the east from whom the Templars learned so much, and later, in Brother Bartolomeo's time, the Italian Giordano Bruno, who lectured at John Dee's secret 'school of the night' in London. The secret emblems the Freemasons use are the same signs and symbols that have come down from the ancient Chaldeans, Egyptians, Indian Brahmins, Greeks, Celts, the Chinese."

"But why would people have risked joining those secret societies if it meant being tortured, burned at the stake?" Brigit wondered.

"Something incredibly powerful must have moved them," said Vanessa.

"Like what?"

The library door opened, blowing in a flock of chattering toddlers and their mothers. Mlle. Durocher smiled at Vanessa and Brigit.

"Now it is story time. We will continue." She brushed a hand, a little self-consciously, across Vanessa's shoulder. "Also, I will have something interesting to tell you... Some news I would like to share."

∆ ∆ ∆

"Why would you think having dinner with Blackbeard would be fun?" Brigit was leaning against the doorway of Gran's bedroom. "I thought you were off men."

"I'm not going to get involved with him—"

"So why go? Why not stay home and finish the translation?"

Vanessa laughed.

"I'll only be out for a little while." Fresh from the shower, dressed only in her underwear, Vanessa was appraising her body in the mirror on the inside of Gran's armoire. "I'm going out of curiosity. I don't know why Edward upsets you and Mlle. D so much. He's a perfectly respectable businessman and maybe he'll have some information we can use, because once that real estate agent sells this house..." She turned sideways. Could it be that to Edward Sanger she really was goddess-like? Maybe Brigit was right: what each of us sees as real is the product of our individual senses—

"Isn't Stewart Hall very exclusive, only a few rooms?" Brigit asked. "What if once you're in there—?"

Vanessa had taken her burgundy silk cocktail dress out of the closet and was holding it against her. It was short, with spaghetti straps, Charlie's favourite—

"You can't wear that." Brigit snatched at the dress. Vanessa flipped it out of her reach, pushed her out of the room, kicked the door closed.

"I am going Brig, so get over it!"

"Why? Do you think he's going to tell you anything? What he will do is flatter you all to Hell, find out what you were doing on Oak Island and then—"

Vanessa opened the door enough to frame her face.

"What? Rape me? For God's sake, Brigit, I'm thirty-three years old!"

"And he's a predator who'll do whatever it takes—!"

Vanessa shut the door again, slipped into the dress, piled her hair up into a loose chignon, checked herself in the mirror.

A predator: powerful, dangerous. Beautiful.

But Athena, goddess of war, could hardly be called prey.

"Don't worry," she said later, shrugging into one of Gran's soft Nova Scotia knit shawls, "I will not say a word about Brother Bart." His diary was locked away, inside its metal box, in her suitcase under Gran's bed.

## IX

THEY EXPLAINED THEIR RESPECTIVE TRESPASSES on Oak Island over scotches by Stewart Hall's sitting room fire: Sanger was a prospective investor; Vanessa was down here cleaning out her Gran's house and had gone sailing to show the island to her friend Brigit, who had just arrived from the west. Not that there was much to see there.

Stewart Hall guests guaranteed their seclusion by renting the entire mansion. The carpets were thick, the light over the dining room table cast by a crystal chandelier. A second fire crackled in the fireplace along the side wall while the picture window at the end of the room looked out over Mahone Bay's patchwork of islands. Above them the setting sun had turned a fleet of fleeing clouds mauve, purple, mother of pearl. Sanger held out Vanessa's chair, draped her shawl over the back of it.

The waitress, 'Marlena' according to the plastic nameplate pinned over her left breast pocket, lit the table candles.

Sanger had taken the liberty of ordering ahead. She didn't mind?

"Depends on what you ordered." He carried such an aura of power; she must not allow herself to be intimidated.

"Lobster Bisque prepared with a brandy and cream sauce to start."

Marlena wheeled in a pail of ice, took a bottle of wine out it, showed him the label. He nodded. "And a dry Santorini white to go with it." He swirled a first sampling round the bowl of his glass, sniffed it, tasted, and then nodded to Marlena to pour.

Nervousness straightened Vanessa's back.

"While we wait why don't you tell me why you call yourself by Blackbeard's name."

Sanger parried with a smile.

"A coincidence, I assure you. In my case 'Teach' stands for teacher." He told her about playing running back on his university's football team, not having much time to study, how in his sophomore year he had cottoned onto the fact that if you told your history professors something they did not know and backed it up, they loved you. So when they were studying the settlement of the west he had quoted Chief Seattle — nobody had heard of him then — and had woven valour and misfortune into the Texans' defeat at the Alamo.

"And now what do you do?" He did not look like a teacher.

"Well," he laughed, "by the end of college it was clear that I wasn't headed for the National Football League so I took up business. Turned out I was pretty good at that too."

Vanessa took a sip of her wine.

"As a running back? Doing endruns?" She smiled.

He sat back, regarding her.

"'Enrons.' So you're clever too." He let the silence play out. Vanessa struggled not to rush into it until finally he allowed his amusement to show. "Okay, sure, I like to win. And show me big business anywhere that doesn't do what Enron did, gild the profit lily a little, give its big clients a few rewards, whatever it takes."

"To make a profit?"

Sanger considered his wine.

"To make a bigger, better profit than the next guy because who knows what tomorrow will bring. But," He smiled, "I've never had to rape and pillage to lay my hands on a prize." He raised his glass, waited until hers came up to meet it. "Here's to the company of a beautiful lady. You grew up here?"

"No, my father did."

"And what did he think of Oak Island?"

Vanessa laughed.

"That it was a big hoax, a way for the island's owners to channel a steady stream of money."

"But you don't agree."

"I don't?"

"If you did why would you have sailed over there so early in the morning?" Quick, deft, leaving no room to duck, to prevaricate.

The bisque arrived. Vanessa took a slow spoonful, waited for it to cool, then another, conscious only of his blue 'hawk's eyes' on her, forcing herself not to react to the cascading realizations that he could have followed them all around the island this morning, could have heard their every idea, every reference to Brother Bart. Another spoonful — maybe two could play the silence card — until finally she dared to look at him. He appeared to be relaxed, still amused.

"The truth is I don't know what I think," she told him. "The Oak Island stories are great but when you keep hearing them, growing up, and nobody ever comes up with anything more than an occasional doubloon, you develop a certain skepticism. Still, there were pirates all over these parts." She watched him eat the bisque, his every sense savouring it. "And what about you? Surely you know how many investors have lost their shirts on Oak Island. Why would you want to join them?"

"Same reason I invest anywhere there's money to be made."

"Here?" She laughed again. "How did you even hear about it down in Philadelphia?"

Will Allen, an oil man, was a brother Mason. His grandfather had found an old map, bought a boat and spent two summers looking for the island on his map.

"He didn't find it and old Will doesn't have the map anymore, but when he heard about Oak Island he figured that was what his granddaddy had been looking for and if Franklin D. Roosevelt had once taken an interest..." Sanger returned to his bisque. "Will lost his money like all the rest and pulled out."

"And you?"

"I reckon he and the others didn't know how to use what they knew."

"Which was?"

"The facts, the finds, the meanings of the symbols. There was a mind at work on that little island." Sanger patted his mouth with his napkin. "And if there's one thing I truly enjoy it's sparring with a great mind."

Pan-roasted breast of duckling with a blueberry Pinot Noir sauce, fresh green beans and carrots, baby potatoes, a bottle of red wine. Sanger filled her glass. The wine glowed red, translucent in the candlelight.

"It's a Gervey-Chambertin. You'll enjoy it." Stated as fact, his confidence complete, unassailable.

The painting on the wall behind Sanger, above the fireplace, had been arresting her attention: a man in a Victorian black suit was leaning across a small circular garden table toward a woman. Her back was all the viewer could see. Her long, white gown flowed out over the grass. The man had a black goatee and black hair swept up in wings.

"Are you sure that's the sort of thing you want a woman to see on a first date?" Vanessa kept her face straight. "Isn't it the devil, Mephistopheles?"

Sanger turned in his chair.

"Oh for Chrissake. I swear to God, someone ought to give the owner of this place a course in art appreciation. You should see the hideous piece they had me sleeping under. I had to take it down."

"Or is it Machiavelli?" Vanessa began to enjoy herself a little. "Both of them were great minds."

"And you know that because you are a writer."

Vanessa sawed into her duckling, cursed the flush creeping up her neck.

"When there's treasure to be had, a smart man does his research." Sanger looked kind. "And my bet is that you know a lot more about Oak Island and the Masons' connection to it than you're letting on."

Vanessa took time to chew. "Well, it seems my great-great-I-don't-know-how-many-times-great grandfather was a Freemason, as were a lot of the Oak Island treasure hunters, not that that's ever done any of them any good. And as you must know, there are a lot of theories about what's buried on the island: was it Spanish treasure liberated from Cuba by the English—?"

"The sack of Havana in 1762?" Sanger shook his head. "There would have been records—"

*Jane Bow*

"Not if the British nobles in charge were early Enronites, and King George was mad, remember. Or what about a British payroll ship liberated by an American privateer?"

"Some drunken seaman would have talked."

"Okay then, what about the Bacon-was-Shakespeare theory based on the Oak Island drill that went through wood and came up with a fragment of parchment? Apparently there is a code in The Tempest—"

"I am negotiating to buy that piece of parchment."

"Really? You're a Baconian?"

"I don't know about that. I do maintain that there's every reason to believe that a) Sir Francis Bacon wrote the Shakespeare plays, and b) he buried them. And as a writer who knows the Oak Island mystery, I'd be very interested in your thoughts on that subject."

Vanessa drank some wine. Was this why he had invited her here? Across the table he was savouring his duckling, eyes lifted as he explored the tastes before washing them down with a mouthful of wine.

"To be honest, I haven't given the Bacon theory a lot of thought. The books on Oak Island tend to dismiss it."

"Sure they do. Who wouldn't rather sell books about truckloads of gold, or the Holy Grail, or the biggest prize of them all these days, the Virgin Mary herself?"

Sitting back now, tummy full, her mind loosened by the wine, Vanessa sensed Sanger's passion for the subject. "What about all the recent books about William Shakespeare himself as author?"

"Money-making edifices built on supposition, every one of them. I'm with Mark Twain who said, how could you have two geniuses fascinated by the human psyche alive and writing in the same place at the same moment in history? If you've studied this stuff you'll know there's evidence Sigmund Freud got his ideas from Shakespeare." Sanger leaned across his plateful of duckling bones. "Also, William Shakespeare had no library. Every one of the plays' plots was taken from existing sources, but the playwright owned no books at all."

"Maybe he borrowed them."

But Sanger was not listening.

"Other indisputable points," Sanger ticked them off on his long, surprisingly elegant fingers. "One: Bacon and his 'father' — because

Francis may have been the Queen and Robert Dudley's illegitimate son — and Robert Dudley were members of Dr. John Dee's secret circle which explored Hermetic and Cabbalistic teachings that go all the way back to the mystery schools in Egypt and used symbols that now belong to Freemasonry. Two: Bacon was a philosopher, also the acknowledged founder of modern science, also a homosexual, so he had all kinds of thoughts that Elizabethan society — which was still uptight about Copernicus for God's sake — would not have allowed. Three: Bacon believed that knowledge would be the salvation of humankind and that plays, by mirroring human nature, could bring knowledge to the common man. Four: Bacon jotted down phrases, thoughts, ideas, lines of poetry in a private notebook called The Promus. In it there are word-for-word matches with lines in the Shakespeare plays." Sanger stopped, smiling. "I could go on and on, about how the Globe Theatre was built round just like the old Templar churches but hey, you're a writer. You already know all this."

"Actually I don't, but I do have to wonder, if it's so obvious that Bacon wrote Shakespeare's plays, why does the controversy go on and on?"

Sanger raised an eyebrow.

"It's a question of irrefutable evidence — maybe Shakespeare knew the secret teachings too. Maybe Bacon cribbed The Promus - the argument will go on until someone comes up with the original manuscripts."

Marlena cleared away the remains of the entree, then slid plates of chocolate raspberry mousse torte onto the table in front of them.

"Oh!" Vanessa's plate, decorated with swirls of red and brown sauce, was a work of art. "I don't know if I have room."

Sanger smiled at Marlena.

"We'll have the Veuve Cliquot with this." His pleasure in Vanessa, in the food, in the chance to indulge in a puzzle that was obviously running his life, was palpable. And to watch the power of his energy focused, to be its recipient, was fun. All she had to do was rise to it.

"Okay, say Bacon did write Shakespeare. Why would he bury the manuscripts over here? In the early 1600's the French were still in control—"

"The tenets of Freemasonry supersede nationality, and who was here to suspect? Also Walter Raleigh, who was Bacon's friend, was a fellow member of Dee's secret society. He knew this coast and he also would have known about the Templar Knight carved into the rock..."

Vanessa toyed with the torte, trying not to betray any interest as she racked her brain: had she and Brigit mentioned the carved knight while they were on Oak Island? Was he tempting her to show what she knew? Was that why the edges of Sanger's smile were turning sardonic? Once, during Adrian's short career as a wobbly high school hockey player, their father had told him that the best defense was offence. Vanessa looked up, frowning.

"Still, two things strike me: first, if Bacon was such a genius, why did he have the manuscripts buried in a way that made them sink into the sea?"

Sanger cut into his torte. "Good question." He took a moment to savour the taste. "I wonder, did he?"

Vanessa smiled. "Second, why you are telling me all this?"

"I haven't told you anything you couldn't find out for yourself on the Internet."

"So now you're up here to capture the big prize?"

Sanger smiled. "Could be there's more than one prize up here."

Vanessa looked out at him from under her eyelashes.

"And if one of the prizes is not available to be won?"

He laughed, put down his fork to drink.

"People say money can't buy happiness, and you know what? They're right. Money buys comfort, luxury, whatever you want, but it's not the money that buys happiness."

"Oh?"

"No. Setting the stakes high and then pitting wits, guts, muscle, whatever it takes to come out on top, that's what buys me the choice to sit here eating delicious food with a lovely lady." Sanger held a forkful of torte out to her.

Vanessa hesitated.

"Take it."

She leaned forward, allowed him to put it into her mouth.

"Feel it on your tongue — creamy, rich — you like that?"

Vanessa nodded.

"Well that makes me happy." Sanger took a bite, rolled it on his tongue, watching her.

"And what if you don't come out on top?" she asked, "what if you lose?"

Sanger's smile was impenetrable. "I'm not in the habit of doing that. But hey, sometimes circumstances shift. So you take stock while the dust settles, find a better strategy."

Marlena served coffee with a tray of liqueurs and two miniature stemmed glasses.

"We'll have the Kahlua." Sanger reached into the pocket of his sports jacket, took out a small embossed leather jewelry case, passed it across to her, smiling.

"For you. Call it a souvenir."

The doubloon they had found on Oak Island shone gold on a bed of burgundy velour. It was mounted on a gold chain.

"Oh." Shock, confusion. "No Edward, I couldn't possibly—"

He reached across the table, took the box, lifted out the doubloon and held it in his palm.

"Why not? You're the one who found it." He got up, came around the table before she could object and fastened it around her neck, taking care not to touch her unnecessarily. "I just had it polished."

Seated again, he admired the way it hung just above her cleavage.

She tilted the coin towards the candlelight.

"Thank you." What else to do?

When the Kahlua was gone he came around the table again to offer his hand.

"Would you like to walk?"

The gold Freemason's ring on his baby finger caught the light. She took his hand, turned the face of the ring towards her.

"So, you and Ben Franklin and Francis Bacon—"

"And Thomas Jefferson." He took back his hand, got out his wallet. "The U.S. dollar is the strongest currency in the world. And see?" He showed her the picture on the back of a dollar bill: a pyramid. Looking out of the summit was the same all-seeing eye Vanessa had seen embroidered on her ancestor Seamus Holdt's Freemason's apron. The stars above the eagle opposite it were shaped into the Star of David. "The Great Seal of the United States is made of Freemasons' symbols." He dropped some bills onto the table as a tip. "We go all the way back to the building of the Temple of Solomon... but I think you know that." He draped her shawl over her shoulders and took her arm.

Marlena was holding the dining room door open.

"Good night, Marlena." He turned to Vanessa. "The question is, what else do you know?"

Light spilling out through the doorway lit their faces. Vanessa smiled.

"Have you read my article, 'Treasure Island North?'"

"I have." Reaching up, he pulled the pins out of her hair. It fell, a golden wave in the light. "Do you have any idea how beautiful you are?"

She tried to laugh.

"Come on, I'll show you something." His arm around her shoulders felt strong, hard, warm.

On the far side of the lawn, past the swimming pool the chokecherry bushes were in bloom. Beside them a chess board had been set into the grass. Wooden kings, queens, bishops, knights were three feet tall, painted black and white. Their rough cut faces looked depraved, malevolent in the twilight. Sanger's arm came around Vanessa's waist. She could not help tensing. But why had she come, if not to know him, to relax with him?

"Maybe one of these days, we'll play," he said.

Inside the Hall someone flicked a switch: Tchaikovsky, a waltz. Sanger walked her back up onto the open lawn, flooded now with light from the dining room. Vanessa dropped her shawl and he took her into his arms under the three-quarter moon. Successful running backs do not lose their grace. She kicked off her sandals and, as the music soared out into the moonlight, allowed herself to flow with him. He moved his hand into the small of her back. She did not pull away.

"I am a great lover," he murmured.

"Oh?" She pulled back a little to look at him. "You're not married?" There was no ring on his wedding finger.

"As a matter of fact I am." Sanger pulled her closer. She smelled the clean, crisp spice of his after shave. "But my wife and I have an arrangement. We go our separate ways most of the time."

When the music ended, she looked up at him.

"I have been living with someone for six years."

"If that mattered, dear heart, you would not be here." He led her back to her sandals, picked up her shawl, walked her to her car, leaned on the sill of the driver's window.

"I'm thinking of chartering a yacht, taking a sunset cruise in the bay." She saw him glance at the doubloon on her chest. "I'd be honoured if you would join me."

∆ ∆ ∆

The tide at the little beach across from the Chester cenotaph was low. High above it the moon laid its trail across the sea. The stones beside the dock smelled of seaweed. If you sat very still, a ticking sound soon started. Nothing moved, there was just the clicking all around you: barnacles. Sun bleached, hard as rock, their edges so sharp you could easily cut your foot on them, the barnacles were closing their stone-shelled beaks against the air world. Waiting for the tide to turn.

Just beyond Vanessa's feet wavelets fingered the beach pebbles. In a few hours, inside the safety of the new tide, these white dead-looking barnacles would open their visors again, shooting out sheaths of curly-ended pink fronds that spread like hair, so delicate, combing the water for the invisible food they needed to survive.

Vanessa fingered the doubloon, thought of Sanger's smile, power harnessed, and the thrill of matching, playing with him, of his hand in the small of her back, of dancing free.

Edward's yacht would be one of those forty-footers with a fully equipped living room... and a king-sized bed.

So? Every invitation did not have to lead to bed. If she wanted, she could just have a glass of wine, dance with him again. This was a man used to getting what he wanted, but 'I don't need to rape... to get my prizes.' He would expect that eventually, if he played the right cards, she would come to him.

The polished doubloon, absorbing the moonlight, directed her gaze out into the darkness where Oak Island lay — where she had gone because of Brother Bart, and had found Edward Sanger.

## X

Brigit was sitting at Gran's desk, staring at the screen of Vanessa's laptop.

"You better come and look."

'Alpha Corporation' The holding company's home page had a royal blue background. Its chief executive officer: Edward Sanger. Assets — Bridget scrolled down through the alphabetical listing — stopped at G:

'Gold International.' Deep gold letters against the blue.

"Yeah, so?" Vanessa sat down to unbuckle her sandal straps. Digging around inside someone else's life, especially when that person had just treated you to such an elegant evening, felt rude.

"Well, didn't you tell me once that Gold International was the company that financed and then cut off your father's work at Altamira's Institute for Studies in Roman Ruins?"

Vanessa looked up.

"That's right." Whenever her family had gone into the mountains exploring her father would pick up stones, examine them, then put one or two not particularly pretty ones into his haversack. "For my boss," he would say. Why, she had wondered, would a gold company care about studying Roman ruins? "They don't, dummy," Adrian had explained, "The Institute's a front so no one'll know they think there might be gold in this area. Dad sends them rock samples…"

Brigit clicked on Sanger's name. Up came a list of his private holdings: entertainment and theme park companies.

"Oh great, look: 'Wild West World,' 'Wagon Train,' 'Amazon Jungle.'" Brigit turned to look at her. "He's going to turn Oak Island into an open pit mine, Van, scoop out its innards, then set it up as Pirate World! Ferris wheels and neon lights, canned music — you'll hear it all over the bay — and there'll be fast food wrappers floating—!"

"Please Brig, give it a rest." But Vanessa couldn't help getting up, coming to look at the screen.

Sanger's favourite charities were UNICEF, Doctors Without Borders, Oxfam, libraries, symphony orchestras—

"You know the type," said Brigit. "His limo is parked in the No Parking zones outside boutiques in Vancouver, Toronto, New York while his wife shops. Meanwhile, back in the office he is authorizing the dumping of 'harmless effluents' into South American, African, Asian rivers, signing the death warrants of hundreds of thousands of people with his gold Cross pen—"

"Oh stop it."

But Brigit was on a roll, searching the New York Times archives now under "Gold International+1988," the year Vanessa's family had had to leave Spain.

## 'Gold Company Manager Disappears From Ancient Spanish Seaport'

She read the article out loud:

"'Sources say Gold International's Institute for the Study of Roman Ruins, which has been instrumental in the discovery of several major ruins that tell the story of the Spain that existed prior to its medieval invasion by the Moors, has had to shut its doors because the company's European manager has disappeared. Also gone is the Institute's operating budget.'"

Vanessa dropped onto the couch.

"His name was Eduardo Hessler. He was a little bowling ball of a man in a black and white checked suit. I remember the day the Hesslers moved into their new house, just down the road from us. They had a little girl so my Mom asked them over for a swim in our pool. Mrs. Hessler brought the little girl all dolled up in a white lace party dress trimmed with red ribbons and it was about a hundred degrees in the shade, and there were Carlita and Paco and Adrian and I doing cannonballs. I felt so sorry for that little girl.

"I've told you about the night after they disappeared, when we broke into the Hessler house..."

It had been after midnight when Santi's voice had called up to Adrian's bedroom window:

"*Los Hesslers se han desaparecido.*" Santi and Paco were going into the house, just to look. By the time Vanessa reached her window Adrian was halfway down his knotted rope ladder so she pulled on her jeans and tiptoed downstairs, after him. Paco was waiting under a street lamp and look! Coming the other way, slinking through the hedge shadows, was a white ghostlike shape: Carlita, still in her nightie. If the boys didn't let them come too, they would tell.

Pieces of broken glass had been cemented into the top of the brick wall around the Hesslers' house but there was just enough room on each side for a foot. One of the tall dining room windows had been left open, the moonlight shining on a long white marble dining table. In the centre was a round crystal bowl. Fresh apple blossoms were still floating in it, scenting the air. Adrian's flashlight ran over walls that were paneled in white wood and apple green silk embroidered with tiny white flowers, but—

"*Mira!*" Someone had driven a knife blade through the silk, high up, and then brought it all the way down. Another slash, and another. Whirling arms must have reached up again and again, ripping. Whose? What person could have contained such hatred? The impeccable *Señor* Hessler? His wife, who had floated the apple blossoms?

Upstairs in the master bedroom a round king-sized bed was covered in red satin. Vanessa and Carlita jumped onto it, were doing shoulder stands when they discovered the mirror on the ceiling above it.

"*Qué verguenza!*" (Shame!)

Paco sat down on the bed beside Vanessa, tried to twist his head upside down to look. She toppled over, slipping onto the floor.

"Look at this!" Adrian called from the ensuite bathroom. "Gold taps!"

Empty brandy snifters, sticky wine glasses littered the white gilt-trimmed bedside tables. *Señora* Hessler's dressing table was strewn with open make-up tubes and jars, hair clips, brushes, a container half-full of purple pills. The air reeked of stale perfume and cigar smoke and rancid bodies.

Carlita had gone into the walk-in closet where, at one end there was a row of evening gowns, summer dresses, at the other, suits and shirts. She came out wearing a fur stole, gold lamé high heels. Vanessa found a purple felt hat with an ostrich feather. Down at *Señor* Hessler's end of the closet, beside a long line of shoes, there was a shoebox. Inside it were videos.

Of *Señora* Hessler. They huddled together on the end of the bed, watching on the television screen as she knelt on this same bed. Naked except for two red tassels stuck to her nipples and a thong. A man's square back and round bum cheeks — Whose? *Señor* Hessler's? — came into the frame. But then Adrian punched the television's 'off' button, said he didn't want his sister watching porn.

Down the hall, in the little girl's pink bedroom, the shelves were stuffed with abandoned teddies.

The next night after dinner Vanessa's father had pushed back his chair and told them they would have to leave Spain. . .

Brigit was scrolling through related articles.

"A year later this same Hessler was found electrocuted in a hotel shower in what is now Croatia."

"No! I didn't know that."

"Suicide, they called it." Brigit read on. "It was one of those primitive showers where the heating element is right there, plugged in beside the shower stall. Hessler's wife and child and the money were never found."

"Good." Vanessa had been struggling to keep her eyes open. "Poor woman."

Brigit turned in her chair.

"But what if Hessler was killed, Van? I'm telling you, predators like Blackbeard will stop at nothing."

Out in the fuzzy reaches at the edge of her mind, Edward Sanger's voice echoed: '...Wits, guts, muscle, whatever it takes...' But scotch, wine, duckling, Kahlua, torte, dancing: there was a limit beyond which a person's brain ceased to function.

"I'm going to bed."

Something in Gran's bedroom was not right. Vanessa looked blearily at Gran's silver hair brushes still lying on the lace runner across her dressing table. There was nothing much in Gran's jewelry case — a string of cultured pearls and matching brooch, a tarnished silver pendant engraved with her and Grandad Holdt's initials — and these had not been touched. So what—?

The edge of the little area rug beside the bed was rumpled. Vanessa knelt to pull it straight and noticed that her suitcase, under the bed, lay on an angle. The little padlock had been pried open.

"Oh no. No no no, Brigit!" She pulled the case out.

It was empty.

"Oh my God, Van," Brigit sank on the edge of the bed. She had been in the living room cruising the Internet all evening, had taken one short walk, just to the end of the road. "Whoever it was must have been watching me the whole time, waiting for me to go out! When I came back the front door was unlocked and I nearly died. I knew I had locked it. But nothing was missing from the living room — the laptop, stereo, my purse was lying right there on the table and the cash, credit cards were all still in it — so I didn't think to look any further. I thought that real estate agent must have dropped by for some reason and I wondered how he could have been so careless." She looked stricken. "I'm so sorry."

Vanessa's brain felt thick.

"So whoever it was must have come specifically for the diary."

"And they knew exactly where to look. Which means they've been watching us. But who knows about Brother Bart except you, Mademoiselle and me? You didn't tell Blackbeard?"

"No, of course not! And anyway, he wouldn't—"

"But didn't you say that he came into the library kitchen the other day while you were showing the diary to Mademoiselle?"

"He only saw the metal box."

"What about this morning then, on Oak Island? He could have been sneaking around, listening—"

"The man I had dinner with would not do that." 'I have never needed to rape and pillage.' But...Vanessa stared down at the broken lock.

'Winning, pitting whatever it takes...' The thought of someone thumbing through Brother Bart's pages, leaving oily fingermarks—

The pan roasted breast of duckling reappeared at the base of her throat. Vanessa ran into the living room but the exercise book containing her translation was still jammed in among the dictionaries in the book shelf, where she had shoved it after their trip to the library.

"Thank God... But," She looked at Brigit, "how am I going to finish the story—?"

She reached the toilet just in time.

Brigit had a mug of chamomile tea waiting in the living room. "You weren't meant to discover the loss tonight. It's just lucky you sensed that something was wrong. And you know as well as I do that the only person who could have done this is Blackbeard."

Vanessa looked into the tea.

'I like to win,' he had said. And: 'Show me big business anywhere that doesn't do what Enron did.' Wasn't that what had drawn her: the sense of raw power that, refusing to be bridled, delivered all the accoutrements of beauty, grace, freedom? She saw him leaning across the table, telling her about Bacon and Freemasonry and the carved knight. He had been testing her, giving her the chance to tell him about Brother Bart. When she had not done so—

How dare he!

"I'm calling the police."

"There's no point, Van. By the time we convince them to get a search warrant Sanger will have sent Brother Bart's diary to Philadelphia to be translated." Brigit got to her feet. "The only thing we can do is steal it back. Now, tonight, before he knows that we know it's missing, and before he can send it anywhere."

## XI

A MIND'S SECOND WIND, loosened by alcohol, sharpened by caffeine, blows free of care, sees only the shape of its objective. Vanessa saw no surrounding colours, no shadows. It was 2:30 am. If he had stolen it, Sanger would still have Brother Bart's diary with him in his room. He would not risk discovery by using the hotel safe.

Brigit parked her rental Jeep halfway up the Stewart Hall drive, facing downhill, out of sight.

"The last thing he will expect tonight is us."

But to decide to take a risk was one thing. To actually do it—

Was to get even. To show him. To use this rage to beat him. To get Brother Bart back.

Still, breaking in—

"Let me know when you're ready." Brigit's hands were resting on the steering wheel.

But how could she drag poor Brigit into such danger? Even though Brigit had been the one to come up with their costumes: the lacy see-through nightie Vanessa had bought on a whim last summer, her raincoat over it, and running shoes. Tight black jeans, a low cut blouse and beret for Brigit, her face heavily made up, a splash of scotch at her throat. If anyone raised the alarm on their way up the drive, Brigit would start calling: 'Scuse me, 'scuse me? She was trying to find her way home — hick! — was there someone here who could help her? Vanessa would hide. The staff would not disturb their prized guest... But now, how to get her legs to move?

Outside the window on Vanessa's side a rabbit broke cover, bounded across the moonlit drive. Right! Vanessa opened her door.

Up through the underbrush to the rose trellis in the side garden. The few wild roses already blooming tossed their perfume into the night, luring whoever passed this way through the trellis archway into the chess kingdom. The black king's phalanx of horses, bishops, castles, pawns and the crazed Queen cowering in a corner looked as if they had been conjured by a moonlit nightmare. Brigit clutched Vanessa's arm.

"Sorry," Vanessa whispered, "I should have warned you."

Across the lawn at the front of the Hall the terrace and the dining room windows behind it were dark. So were the two big sea view bedroom windows on the second floor.

"He'll be in one of those," said Vanessa. They came back around the side of the Hall towards the kitchen at the rear. The air was as still as it gets in the small hours, the birds and bugs asleep, the grass wet with the night dew. Nothing moved.

A patch of yellow light came through the panes of the kitchen door. It was still unlocked. Inside they could hear the staff finishing the evening's dishes. They looked at each other.

"Remember," Brigit whispered, "we're brazen."

Vanessa took a breath, opened the door, moved quickly past the dishwasher, the fridges, guessing her way, trying to control her chattering teeth, trembling limbs.

"Evening, Marlena."

Brigit sidled along behind. There was a pause in the kitchen conversation, then—

"Excuse me, Miss—"

But by the time Marlena reached the kitchen door, Vanessa and Brigit were halfway up the oak staircase to the mezzanine. Vanessa put her fingers to her lips. Marlena blinked, and suddenly it was as if Vanessa had split into two people, one pulling open the raincoat to show off her nightie, winking and pointing to the two bedroom doors on the mezzanine: which one? The other watching, amazed.

The waitress pointed right. Hussy-Vanessa gave her a lascivious thumbs up. Marlena withdrew.

They needed an empty room close to Sanger. They would wait in it all night, until he left his room for his early morning run. He had rented the entire Hall so it was unlikely that he would lock his door.

"Anyway we can get a key." Vanessa had seen the hotel's duplicates hanging behind the reception desk.

They stopped outside the two bedroom doors. Was the second sea view room, beside Sanger's, empty? Yes. CEO's do not allow their servants to have equal status. Vanessa held her breath, looked at Brigit and turned the knob.

The curtains were open, the moon showing them the empty bed, a dressing table, their faces ghostlike in the mirror above it. There was a stuffy unused smell. Vanessa shrugged off her raincoat, unlaced her running shoes, tried not to breathe — there must be no sound. Then, as her eyes adjusted, she could see the closet and a painting over the bed head. It was in shadow. Just as well, no doubt.

They sat side by side on the bed. After awhile Brigit whispered:
"I have to pee."
"You can't!"
"I can't help it, Van. This always happens—"
"Well then, find some faraway bathroom. And hurry!"

Vanessa sat alone, listening to her heart pounding out the seconds. She should have gone with Brigit to show her the way because what if she opened a squeaky door, what if—

Alone, she was just one Vanessa, terrified. She came to her feet, pulled open the door, needed to be with Brigit. She was halfway down the mezzanine hallway when the overhead light came on. Sanger's driver appeared at the other end. Reading glasses, slippers, a white terry towel bathrobe made him look more like a professor than a bodyguard/dogsbody. He stopped, surprised, took in her body in the shameless nightie—

Hussy-Vanessa glanced towards Sanger's bedroom door, put her finger to her lips, mouthed the question: "Another bathroom?" as if she did not want to wake him now.

The driver pointed to a door on the other side of Sanger's. Brigit appeared behind the driver, then disappeared again. Vanessa opened the bathroom door and went in. Stood waiting for the driver to go away.

*Jane Bow*

But now there came a scuffling sound. She opened the door a crack. The driver had Brigit by the wrist.

"Yeah, well 'scuse me! I was just tryin' – hick! – to find —"

"Shut up, bitch." The driver hauled Brigit down the stairs.

Oh dear God—

Sanger's door opened.

"That you, Harvey?"

"It's okay, Mr. Sanger. Don't disturb yourself, sir."

But he was already leaning over the mezzanine railing.

"Who is that? It's not—?" He went back into his room, came out wearing a white terry towel robe — they must belong to the hotel — and went down the stairs.

His door was not locked. It would take less than a minute to slip into his room. But Brigit was being held, Sanger descending, and it was the middle of the night and now Vanessa saw Eduardo Hessler, his short, naked bowling ball body hanging—

She slipped into the second bedroom, grabbed her runners and—

"All right, I've had it!" She stamped down the stairs. "We were just trying to bring a little fun into your life, Ed—"

Sanger looked up, startled, took in Vanessa's see-through nightie. The driver was still holding onto Brigit, the telephone in his free hand, but now his attention too fastened itself to Vanessa's body.

"What the hell do you think you're doing?" Vanessa took Brigit's other arm.

"He's calling the police, Van!"

"Oh for pity sake, Ed, where's your sense of humour?" She yanked Brigit's arm out of the driver's grasp. Sanger was still staring at her nightie, but now she could see his brain switching on. "As for you, Gorpo," she told the driver, "do you want me to tell your boss what your dirty little mind's been ogling? Come on, Brig."

They were pushing the kitchen door open when the voice with the power to destroy entire corporations, to make or ruin the lives of hundreds of thousands of people across the globe, sounded.

"Just a minute."

But then Marlena appeared in the doorway.

Thank you, God. Vanessa looked over her shoulder at the two men.

"You go ahead and call the police if you need to, Ed. You know where to find us. And then, since beauty sleep seems to be your preference, I guess you better get back to bed."

Past Marlena, through the kitchen, a minute spent jiggling the back door lock open, then down through the bushes into the night.

Δ Δ Δ

They kept their hands steady enough to pour the single malt scotch Gran had kept for Christmases, then collapsed, Brigit onto the living room couch, Vanessa into Gran's wingback chair, nerves exploding.

"Oh God Van, you should have seen yourself: 'Oh for pity sake, Ed!' and 'As for you, Gorpo—!' I couldn't believe it!"

Vanessa looked into her glass, swirled the golden scotch, pride and disappointment and the censor jostling for the centre of a stage that did not seem to contain any Right Choices.

"If only I could have searched his room—"

"You should have."

Δ Δ Δ

Dream and memory often sprout from the same roots, twisting, curling, growing one into the other in that fertile movieland between sleep and consciousness: pan to a man in a black Victorian tail coat, black hair swept up into wings, with a goatee, and dead eyes: "I never lose—"

Cut to Carlita's grandfather taking them out onto the sea in his red rowboat, lowering his glass-bottomed box.

"*Mira.*" His old face broke into a million wrinkles when he grinned. "See my treasure?" Shiny blue, orange, yellow striped fish, a plump red snapper then suddenly, right near the surface, a bulbous grey jelly fish streaming poison-filled tendrils glided into view.

"The Portuguese man-of-war," said the old man, "if it wraps itself round your thigh it can make you very ill, maybe even kill you." He pointed to his eye: *"Tienes que tener cuidado—"*

Dissolve to Vanessa's father's face, a close up, jaw muscles tight as he told them they would have to leave everything they knew—

Wind rattled the window. Handfuls of rain became shards of glass shredding the image. How, she wondered on waking, had this headache let her sleep at all? Out in the living room the telephone rang.

"Good morning, doll." A low, guttural American chuckle.

"I'm sorry Ed, I really don't want to talk to you." Vanessa hung up.

The telephone rang again, again, again. Vanessa held her head. Brigit came in from the kitchen to snatch up the receiver:

"Hello... No, I'm sorry Mr. Sanger, she's in the shower... Yes, I'll tell her." Brigit hung up. "He wonders why you would come across so lovey-dovey last night then not even—"

"Did you tell him I don't make love to thieves?" Vanessa closed her eyes.

"Van listen, I've been thinking—"

"God help us, not again," Vanessa dredged up the semblance of a smile. "Because really, Brig, what do we think we're doing? How likely is it that we two are going to find a treasure that men with drills and backhoes and millions of dollars have not been able to bring up—?"

"We have to go back to the library, Van, this morning. We still have the translation and if Brother Bart's treasure is here, we need to find it now, before Sanger buys the island. That way he'll lose interest."

Vanessa squeezed her eyes shut.

## XII

"Brother Bartolomeo's journal is gone?" The library's fluorescent lights sapped the colour out of the old librarian's cheeks. "But how?"

Outside the wind had died. Vanessa watched the rain drops dribbling patterns down the library windows.

"Blackbeard had someone remove it from Vanessa's suitcase while she was having dinner with him," said Brigit. "Whoever it was waited until I went out for a walk. They took nothing else—"

"Please, I feel badly enough!" Pills were just beginning to dull the pain slicing through the back of Vanessa's head.

Mlle. Durocher stared, blinking, then gestured towards the kitchen.

"We will make some tea." As they sat around the kitchen table there was no place in the old lady's psyche for recriminations. "How far had you translated?"

"Not far enough." Vanessa took out the exercise book, then got up and jerked open the door into the library.

"It is all right today," said Mlle. Durocher. "The rain will keep the adults at home. The children will come a little later. Tell me."

Vanessa sat down again, opened the exercise book.

"Brother Bart was here, Mademoiselle, and on Oak Island," She found her place. "Remember they had taken his rings and then buried him? Well now listen:

*"Hauled up out of the earth after I know not how long, naked and pale as a grub, my eyes were blinded by the light as they washed me*

and then, dressed in someone's clean white shirt and breeches, I was inducted through an elaborate ceremony involving swords and incantations I could not follow into the pirates' secret society. An extra ration of rum all around, back-slapping, huzzahs followed. I knew not what to make of it all.

"'Goodness and love lie beyond the religions,' the advisor told me, 'You find them in your own heart. That was the real teaching of Our Lord Jesus Christ.'"

Vanessa looked up. Mlle. Durocher's head was bobbing, quick bird-like nods in time with her blinking.

"How, I wondered, did that justify the pirates' shooting people down in cold blood? But then I wondered that of You too, Father. Did you have me fall in love so that you could rip Mia out of my arms, murder the very beauty You had created? If that is the kind of God You are, I want nothing more to do with You.

"Life went on. Captain St. Clere kept going off in one of the pinnaces to explore, until one day at the end of July. The captain returned to camp so happy. He tried not to show it and there was no explanation given, but there was extra rum that night. The next day we set sail, just a short way, to anchor off one of a handful of islands on the west side of the bay—"

"The west—?" asked Brigit.

"The inland side, where Oak Island is." Vanessa returned to the book.

"I then spent several weeks cooking for an endless stream of silent men on the island. They were working in shifts, sleeping on the ships, then working again, all day and all night. Some were soaked to the skin when they came to eat, others covered in dirt. But no one knew what, exactly, was going on. Anyone caught speaking would be shot."

Vanessa's reading voice was hushed in a kitchen silence counterpointed by the clock's ticking.

"One afternoon I found myself with a few rare moments of peace. I took the liberty of strolling along the beach. I had noticed a place in the centre of the island where the terrain was lower, given more to grass and scrub than to forest. I turned inland. Jesus stepped out from behind a bush. He was holding a musket.

*"'Stay back, Brother,' he whispered, 'I am under orders to shoot.'*

*"'Why? What are they doing?' Was it Mia's people's treasure they were burying? It was the only thing I cared about.*

*"Jesus looked over his shoulder into the woods, then behind me at the beach.*

*"'I don't know, they seem to be digging everywhere,' he grinned, 'but if they are leaving gold here, we'll know where to come back for it, won't we?'*

*"Did he not realize that so would all the men, unless our captains did something about that?"*

Vanessa looked up, stricken.

"That's as far as I got."

What had happened next? The question hung in the stillness of the library kitchen. How had Brother Bart and his diary survived?

"It was a Spaniard who gave the diary to your Uncle Seamus," offered Brigit.

"That was two hundred years later."

"And pirates were bound by an oath of secrecy," said Mlle. Durocher. "To break it was to risk death."

"Which Brother Bart did by writing the diary."

The silence became a requiem until Vanessa, wriggling in her chair, looked defiantly at them.

"I'm going to get the diary back."

"Well," Mlle. Durocher got up, pushed open the kitchen door. "In the meantime there is lots we can explore." She had a tower of books waiting on the reading room table. "We have established links to Freemasonry—"

"Which could include just about anybody," said Vanessa.

"—and in Scotland the source of Freemasonry is clearly rooted in the medieval Knights Templar Society. You remember I mentioned the Templars yesterday?"

Brigit nodded. "They were excommunicated and tortured and burnt... Do you think those hands I saw on Oak Island yesterday, at the headstone, could have belonged to a Knight? If I could just get back there..."

Mlle. Durocher smiled. "You will. In the meantime, perhaps you will find your ring in one of these books."

Vanessa opened one of the volumes. The Knights Templar had built their first castle on the ancient site of King Solomon's Temple. A page of Templar symbols showed the same Star of David that Sanger had showed her on the American dollar bill, and that had been embroidered into Seamus Holdt's Freemason's apron. Mlle. Durocher pointed to it.

"The star is made of two triangles, one pointing up, the other down. You will recall that recent books make much of these: the one pointing up as the male thrusting blade, the one pointing down as the female chalice, open, waiting. But the point of the symbol is that the two triangles are linked, part of the same whole."

"Like the Taoist circle symbol where the female yin, cool, moist, passive, and the hot energetic male yang are one," said Brigit.

"Exactly," the old librarian smiled. "All the world's great philosophies point in the same direction..."

Towards something incredibly powerful. Something that defied reason and the usual defenses in a person's life, that formed the basis of secret outlaw societies people had risked their lives to belong to. Suddenly Vanessa saw herself on the Canary Island beach, the lump of tomato landing on her breast, herself looking down at it, then into Charlie's eyes as a lush new feeling erupted, deleting the need to question, to guard, to doubt, so certain had she been of the joy and the glory that came with nakedness and sunshine and Charlie in the warm sea... Something incredibly powerful—

"Love." The word had landed in Vanessa's mind. She looked at the other two. "That's why they joined the secret groups. For love."

"Love?" Brigit yelped. "Brother Bart's secret group and the pirates who shot them without a second thought were in love? With what?"

But Mlle. Durocher looked as if she had just been given a gift.

*"Oui chérie,* I believe you are right, because when does human behaviour make no sense? When love is present. The crusaders for Christ who massacred thousands of Moslems in 1099, so that the streets of Jerusalem were running with blood, these knights, who became the Templars, came to worship at the same font as the Arabs. They learned ancient eastern astrology, mathematics, sciences, architecture from them.

This is the knowledge that built Chartres Cathedral and hundreds of others in Europe and England during the 1100's. The Templars did map-making, surveying, navigation, road building. By the end of the 13th Century they owned huge tracts of land, had their own hospitals and doctors. They even knew about the antibiotic properties of mould extracts." Mlle. Durocher smiled. "Believe me, an educated Templar would have had no trouble digging the Oak Island tunnels."

"So what happened to them?" Brigit asked.

"Ah, love may have been present, but it could not conquer. The great Turkish Muslim, Saladin, finally defeated them in 1291. They had to leave the east and then in 1307 the kings of France and England, who were heavily in debt to them, had Pope Clement V order their arrest and torture for worshipping heathen eastern symbols."

The voice of her Cornish Grampa came out of Vanessa's memory. She echoed it, singing:

*"Frère Jacques, frère Jacques, dormez-vous?'"*

"That's right!" Mlle Durocher smiled. *"Frère Jacque* may have been Jacque de Molay, the head Templar. You remember," the old librarian's voice trilled: *"'Bon voyage, Monsieur de Molay. A Saint-Malo débarquez sans naufrage.'* Saint-Malo is an Atlantic seaport. According to the legend the Templars were warned that the King's men were coming. They loaded their ships with money and treasure in the dead of night and sailed them down the river to the sea. Everyone in the Catholic Empire had orders, on pain of death, to turn in any fleeing Templars but some of them made it to Scotland where King Robert the Bruce had already been excommunicated." She looked at them, her smile enigmatic now. "And who did these men worship, that caused them so much grief, but Sophia."

"The great goddess?" Vanessa was jolted out of her stupor. "I thought they were crusaders for Christ."

"Ah, here is where the water becomes deep. Because you see, over time, as they studied with them, they became very like some of the Arabs, wearing white robes with a red cord, for example. Later, when the Pope rounded up and tortured the Templars, he said it was because they worshipped a severed head called the Baphomet. And this word 'Baphomet' turns out to be an old Essene code word for 'Sophia,' which is Hebrew for 'Wisdom.'" Mlle. Durocher smiled again. "As I said, signs and symbols aside, all the world's philosophies come down to the same thing, hence the word 'philo-sophy': love of wisdom."

"And these Essenes?" The name was familiar to Vanessa. "Didn't Jesus study with the Essenes?"

"That is right. The Essenes — who also wore white robes with a red cord — were healers who believed there was no wrathful, all-powerful God, that the fountain of wisdom was within the human heart, and their message is there again and again, hidden in King Solomon's beautiful Song of Songs, in the gospel according to Thomas." Mlle Durocher's old blue eyes were alive behind her glasses. "Did you know that Jesus also went to Egypt? The Arabs, Egyptians, Essenes, early Christians, all of them knew that completeness arises out of unity of the individual with the creativity of nature, out of love, that the initiate had to die to the world, to his distractions and the tyranny of constant thinking, grasping, wanting, hating, had to be plunged into the black depths of nothingness—"

"Sounds like enforced meditation," Brigit commented.

"Or alchemy," said Mlle. Durocher. "Plunging hot metals into the cold depths."

"Gold, the heaviest, would sink to the bottom!" Brigit was excited.

"Sanger was talking about the Hermetic teachings that go way back to Egypt last night," said Vanessa. "Didn't they include alchemy? He ascribes to the Bacon-wrote-Shakespeare-and-buried-it-here theory, by the way."

"So he would have you believe." Brigit looked at Mlle. Durocher. "Do you think the initiation burial could have been an alchemical process, a transformation of energy within?"

The old lady was already nodding.

"The purpose being to find Heaven. This is the key, I think." Her voice quickened. "We know that the Bible's gospels, upon which the Christian churches are based, contain only part of what Christ was trying to teach. Heaven is in the heart, said Thomas, just like your pirates' advisor. Indeed, is this not what Buddhism, Islam, Christianity, all religions are about, *au fond*?"

"'The meek shall inherit the earth.'" Vanessa looked at them. "Brother Bart was right, Christ would have been horrified to know what's been done in his name through all the years. But," Her headache was receding, not so the cloud of despondency, "what does any of this have tell us about the treasure on Oak Island?"

"Well for one thing, the men who left the Oak Island clues, who professed to worship at a deeper level than the established religions, were users, takers, and as twisted as their ancient teachers." Brigit was tracing the wood grain in the table top.

"Ah, but this has always been the case, *chérie*." Mlle. Durocher got up. "Three hundred years before Christ Aristotle knew that alchemy was a metaphor for the transformation of leaden feelings into golden ones. Why? Because the leaden behaviour is always there. The gold, on the other hand..." The old librarian disappeared into the library stacks. She came back to hand Vanessa a tattered little book.

"Take this home. It will tell you the first story of love, upon which so much is founded: the story of Isis." Mlle. Durocher had been old for as long as Vanessa could remember, but always quivering with energy, delighting in new discoveries. Now, though, something in her seemed to falter. Holding onto the table, she let herself back down into her chair.

"Mademoiselle? What is it?"

"Oh," the old librarian shook her head, "it's just..." She looked sheepish. "All this talk of love. I have been wanting to tell you, my Robert has asked me to marry him."

"Oh!"

"When?"

"When did he ask me? Last night. I had made us a little dinner. I was so surprised. He went right down on his knee just before the coffee, and he has such creaky knees. I did not know if he would be able to get up again!"

"And you want this," asked Brigit, "to get married?"

"Oh yes!" But something — was it apprehension? — flickered behind her glasses. "It is only that living with somebody else every day will be new for me. He is English you know." Mlle. Durocher chuckled a little. "Well, originally he was. He has been here for forty-five years."

She looked at Vanessa. "Also, you have shared so much with me, *chérie*, now it is my turn. I have bought a little lot," she leaned towards them, whispering, "on Oak Island. The treasure hunters are always in need of cash and I have my savings, so a few months ago I talked to one of them... Now Robert and I will build a little cottage just down from Joudrey's Cove. No one knows about this. We will marry next weekend. Why wait, said Robert? We do not have any time to waste. We will start the building right away."

"Oh Mademoiselle!" Vanessa came around the table to hug her old friend. The old lady's shoulders felt as delicate, under the silk, as bird bones.

"When can I meet this Robert?"

Mlle. Durocher looked out the window.

"The weatherman says the sky will clear. Perhaps you two will meet us at the Oak Island causeway the day after tomorrow, shall we say at one o'clock? I will introduce you, then we will take the boat around to our new property. It will be quiet on the island and we will make some sense of all these symbols. And then," she looked from one to the other of them, "perhaps next Saturday you will be my bridesmaids there?"

"On Oak Island?" asked Brigit.

"Of course, where else?" Vanessa smiled. "Because doesn't gold stand for love?"

The rain had stopped, leaving the air heavy with the smells of fecundity and the sea. Mauve lilac, red quince and white chestnut blossoms drip-chatted with the new green trees along Gran's road. The real estate agent was parked at the end of the front walk. He rubbed his hands, excited: there was the possibility of an offer, but now a second prospective buyer wanted to view the house. There could be a bidding war. So when could he have the next showing?

Vanessa got out her house key.

"I'm sorry Mr.—?" Who was this man? Could he have taken the diary? He had a key... but how would he have known—?

"De Carlo. Frank DeCarlo, and Ms. Holdt, your uncle wants me to—"

Beside Vanessa Brigit suddenly crumpled to the ground. Vanessa's gasp was real. She knelt beside Brigit, felt for a pulse. Looked up at the agent—

"She seems to have fainted! Can you unlock the door? Brigit!"

Brigit's eyelids fluttered, swiveled to follow the retreating agent. Winked.

The agent helped Vanessa settle Brigit on the couch. Vanessa struggled to keep her voice level.

"I'm sorry," She took the agent back to the front door. "You can see, she's not well."

Δ Δ Δ

"You up for that sunset cruise, tomorrow? They say the weather's going to clear." Sanger's voice on the telephone was pleasant. As if the theft and her snub of him this morning had not happened.

"No." Vanessa looked out the window to where Brigit was wandering down through Gran's back garden to the dock. She had not heard the telephone.

"It'd be just you, me and the skipper. That's what you wanted last night, wasn't it? You and me alone?" As if he suspected nothing.

"No thanks, Ed. What I want is the return of my stolen property."

"Your what?"

Vanessa looked at the telephone receiver. Did he want her to name the diary, admit its existence, turn it into a game token? Was he a psychopath, devoid of conscience? She had recently heard on a radio program that the number of psychopathic businessmen was frightening. Or was he genuinely unaware and innocent of the theft?

He had ordered dinner on the yacht. Wouldn't she join him for just an hour or two?

"Why would I want to trap myself on a yacht with a man who steals from me?"

"Listen, sweetheart," Sanger was undeterred, "I don't know what's clogging up your mind right now but whatever it is, I think you know

I'm a gentleman. So come out sailing with me. You can tell me all about this theft. And who knows, maybe I can tell you something you don't know about Oak Island."

By the time Brigit returned, Vanessa had hung up. She would not tell Brigit about this. Because why not cruise with Sanger, let him think she was still interested? If she could get Sanger to admit to 'borrowing' Brother Bart's diary, maybe she would be able to talk him into giving it back, letting her translate it for him. And really, what was she risking—?

Your life, Brigit would say.

But that was ridiculous. What could he do to her on a chartered boat?

## XIII

THE EVENING WIND WAS A brisk westerly, the yacht a floating palace: forty feet of plush couches, crystal chandeliers, picture windows letting in the late afternoon light and the panorama of flying clouds over the white capped sea. Brigit had been out buying groceries when the yacht dropped anchor and the uniformed skipper lowered a little skiff to row into Gran's dock. Vanessa had jotted a quick note:

'Out cruising. Don't worry. Back by midnight.'

Cruise-wear in Sanger's world would involve designer track suits worn with one-of-a-kind earrings but, sitting in the yacht's salon sipping champagne, Vanessa was wearing jeans torn at the knee and a t-shirt.

Sanger offered her a plate full of green grapes and wedges of Camembert. Vanessa accepted, nibbling, smiling, trying to set a solid, equitable stage from which to question him first about Gold International's involvement in Altamira. The floor tilted as the skipper changed his tack.

Sanger sat down beside her. His arm, stretched across the back of the couch, came close but not too close. Her research of him was impressive, he said, so she should know that he had bought Gold International ten years ago, when its first British Columbia mine had started to produce. By then the Altamira Institute for Studies in Roman Ruins was defunct. He pressed the play button on a built-in compact disk player. Billie Holiday's gravel and honey blues backed the conversation with a sultry beat.

"Studies show that food tastes better at sea." Sanger plucked a handful of grapes from the plate on the coffee table, held one out to feed to her.

"Is that right?" Vanessa took the grape in her fingers, sipped her champagne.

"I think I owe you an apology," Sanger smiled. "Your little night visit surprised me. I'm afraid I was a poor host."

Vanessa watched the bubbles rise in her champagne glass.

"Maybe you'll let me make it up to you."

"No thanks, Ed." Had it come out a little too quickly? And how to keep cool with the dreaded flush rising again? Offence, that was it. Vanessa trained her eyes on Sanger. "I'd rather know why, if you wanted something from me, you didn't just ask instead of having someone sneak into my house while we were having dinner."

"You keep talking about this theft."

"Come on." But where would anger take her except into a corner? She tried to smile. "Anyway, I doubt the diary's going to tell you anything you don't already know."

The diary. Named now, its existence tangible, the word vibrating between them.

Sanger reached across to brush back a strand of her hair that had fallen forward and stuck to her cheek.

"But you can't be sure of that, can you?" Vanessa continued, "because you can't read it." She smiled again, skating strongly now, flush be damned. "I can, and news flash: finding anyone else who translates ancient Spanish is going to take longer than you'll want to wait. So why don't you give it back and let me read it to you?"

The floor tilted again. Sanger put down his glass.

"A man could start to feel a little insulted, Vanessa. A couple more days and I'm going to own Oak Island." Sanger took another wedge of Camembert. "We'll be neighbours — and I have to tell you, the thought of that makes me very happy — so why would I jeopardize anything by stealing something that's not going to tell me anything new? Also, for the record, I know there's treasure on Oak Island. I know who put it there, and I have a good idea how they did it."

"I thought Shakespeare's manuscripts were what you're after."

"True, but you know as well as I do that those holes were dug a lot earlier than the early 1600's." He held the cheese out to her. Vanessa took a piece.

"So you think more than one person buried treasure on Oak Island?"

Sanger smiled. "I also think that if you want to collaborate on this Oak Island thing, I'll say great, because it's a chance to get to know you." The skipper's head appeared at the top of the hatchway:

"Oak Island, sir, dead ahead."

Sanger poured more champagne and they went up onto the bow deck. The wind picked up Vanessa's hair, whipped it across Sanger's face beside her. Putting her hands back to trap the hair in an elastic, she saw him focus on her lifted breasts, the cotton tightening across them, and now her nervousness dissipated. It was as if she were sailing free on a stiff easterly, holding the tiller in one hand, the sheets in the other, feeling the wind's power as the boat that was her life cut through the whitecaps. Sanger was leaning on the ship's polished wood railing, looking at the sky where a last shaft of sunlight was piercing a yellow peach purple cloudscape.

"Isn't that something?" The wind tousled his hair. "The touch of God."

She stood at the railing beside him.

"So you're a believer?"

"A what?"

She shouted over the wind: "You believe in God," she grinned, "like the Spanish *conquistadores.*"

But as suddenly as it had appeared, the glory leached out of the sky. They sailed by the mess in Smith's Cove, the Joudrey's Cove bungalow, the line of scrubby trees and the pebble beach.

"Picture fireworks every colour of the rainbow lighting the night sky, every yacht on the eastern seaboard anchored right here," Sanger gestured at the sea, "around an exact replica of a Spanish galleon, except that inside there's a restaurant, a casino, entertainers brought up from New York City. On shore, where it looks like a strip mine now, picture a landscaped network of tunnels with clues—"

"About where to find Francis Bacon's Shakespeare manuscripts?"

Sanger looked at her, sardonic, appraising. Vanessa laughed.
"Won't all that cost you a second fortune?"
She watched him shrug.
"Give a paying public what it wants, set up the right websites, links, plant articles in the right newspapers, magazines, get on the talk shows, and then guarantee investors a five-year return... Then there's the potential for video and computer games—" Sanger squinted at the wall of trees lining the Oak Island shore.
"What?" Vanessa tried to follow his line of vision.
"There, behind the trees in the bush. Looked like a tent."
Vanessa looked at the island sliding by. "I don't see anything, but the treasure hunters could be working anywhere on the island." She laughed at him. "Or maybe what you saw was one of Oak Island's ghosts. Was it an old man beckoning with his crooked finger? Or a dog?"
The island slipped past their stern. He took her hand.
"I'll head north-east now, sir," The skipper, calling from the ship's wheel at the stern, pressed a button, letting out the sails. His face was expressionless. "Then we'll make for Chester Basin. It's a sheltered spot."
"Come below," Sanger's hand felt warm, firm on her back, "and I'll tell you something you might want to know."
Billie Holiday's voice was still wrapping itself around long slow notes. Sanger's arm came around Vanessa's waist. She let her body follow his dance. Why not? The closer she got, the deeper she could dig. Besides, there was a thrill to dancing free. His cheek came to rest lightly against the top of her head.
"You were going to tell me something?"
He hummed to the end of the song, then moved them back to the couch, topped up her champagne glass, raised his—
"Here's to you, Vanessa Holdt." He sat down beside her. "Tell you what, to prove how much I like you, I'll let you in on something about Oak Island very few people have figured out."
Vanessa tried not to look interested.
"The ancient Arabs, the Knights Templars — precursors of my own Freemasons — knew advanced architectural techniques and hy-

drodynamics. Just look at Plato's lost city of Atlantis, which he heard about from the Egyptians. All kinds of people throughout history have known how to work with water pressure, compasses, angles."

"Yes. And?"

"The answer to Oak Island," Sanger continued, "has to do with the sea level."

"The sea level." Vanessa sipped her champagne.

"It gets higher every century as the ice caps melt." He sat back, watching her, his arm across the back of the couch. "So several hundred years ago it would have been several feet lower."

The chandelier's crystal chimed as the boat bucked on a wave. One of Sanger's arms slid down behind her back. To stay seated would be to go with the flow, to feel his mouth hard on her own in another minute, to lie back, to let go—

"Give me a break Ed, the sea level thing is in the books. Some people think that in the distant past people lived in limestone caves that are now underwater along this part of the coast." Vanessa got to her feet, asked for the washroom.

Took a few breaths, trying to think, to order her gaggle of feelings ideas sensations fears. She looked into the mirror. The wind on deck had made her skin glow.

Maybe he's telling the truth: he didn't take the journal, she told her reflection. When she'd mentioned it he had not batted an eye and why, if he was going to own the island and could dig up every inch of it, would he need to resort to theft?

He was a taker, that was why. He wanted it all: the island, the diary, the treasure. Her.

As for her, what was the difference between what she was doing and whoring? Where exactly, with a head full of champagne, did you draw the line?

When she came back, he was standing. The liquid tones of Billie Holiday's blues closed around them as he took her hand in his. Vanessa lifted his hand to look at it but now he was moving closer, kissing her, confident that his body pushing against her, his tongue inside her, would induce her to yield.

She worked her mouth free.

"Ed?"

"Hmm?"

"First admit to me that you have the diary, by way of trust."

Instead he found her mouth again, his eyes closed, his hands moving down her back and now, as the yacht slowed, he was undoing the leather belt at the top of her jeans, unzipping the fly, pushing them down. Trapping her in the jumble of denim at her feet. She stepped out of it. And now his arms were pulling her closer again, his hands exploring her bottom and up under her t-shirt, and there was part of her that thrilled to his touch, that whispered why not? But:

"Ed wait—!"

He did not appear to hear as one of his hands came around to cup her breast.

The yacht turned up into the wind, shuddering, the salon rocking. Somewhere out of sight in the bow the anchor chain rattled. And suddenly the chaos inside Vanessa — illusions, delusions, sex, the smear of fear — cleared and she was breaking free, running up the steps, out onto the deck.

Δ Δ Δ

By the time Brigit arrived home to find Vanessa's note, the yacht was a distant glimmer of white sail against the setting sun.

Damn you Vanessa — Brigit crumpled the piece of paper, threw it onto the floor — one minute you're shut down, such a Cautious Cathy, and the next you flip right out! If only she'd carry a cell phone.

Five minutes later Brigit was pushing Dancer away from Gran's dock. Daniel had taught her to sail on Shuswap Lake and the sea couldn't be very much different, especially here in the bay where she had just been sailing with Vanessa. She would follow the yacht, to know where it was, then she'd do some sailing of her own, to Oak Island. Always follow the energy, her Indian Maharishi had told her. Even if it appears to make no sense, the energy has something to tell you. She would go back to the headstone.

The wind was strong but she had on a sweater, jeans, the red rubber weather gear Vanessa kept in the boathouse and her multi-coloured cotton hat.

Gooseberry Island slipped by and now suddenly the wind was stronger, tossing Dancer's bow up towards Heaven then dropping it. She was on too tight a tack, sailing too fast. Sanger's yacht was slicing through the sea way off to her right now, and there were no other sailboats in sight.

Ocean swells come in cliques. Murmuring grey-green waves slap the boat's hull then roll on, indistinguishable, until suddenly a leader wave rises, undulating, gathering strength.

Brigit pulled on the tiller, yanked the mainsail and jib lines free of their clamps. The wind pushed Dancer's boom and her jib sail way out over the side of the boat as the bow veered right, toward the other end of the bay. But the leader wave was a wall of water now, too close, looking down on her, blocking out the eastern horizon, flinging spray. If, rolling under her, it caught the edge of the boom she would capsize. Out here, alone.

To succumb to terror was to die in its grasp.

"Prepare to jibe!" Brigit pulled the tiller hard towards her and waited, breath stopped, fingers stiff with cold now. Jibing, she remembered, turning away from the wind, was the most dangerous sailing manoeuver. The boom, swinging with the mainsail across the boat's cockpit, had the full force of the wind behind it. Brigit hung onto the lines, did not look back as Dancer, beginning to turn, dropped stern-first into the leader wave's trough. Began to rise. The wind snapped at the mainsail, tossed the mast, tore the lines out of her hand, searing her palm. The boom flew across. Brigit ducked just in time, then lunged after the mainsail line, hauled it in, insensible to the pain in her hand, before the wave could catch the end of the runaway boom.

Dancer's stern rose higher, higher until, leaning out over the back, feet braced against the centerboard well, pulling on the lines, Brigit was nearly erect.

The wave rolled out from under her. Harmless. The wind was behind her now.

"Let out the jib. Also your breath." The sound of her voice comforted her. "Now the mainsail. Carefully."

'Running,' pushed by both wind and waves, was deceptively fast and, hanging onto the lines, Brigit felt like a tiny human link between the mighty powers of wind and sea. She was safe now as long as nothing changed. She flexed her stinging left hand. The rope burn was an angry red line across her palm, oozing blood. She numbed the pain by trailing it in the cold salt water. When finally she dared to look back, she saw the blue yellow pink sunhat that was all she had left of a special day in Boston — when she and Daniel had slurped fresh oysters out of the shells, drunk cold beer in Israel Putnam's tavern, strolled around the Trongate licking ice cream and watching buskers — bobbing up the side of a wave. After Daniel had bought her the hat they had gone back to their room to make love. Now it was a multicoloured flower bobbing on a blue-green field of water, receding. Soon it would sink, but Brigit dared not risk trying to turn back.

The bay's scattered islands reappeared on either side of Dancer. The early evening light broke the surface of the sea into patterns of gold, peach, silver on black, one leaking into the next. Ahead of her, she could see Sanger's yacht coming north now, past Oak Island, heading toward Chester Basin.

Brigit sailed in close to Joudrey's Beach just as Vanessa had done—

What was that? Something light coloured, green — a tent? — in a clearing behind the shoreline jack pines.

"Coming about!" She pushed the tiller away from her but she had not been paying attention, had thought that because the wind was lighter in here she was safe, did not know that westerly land winds are fickle, squalling then shifting directions, catching the back of a sail. Dancer tipped too much as she came up into the wind. Brigit leaned way out over the side.

"Release the jib!" She reached forward to yank the line free. The cleat did not give. The line slipped out of her hand. And now Dancer's cockpit was vertical, perpendicular with the sea—

"Lean out!" She was pulling with all her strength, trying to bring the mainsail in, to come up into irons, to dump the wind out of her sails, to stop, when a new gust filled the jib.

Capsizing happens in slow motion. The boom skidded across the water, caught the top of a wave, pulled the mast down. The mainsail lay on the water, the bailing pail floating, tied on, thank God. Brigit lost her footing and slid down into the sea.

Down, down. Her rubber-soled runners, jeans, sweater, rubber rain jacket heavy as a shroud, dragged her under, deeper, eyes open, hair floating above her, bubbles mumbling upwards. Deeper. But it was not too bad, not like the Pacific where, fall in and within two minutes your bones ached, muscles stiffened, brain ceased to transmit—

Her feet touched the bottom. Her knees buckled. She pushed off, popped up to the surface, Dancer's cockpit teetering, vertical, above her. Ropes swirled in the water. The wind whined through the top side rigging.

Do not get tangled. Do not let the boat slam down on top of you. The lessons she had learned from Daniel came back. She kicked around to the other side of the hull. The centerboard was a horizontal step, just under the water. Gingerly she clambered onto it. Stood up, hanging onto the boat's gunnel, bouncing on the board, trying to use her weight as a lever to pry the sail on the other side off the water's surface, to right the boat. Dancer was too heavy and the sail was stuck to the water and all she could hear as the wind beat against the upturned hull was the short ragged intakes of her own breathing. Her feet slipped. She hung on, tried again, again. Again. But the swell was too high and the mast was underwater now.

Should she swim back around to the other side in all these clothes, scrabble around under the teetering cockpit, in among the ropes, to find the flares Vanessa kept in the emergency kit somewhere in the bow? How did you light a flare?

Or should she leave Dancer and swim to shore? Oak Island was only a few metres away.

A skipper never leaves her boat.

A skipper who does not leave her boat will die of hypothermia in Mahone Bay in June.

"Ahoy there!" An elderly man was standing in the water at the shore, his pant legs rolled up to his knees. "Are you all right?"

"I think so, yes." Brigit was treading water, not easy in clothes and running shoes and rubber pants and jacket.

"You're not far off-shore," the man had to shout over the wind. "Can you manage to tow her in to me?"

Brigit blinked the water out of her eyes. Cold was seeping in through the rubber now.

"Okay." Two minutes later the sea bottom was under her feet, the warmth of the man's hand steadying her as she waded in. Together they hauled Dancer into the shallows, righted her, then Brigit pulled up the centreboard and they beached her.

"Why not leave the sails up, to dry?" The man's accent was British, from the north, Brigit thought. He was not much taller than she was, a stolid gnome of a fellow, the remains of his hair, wispy grey, usually combed across his baldness, now flying in all directions. And there behind him, looking impossibly different — younger, rosier — in brown slacks and a sweatshirt with a multi-coloured native print on the front, shifting nervously from one new-looking white running shoe to the other, was Mlle. Durocher.

"Brigit, my dear!" She held out her hands. "May I introduce Robert?"

In a clearing just behind the beach, where Brigit had seen the splash of colour, freshly-cut saplings were scenting the air. The tent Brigit had seen was surrounded by a carton of food, a camp stove on legs, a bundle of dry firewood, two fold-up camp chairs set out in front of a newly dug firepit with rocks laid carefully in a circle and twigs stacked in a teepee around scrunched-up paper.

"Why don't you light the fire, Lily, and put on some logs while I get Brigit some dry clothes." Robert disappeared into the tent, came out to hand her a pair of faded red track pants and matching sweatshirt still creased from the package, and woolen socks, then held the tent flap for her to go in. "You won't win any fashion prizes, but you'll be cozy enough, I reckon."

∆ ∆ ∆

Vanessa ran up to the bow, pulled her t-shirt over her head and, holding onto the jib stay, climbed the yacht's railing. The skipper was anchoring out of the wind behind Borgel's Point in Chester Basin. This was where Brother Bart's pirate ship had anchored. His burial pit must have been right there on the bluff. There were cottages on all sides now, most of them empty this early in the year.

"Hey doll!" Sanger had just reached the deck.

But poised on the ship's rail wearing nothing but her blue silk bra and thong, arms outstretched, toes gripping the polished wood as the air chilled her midriff, Vanessa felt a rush of joy. The clouds were so close, if she reached up she could touch them. Twenty feet below the sea was playing with the remains of the pink and mauve early evening light, winking at her. How long since she had felt so feather light, so free of thought—

"Vanessa!" He was moving towards her when her body rose, balancing on the balls of her feet while her eyes picked their point. Then her knees flexed, sprang and she was flying. Time stopped. Until, arcing now in descent, she pointed her fingers, thumbs hooked together, and cut cleanly through the surface of the sea.

She came up gasping, rolled over onto her back, grinning, ignoring the water's icy fingers.

Up on the deck Sanger and the skipper were leaning over the railing, looking worried, annoyed.

She laughed. "Come on in!"

Her stomach, as she turned over again to swim, was numb — it was, after all, still early in June — but the shore was no more than a hundred metres away. She began to stroke, face in — it was faster — head turning, reaching for breath. But now her arms were stiffening in the cold. She could no longer feel her feet. Her pace slowed.

∆ ∆ ∆

Brigit had been fine in the water, all her attention keyed to surviving, but now, sitting on a log by the fire, Robert's faded red sweatshirt down to her knees, his track pants bunched at her ankles, she realized she could not feel her feet. Smoke swirled up into the wind as Mlle. Durocher poured water from a pot she had boiled on the camp stove into three mugs of hot chocolate powder. Brigit could not get over how different she looked here.

"So there I was, standing up to my waist chopping saplings when I looked up." Across from her in one of the camp chairs, Robert was wearing his pajama bottoms, his ankles white above running shoes that looked as new as Mlle. D's. "And there was a sailboat, heeling, heeling. 'It's Dancer!' Lily cried. We watched you go over."

"Vanessa is not with you?" Mlle. Durocher handed them each a mug.

"No, she's... out cruising with Sanger." Brigit pulled her knees up, hugged them. The fire crackled, flames dancing crazily in the wind. She started shivering again as above the trees the sinking sun painted the bottoms of the clouds a dusky last minute pink. The shadows were deepening but she got up.

"There's something I came to do," she looked apologetic. "Now, before it gets dark."

Mlle. Durocher and Robert walked with her down to the beach where Dancer was chattering in a wind that cut through Brigit's sweatshirt. She looked out at the darkening sea. Vanessa was out there.

"Would you allow Robert to accompany you?" asked Mlle. Durocher.

Brigit looked embarrassed.

"It is all right. He will not speak if you don't want him to, isn't that right, *mon amour?*" Mlle. Durocher smiled, knowing, understanding. "I would like you to be safe."

Brigit was afraid she would cry.

The treasure hunter's boat was not in Joudrey's Cove. They walked up through the twilight, past his bungalow.

"Vanessa says this land used to be swamp, till they drained it," Brigit said. Robert was so gentle. It was nice to chat. "When they did, they found all kinds of things: part of a wooden runway, what might have been an ancient gold branding iron, the hinged piece of a chest, part of a ship's gunwale, drilled stones and markers, even a heart-shaped stone. But you probably know all that. This can't be where the treasure is, though." She glanced around into the twilight. "Still, the guy who bought this land from the original finders of the treasure shaft, Anthony Graves, lived right here. He never took the slightest interest in treasure hunting but Vanessa says he paid for his groceries with doubloons. Interesting, eh? What we're looking for is a place where the limestone part of the island ends." She pushed into the undergrowth. "Come on, I'll show you the headstone."

Scents of spruce and sea and the coming night; Brigit walked ahead of Robert, slowly, stopping, listening, then walking on, her body a diviner's rod now, quivering, pointing, the images so vivid, so clear by the time they reached the headstone.

The skin on the hands chiseling the headstone was rough, reddened by chilblains, fingers not short. It was the whole hand that was small. The whole man was small, dark, smelling of pine resin, a man from an era much older than Brother Bart. He was concentrating, worried. Alone. There was something near here, she could feel it. But not right here.

Robert was standing a few feet away when Brigit stood up, turned her head towards the east, then towards the west, along the lines of the cross's arms. East-west: the axis of the mind. East led to Joudrey's Cove. West?

Swamp, trees thick now: fir, spruce, oak, beech, aspen. Alders, chokecherries crowding between them, blooming white. The trace of a path wove through the shadowy undergrowth. Mosquitoes and no-seeums buzzed past her ears, landed on her neck. A road, overtaken in places by weeds, wound along the shore behind South Cove, on the island's landward side. To their right, just down the shore near the causeway, the lights were on in the treasure hunter's bungalow.

The sea lapped at the stony shoreline here. And now Brigit heard the rattle of bygone bulldozers, men in hard hats moving rocks, behind them other smaller men disappearing into the sea, a chaos of images superimposed.

Robert stood on the rocks pointing along the shoreline to where a cedar was tilting towards the water, its roots straining to keep it from falling in.

"Erosion." He looked at Brigit. "I wonder how much that's changed this shoreline in the last four hundred years."

Brigit looked stunned.

"Erosion?" And then saw, suddenly. "Erosion, of course!" Cedars, pines, birch trees lost their footing in a wind, uprooted the earth. Snakes, crabs, beetles, worms toppled with them into the water. Winds and the rising and falling tides teased them loose until finally they floated off to some other beach where they became white sun-bleached tree bones. You could see them on any of Vancouver Island's beaches. And no longer anchored, the earth and stones they had left behind slid down into the water. New green shoots sprouted in the opened earth. Hundreds of years ago what was now sea would have been land.

"You there!" Two men were standing on the road near the treasure hunter's bungalow. Robert pulled Brigit back into the undergrowth.

Δ Δ Δ

The skipper must have recognized the signs of hypothermia and lowered a dinghy because now Vanessa was back in the cabin. Edward must have taken off her dripping underwear, toweled her down, ordered an electric heating pad — her skin was cold as a corpse's — tucked her into the queen-sized bed in the bow, given her something to drink because everything, voices, memory, thought, fears, all her senses were muffled now, as if by cotton batting. She closed her eyes, saw a knight riding a horse, a white tunic with a red cross worn over his armour, visor down, face hidden: a saviour or a predator?

And now, look! Here were Carlita, Paco, Adrian and Santi hiking with her a few days before Vanessa's family had left Spain, up a stony path that led through the olive grove on the lower reaches of *La Montaña,* the rib of rock behind Altamira. A few people still lived in *La Montaña's* creases, in caves, their painted wooden window frames and curtained doorways set into the dusty mountainside. Faded blue and red and white cotton shirts and pants and nightgowns flapped on lines stretched between poles set into the hill as they passed by.

*"Donde van?* Where are you going?" A grandfather, crooked as the branches of his olive trees, called out from his stoop.

"To the stone hut at the top."

*"Cuidado niños."* It was August. "The temperature is high enough to fry an egg on the rocks."

The heat wrapped itself around them. Sweat trickled down past their ears. No one spoke. The path, a narrow goat track, crisscrossed the face of the mountain as they climbed. A donkey and a few skinny goats munched on the tufts of grass struggling for sustenance among the rocks and dust and a few scrub bushes.

Finally Santi and Adrian, who were in the lead with Paco close behind, called a halt. The path ended just above them at the foot of a ten-metre tower of yellow-grey rock. All you could see beyond it was the sky.

Far below in the ancient Altamira market square ant-sized people were milling about. Down by the harbour the fishing nets were spread on wooden frames to dry. There, drawn up at the end of the beach was Carlita's Grampa's red wooden dory, also the others, blue, green, brown, that had gone out on the tide at dawn while the sea, azure against the sky, broke into innocent lacework at the shore. Vanessa imagined the galleons laden with treasure lying just offshore, and Santi's and the other great-who-knew-how-many-times-great grandfathers rowing out in their dories under the cover of night—

"Why do the boys always think they're so great?" Carlita was sitting down, licking her finger to paint a face in the dust on the canvas top of her running shoe.

"What?"

Carlita spat on her finger, started on the other shoe top.

"They always think we'll do exactly what they decide, even if it's stupid."

She was right. When they were alone Paco would come and take Vanessa's hand, make a present of his smile. But as soon as the other boys were around it was as if Vanessa did not exist.

"We don't need them," said Vanessa. "The stone hut must be up behind that rock." To their left the pitch was nearly sheer. To their right the scree was steep, but a few bushes had found purchase. Tiny white flowers held the ground between the stones.

The idea came to both girls in the same instant. Jumping up, they edged out onto the scree.

"Don't look down," said Vanessa.

Carlita called to the boys: "What are you waiting for?"

Vanessa was concentrating, digging the inside edge of her soles into the shale, testing her weight, Carlita's breathing close behind her, when a sickly sweet stench reached her. Thumping beat the air right over her head. She looked up as something huge, brown, swooped too close, its wings blocking out the sun, its talons dragging, glistening sharp. Vanessa flung up her arms to cover her head as two of the largest birds she had ever seen sailed out over the mountainside towards the sea.

"Owls," said Santi. Their brown tails were fan-shaped, tipped with white.

"That smell," Carlita wrinkled her nose.

"Rotting flesh, mouse carcasses probably, or rabbits. They'll pluck up a baby, then bring it back and rip it to shreds—"

"Stop it!" cried Vanessa.

"Their nest must be up there, behind the cliff." Adrian made his way to the girls, watching with them as the owls paused over the valley, riding the updrafts. Such grace!

"They must be hunting," said Adrian.

But the owls were not hunting. They were circling back, coming in straight and low, so fast, their wings silent, so close suddenly that instinctively Adrian shoved Carlita and Vanessa down. Both girls lost their footing, began to skid, half sitting down, hands scraping across the scree, faster, rolling onto their stomachs, searching for something to hold onto, until finally their running shoes hit the path at the crisscross below.

They were standing, bent at the waist, knees, hands, chins scraped when Adrian slid down to them:

"Nessy, Carlita, I'm so sorry! Are you hurt? I didn't want them to get you..." He looked as if he would cry.

Vanessa searched the sky. There was no sign of the birds.

"Owls." Her father confirmed, sitting on the end of her bed while she told him about it.

"They were beautiful."

"Predators usually are." He had sounded so tired…

Now Vanessa wriggled deeper under the duvet in the yacht's master bed. Safe now, as long as she stayed asleep, she would just wait, ride this bed to wherever it was taking her.

∆ ∆ ∆

When Mlle. Durocher's white Oldsmobile pulled up to the house, Sanger had the key in the lock. His free arm was around Vanessa, who was standing but looked limp. Brigit slammed the car door.

"Excuse me!" She pushed past him to face Vanessa. "Van are you all right?"

"Brigit?"

"What happened?" Brigit opened the door. Watching as Sanger brought Vanessa in and deposited her in Gran's wingchair, she was unaware that, her hair standing in salt spikes, her red sweatshirt three sizes too large, she looked like a demented pixie.

"She took it into her head to go for a swim." Sanger's voice was polite. "God alone knows why."

## XIV

THE DAWN'S FIRST GLOW SHOT across the silver-black sea and was gone as Sanger jogged down the Stewart Hall driveway. He turned right onto the coastal highway towards Chester.

Vanessa Holdt was a beautiful maniac. Certifiable.

Not. Sanger turned right again, off the highway down towards Chester's Back Bay. She's been playing you, Teach, coming to dinner, dancing with you, letting you know she will be yours, just give her time. Coming to you in the night even, wearing that sexy nightie. To screw with your mind, man. Calculating, cockteasing bitch. Champagne, sunset, big bed bobbing on the evening tide: she had been interested. Oh yes, he'd been around long enough to know a woman's pleasure when he smelled it. And her body was so smooth, so ready—

So what in hell had she been trying to prove by jumping into the freezing Canadian sea and then smiling up at him: "Come on in!" Was she trying to give him a hard-on or a heart attack?

Sanger's feet struck the pavement in time with his breathing. Sweat dripped off his chin. The breeze along the bayside road carried the scent of lilacs. Above his head chestnut trees shielding some of Chester's prettiest white clapboard houses were clouds of white orchid-like blossoms. Ahead, past the cenotaph, a little road led out onto the peninsula where her house was.

When Vanessa's little pixie bitch friend had pushed past him last night the red sweatshirt she was wearing had smelled of salt and smoke. From where? The white Olds she had gotten out of belonged to the librarian. Which meant that—

Christ where had his brain been? Vanessa, her friend and the librarian they spent so much time with were plotting against him. Sanger's feet pounded the road.

So let them scheme. By the end of today he'd own Oak Island. He should go up to the house now, bang on the door. Vanessa would open up, stand there half asleep in her nightie, so surprised, and before she could say anything he'd come right in. Get her into her bedroom, lock the door, take a handful of that nightie and do what he'd planned last night, what they had both wanted. Shut her up with a kiss before the pixie bitch disturbed them and this time there would be no "Ed?" No polite backing off.

Sanger's breath was coming in short bursts now.

Her breasts were so round and full. She'd be shocked but she'd love it and the pull of his lips would turn her nipples into little soldiers. He'd bend her over the bed, away from him, bum up and maybe he'd be a little rough. Some women liked that. And it might remind her that nobody plays Teach and wins.

Ahead on his right, past a clump of bushes and an overhanging maple, was her front walk and the For Sale sign.

The door opened. Sanger stopped. Watched the pixie bitch close it quietly. Turned away as she came down the front walk towards a rental Jeep parked in the road. He jogged back the way he had come.

Christ, was the pixie bitch Vanessa's guardian angel?

Your guardian angel more likely, Dumb-ass, because think it through. You want to wind up in a Canadian criminal court?

He turned right at the cenotaph, up towards the bay on the other side of town. Pixie Bitch would not drive this way.

The road back to the highway was uphill. Good. He pushed himself. Get a grip, man. The woman has been blinding your mind, clouding your vision from the get-go. He increased his speed. Get the blood flowing up instead of down for Chrissake.

The deals he had made yesterday had secured his ownership of all of Oak Island — except one lot. Last night one of the treasure hunters had admitted to selling it last month to the librarian, had not told him for fear of skewing the sale, damn him to hell. Still, the librarian's purchase offer had been accepted but the sale would not close until the day after tomorrow. The treasure hunter would own the lot until it did. So stop being distracted by a siren's golden hair and silky body. Talk the treasure hunter into closing your deal now, today. Then let the old lady fight it out in court, if she can afford to. In the meantime who would stop him from putting a fence and gate across the whole approach to the causeway, from forbidding any water access? The highway ahead of Sanger leveled out, a short respite before the last push up the driveway.

Back in his room Sanger blotted his face with a towel. He had a meeting set for Monday morning with the government players in Halifax. He would show them signed deeds of purchase. And if they asked to sponsor a federally controlled archeological program on his land?

No problem. Deliver it in a nice tight time frame and he would cooperate.

Ownership of all treasure found by the program to be held by the people of Canada?

Sure, just give me a guaranteed tax exemption in return. Sanger chuckled. Because by the time the bureaucracy had finished churning out the necessary forms, what two-bit Canadian government archeologist was going to dig up anything that Sanger wouldn't already have taken out of the ground?

As for Vanessa Holdt and her little conspiracy—

Inspirations, solutions come in flashes. Sanger lifted the telephone, gave his morning orders. Then, humming, he headed first for the shower, then downstairs where a masseuse and his breakfast were waiting.

△ △ △

The dawn's first glow shot across the silver-black sea and was gone as Brigit pushed the duvet back, swung her legs out of the bed. She could not sleep. "You could have been killed!" she had shouted last night, once Blackbeard was out of the way. "Just what kind of a menace have you become, Van, first throwing things, then jumping off ships into the freezing ocean?" Vanessa had always been the careful one.

Now she was a derailed train running full tilt, all communication lost. So how could Brigit sit across from her sipping morning coffee as if nothing had happened? Also, she looked at her hand. A thin pink scab had formed across her palm, the skin around it taut, sore. How could she not admit to taking Dancer out and capsizing her? Although Vanessa would find that out soon enough, when they met Mlle. Durocher today.

Brigit pulled on a heavy woolen sweater and jeans and tiptoed out to her car. She would use this early hour to sneak onto Oak Island, to sit by the headstone again. Yesterday the energy had been immediate. Today she would focus on it, and on erosion, and see what came.

Mlle. Durocher's boat was padlocked to the jetty. Brigit was standing at the causeway, screwing up her courage to run across, when a man came out of the treasure hunter's bungalow, walked over to the old museum building and disappeared inside. Damn! What was he doing up this early?

Brigit took a deep breath. Everything that happens in life has a part to play in the whole, that's what the Maharishi had said. So what was the meaning of this? She looked at the sea, still rippling black on this mainland side of the island. Another hour would pass before the light reached it.

"Erosion," Robert had pointed to the Oak Island shoreline there, at South Cove, beyond the treasure hunter's bungalow. She was turning away when the answer came, sudden as the glow across the dawn.

Of course! Erosion, of so many things. Brigit moved off into the weeds facing the island, sat down and crossed her legs, closed her eyes.

∆ ∆ ∆

The dawn's first glow shot across the silver-black sea and was gone as Vanessa lay dreaming of her Dad leaning over her shoulder, poring over the pages of the diary with her, both of them so happy—

Until something percussive — a bird striking the window? A branch knocking? — snatched away sleep.

A note from Brigit was leaning against the kettle. 'Meet you at the causeway at 1 pm.' Last night she had been so angry. Vanessa pulled her bathrobe closer, made tea, took it in to sit, legs tucked under her on the couch: alone.

Again. Alone with a full, spent, lunatic's moon hanging just above the treeline on the other side of the bay. Was that the real reason she had gone sailing with Sanger? Because when you are alone what is there left to lose?

Still, she could not help smiling a little at the memory of flying off the yacht's railing. Free—!

Of what?

The thrust of Sanger's kiss, the power of his desire, the strength of the purpose in which he'd lost himself, her fear.

Face it Vanessa, all men — Ed, Brigit's Daniel, Charlie — attracted women for the purpose of getting what they needed. 'I love you,' Charlie had told her. And meant it. But what exactly was love, to him? Breasts, a vagina, a sense of humour: men used women to salve their wounds, replenish their energies for the ongoing take-what-you-can battle they called making a living.

So now here she was again, sitting on one of life's park benches, pigeons pecking at her feet. Alone.

Don't fight the pain, Brigit would say. Don't try to rationalize or make sense of it. Don't make a plan. Just breathe: in, out, sitting still, hands in lap.

Sorrow Grief Fear gathered strength, tightened her jaw. In... Pain building, squeezing the cords in her neck, knotting her stomach. Out: echoing, shaking her bones, rattling her teeth. In...

Cresting. Out—

Breaking into white plumes of memory:

The Altamira fishermen's widows, dressed all in black, were statues standing at the end of the beach beside the red blue green fishing dories drawn up on the sand, staring out at the careless sea. The wind teased their black wool skirts, plucked at their shawls but still, waiting for the husbands who would never come home, they did not move. If you crept close, you could see in their eyes that they had removed all but their bodies to some other place. In...

Out: Now Vanessa was back in her classroom in Spain, dirty windows gummed shut, uniformed students confined to their seats, working silently in the heat because the nuns would tie you to your chair if you misbehaved. In...

Out: When her father had brought the family back to Canada Vanessa had gone to a high school where teachers assigned group work, nobody checking to see who was concentrating and who was wandering, exchanging notes, making dates. There had been no strappings, no expulsions. No nothing. Failing, lying, raping, killing: everything here in Canada happened behind closed doors, in boardrooms and bedrooms in the dead of a winter gale while the television blared and shoppers streamed, glassy eyed, through the malls. In—

Where was the passion, the real, the cruel, the glorious mesh of mind and voice and body—?

Return to the breath. Meditating is not thinking. Out:

Passion, on a Canary Island beach five years ago. On Brother Bartolomeo's Columbian mountainside four hundred years ago:

*Could there be a greater sweetness? I could not bring myself to believe that such gentle loving, the touch of her fingers light as a butterfly's wings, such towering, shuddering, monumental joy was wrong.*

Love as passion, was that what she had lost with Altamira, and again with her father's death, and finally with Charlie? Passion: the spark that ignites life, that pours colour into a page of research, immortalizes as memory the moments you share with someone you love. 'Gold stands for love,' Grampa had said. That's why it was there in all the stories.

But where was passion here? In the gold that lay buried on Oak Island? Was that why everyone who went there got caught up in the Oak Island hunt, treasure hunters sinking their fortunes into it, losing again and again, sometimes even their lives? Because somewhere inside themselves they knew that the source of life was what they were looking for?

Greed, Brigit had sensed 'layers upon layers of it' on Oak Island. Was that why the gold had to stay buried?

Thinking again. Breathe: in...

Out: Waves of thought pushing, tails of thought tugging: she watched them, trying to stay her course, to link heart and mind, to reach the fishermen's widows' place, the still centre. But trying was thinking, wanting— 'Don't try,' Brigit had told her the other day on Oak Island, 'Just breathe.' In...

Out: Surrender. Thoughts are electrical impulses, let go of them. In...Out:

*I lay very still, listening to my breathing. Pictures came: Mia in the meadow. I felt her body, her love, and how I cried. Then watched again as the pictures rose, then faded. A life lived.*

Everything in life is connected, Brigit said. Brother Bart's diary had been waiting here in Chester and she, Vanessa, had been the right person to find it, to know how to translate it, how to do the research—

Thinking. *I lay very still.* In a grave the pirates had dug for him: a Chamber of Reflection, the Freemasons' symbolic coffin watched over by the skull — the ancient Baphomet, Wisdom — and by two crossed human bones, the dark place in which, immobilized, silenced, they must enter the dark terrain of their own interiors, must search beyond prayers and plans and weapons for the place where 'purification came through unity of the individual with the creativity of nature—'

Thinking. In...

Out: thoughts dissipating now. Into no place, a light place. In...

Out: "...The story of Isis," Mlle. D.'s voice: "The first story of love."

The book had been lying on the coffee table, forgotten, since yesterday afternoon. Vanessa opened her eyes, abandoned the meditation. She did better with books.

Isis, Osiris and Seth were all descendants of Egypt's Atum, 'the complete one' who, rising out of the Nile, was symbolized in the pyramids. Isis loved the virtuous Osiris who was the first king of Egypt. One day Seth, who was jealous of Osiris, had him measured while he slept, and then had a sarcophagus built to fit him. At a feast Seth offered the richly adorned coffin to whomever it would fit. When Osiris lay down in it, Seth had his men nail the coffin shut and sent it off floating down the river. Isis searched all over the earth for her beloved Osiris. When finally she found him in the sarcophagus, she was so happy that a son Horus was conceived. Isis then hid Osiris in some marshes while she took Horus to a relative.

In the meantime Seth, who was out hunting boar, found the chest with Osiris in it and tore his body into fourteen pieces which he threw away. Isis found all the pieces except the phallus which had been swallowed by a fish. Fashioning a wooden penis for Osiris, she fanned her bird's wings over him, bringing him back to life. Horus grew up to avenge his father, but in battle with Seth one of his eyes was torn out. When finally he triumphed over Seth, Horus found his eye and gave it as protection to Osiris, who became Ruler of Eternity.

"The bond between Isis and Osiris is the creative force of life," Vanessa read, "for together they represent the universal soul. He is the flooding of the Nile, she is the earth the Nile covers, the 'Green Goddess.'" Horus, their son, was worshipped by the Egyptians for thousands of years.

Vanessa's thoughts tumbled one into the next.

The forces at work in nature and in human love were exactly the same. The active, thrusting male energy in all humans was virtuous but also prey to the desire for gain, for the golden sarcophagus. It could not, then, see beyond the confines of what resulted. The fertile female energy, meanwhile, would go to the end of life itself in order to find and receive the love for which she yearned. And the ancient Egyptians had figured all this out five thousand years ago!

Love: the creative force of life, the feeling you got when a butterfly danced across the afternoon light, when a tiny violet caught the light in the woods, when a Beethoven sonata reached into you. When you looked the right man in the eye, love rearranged the shape of your universe.

Interesting about the loss of Osiris' phallus. Did the Egyptians equate machismo, greed, vulnerability to destruction with the male genitalia? And yet without the mighty phallus there could be no physical connection, no 'flooding,' no new life.

A photograph of Osiris showed two large painted eyes above him: the eyes of Horus, who was the product of perfect love. The eye on the American dollar bill. Above a pyramid.

Vanessa clasped the book close to her in excitement, remembered the smile with which Mlle. Durocher had given it to her.

And Seth? He represented the opposing principle to Osiris, blind force, unregulated, unpredictable, ungovernable, everything that was destructive, that diminished life or took it away, ripped out what was: storms, lightning, and in people—

Hitler, Saddam Hussein. Her own arm flinging Flamenco Dancer.

"Seth has to be mastered, continually brought into the rule of the good..."

Vanessa jumped up:

I get it, Grampa! Love, the force of growth: golden wheat growing by the Nile, golden love. Now if she could match the Oak Island clues to the thinking of the people who had laid them... Vanessa looked at her watch. The Halifax library would open in an hour. She would have plenty of time to drive there and back before one o'clock.

## XV

THE LIBRARY WAS NEARLY EMPTY this early in the morning. Vanessa settled at a computer terminal at the end of the open stacks, under the window. Bringing up the Google search engine, she heard her father's voice, the way she always did in research libraries and archives:

"The more specific you can be at the outset of your research, the deeper you can penetrate your subject." Vanessa typed in "Isis+Osiris+Horus" and clicked on Go.

"Here's to you, Dad."

Horus' eye, given as protection to Osiris, was called the Eye of Eternity and although Alexander the Great had conquered the Egyptians in 332 BC, the story of Isis' love had lived on, hidden in the Greeks' secret Eleusinian Mysteries and later in King Solomon's songs. Born of perfect love, the seeing eye appears in cultures around the world: as the eye of the Hindus' Vishnu, the eye of the Christians' Holy Spirit, the seeing eye Sanger's Freemasons, whose roots went back to the Knights Templar, had put on the American dollar bill, above the pyramid, which was triangle-shaped. But what was the connection to Oak Island?

Vanessa recalled the ancient knight carved into the cliff down the coast, and the ancient foundation that had been discovered at New Ross, up the Gold River which emptied into Chester Basin, where she had taken her swim, and where Brother Bart's pirates had camped. She typed "Scottish Knights Templar+Pope Clement V" into the computer.

"This one's for you, Grampa."

The Templar cross appeared on the screen. "The Scottish Knights Templar continued to exist after Pope Clement V's purge, led by their Grand Master William St. Clair—"

St. Clair. A different spelling, but the same name as Brother Bart's captain! Vanessa hot-linked into a history of the St. Clairs:

William The Blond of the Norman St. Clere family had been the first—

There, the French connection: St. Clere, the same spelling as the name of Brother Bart's pirate captain.

Something — a tremble of air, a ripple through the library's silence — made Vanessa look over her shoulder. A man in a beige windbreaker, with a night's growth of whiskers sprouting, was standing right behind her at the end of the stacks. He was absorbed in a book.

Vanessa stared at the computer screen. 'He's Blackbeard's man,' Brigit would declare if she were here. And then she would do something. Suddenly Vanessa became two people again, one paralyzed: shut up, put a lid on it; the other one clicked out of the site she was reading, then got up, went over to the man, raised her voice:

"Excuse me." Whiskers turned his head, blinked. Vanessa smiled. "Forgive my bluntness, but what are you doing here? You're obviously not reading."

The man said nothing.

Vanessa returned to her computer. The websites the last person on a computer has visited are not difficult to trace. Vanessa clicked through a series of home pages, laying a false trail through sites on protein supplements, abdominal exercises and the origins of the expression Fuck You. Then, turning off the computer, gathering up her books, she repaired to the women's washroom downstairs where she sat marveling at her brashness. What if she was wrong and he was just some poor mature graduate student getting away from his wife and baby for a few early morning hours to study?

When she doubled back to peek through the stacks, Whiskers was sitting at her computer. 'Coincidence:' a word used by people who did not know any better.

So who was the bastard? Ed's lackey? Some unknown third party?

No unknown third party could have known about the diary, and why would anyone take an interest in what she was doing here unless they did know?

She saw Ed kissing her, no longer hearing. Greedy.

So? Aren't we all greedy? Why else was she here?

The only person in the technology section was the librarian. Vanessa turned on a computer and called up the Scottish Templars again. The door opened. Vanessa could see, in the reflection on her screen, who had come in.

Fear, a close cousin of greed, knocks everything else out of the mind, destroys concentration and the fragile tendrils of new thought, erects crude scenarios of what could happen—

Vanessa forced herself to stare at the screen. Clicked away from the site she had just entered.

Whiskers took a seat at a table across the room and began to read a magazine.

Vanessa slapped her hand against the top of the desk.

"That's it, I can't do this anymore." Her voice startled the librarian, who was sorting request forms behind the counter. "This man," she pointed at Whiskers, "has been following me all over the library, eavesdropping on my research."

The librarian's rabbit eyes darted from Vanessa to Whiskers. Behind him, through a doorway into the closed stacks, Vanessa could see a desk. There was a computer on it.

"I'm sorry Miss," the librarian whispered, "but I don't see what I can do—"

Vanessa leaned close to whisper back.

"Look, this creep frightens me. Do you think you could give me access to a secure computer?" She nodded towards the doorway behind him. "Nobody else is in yet today, right? Could I go in there?"

"Oh no." The librarian's head shook. "I'm sorry."

Whiskers turned a page in his magazine.

"Please? I've got to get this research finished. I only need to check a few more websites. Please?" She tried to smile. "I promise I'm not a hacker or a terrorist. You could come with me. Just for a few minutes? He's followed me all the way here from Chester and I'm scared. Please?"

The librarian took a thousand years to look her over, weighing the relative consequences, then finally he stood up:

"Ten minutes." He led her through a doorway marked 'Employees Only' to a cluttered desk set in an enclave surrounded by metal floor-to-ceiling shelves stacked with books, video tapes, CDs, boxed disk sets. Vanessa sank into the chair.

"Thank you!"

"Yeah, well I could get fired you know." But in here, out of the public domain, amongst the shambles of his desk life, he had power. With it, as he turned on the machine, came magnanimity. He tilted his head towards the door. "Did you cover your tracks out there?"

Vanessa grinned. "Yes."

A tinge of colour came to life in his cheeks.

"I'll go back out. Keep watch for you."

Vanessa resumed her search, took notes:

1. The Templar who had sailed to Nova Scotia was a Scot called Henry Sinclair, Earl of Orkney. By 1398 trade was taking place across the Atlantic. North American buffalo furs had been appearing in Florence long before Columbus sailed, and Greenland ladies were wearing the latest fashions from Burgundy.
2. Henry Sinclair had crossed the Atlantic with a fleet of twelve ships. He had taken with him two hundred men-at-arms, Knights Templar, soldiers, carpenters, shipwrights, sail-makers, armourers, and Cistercian monks, who were farmers. Apparently he was planning to found a new Templar empire.
3. Henry Sinclair was exploring the wilderness coast to the south of Nova Scotia when his best friend and fellow Knight, James Gunn, died. Henry had his men carve a huge outline of a Knight Templar in a rock face on what is now the Massachusetts coast.
4. Henry returned to Scotland in 1400 and was killed by English marauders the same year.

Vanessa stared at the words. If Henry had come to Nova Scotia to found a new Templar Empire, why had he gone home again?

Mlle. Durocher's voice came to her: "With history you must think it through, Vanessa. Put yourself inside the skin of the one you are researching."

Brother Bart's St. Clere was looking for something. And the Templars had fled France with a huge treasure. Was that what Henry had brought here? Or was it the books of Templar wisdom? But if Henry Sinclair had felt the need to bury something ninety years after the Templars were dissolved, why wouldn't he have done it back home, on one of his own remote Orkney Islands off the northern coast of Scotland, where he could keep an eye on it?

Because the treasure and the books of knowledge would have been priceless and the Orkney Island waters were swarming with Vikings. Also, someone might have talked.

Someone had talked. How else had Brother Bart's Captain St. Clere known to come looking here? And what had he found? What had happened to Brother Bart? If only she could have finished the translation.

Vanessa scrolled through the St. Clere site. Maybe there would be a picture. There was. An ancient Templar ring, flat topped, had an insignia: two knights mounted on one horse.

Outside a brisk west wind had come up. The sun was shining but a tower of grey cloud was building out over the sea to the east as Vanessa slid into the traffic flowing south.

"Gold stands for love."

The Templar, Henry Sinclair, who had come to Mahone Bay in 1398 was connected to Brother Bart's pirates. However, carbon dating of the Oak Island finds put the treasure much later, in Brother Bart's day. So, had Brother Bart's pirates liberated the Templar treasure from Oak Island? But they were already carrying Brother Bart's treasure.

Mlle. Durocher's voice: "If they found what they were looking for, they would have had to leave something behind…"

Vanessa checked her rear view mirror. No sign of Whiskers.

Could she have been wrong about everything that had happened in the library? Because if Whiskers was Sanger's flunky, it meant that Brigit was right. Edward Sanger was Blackbeard: Seth. What else, therefore, might he do?

Ahead of her, the traffic slowed. Vanessa took her foot off the accelerator, glanced into the mirror again and there, moving in from the other lane, two cars behind her, its grill glinting in the sunlight, was a no-name blue car with Whiskers at the wheel.

Vanessa slowed so that the car behind her would pass. Then, braking hard, she dared Whiskers to hit her, to give her an excuse to get out, to go back, to call the police, have him charged. He came very close. She watched his jaw tighten, his body jolt, but his car did not touch Gran's old Ford. She wished she had time to slow to a crawl, to keep him here all morning, to see where he would turn off, but she needed to get home, to review her notes. When they reached Chester, she gave him the finger. Whiskers stayed on the highway.

Vanessa slammed on the brakes, did a U-turn, re-entered the stream of highway traffic just in time to see Whiskers' blue car pull off at the turning into Stewart Hall.

Δ Δ Δ

She spread her notes on the dining room table.

Now focus. Forget Whiskers, Sanger, the loss of the diary. Maybe Brigit was right about energy. She had been driving peacefully, mulling over her research, thinking with love about Grampa. But on the sight of Whiskers' po-face in the car behind rage had consumed her, malevolence a contagion as silent, as destructive as any bacterium.

To expunge it from her mind was the only way to reach the place where the treasure was. Because somewhere between the Scottish Templars, Brother Bart and the Oak Island discoveries lay the key to this puzzle, every nerve ending was telling her so. She took Gran's exercise book out of the shelf, found the place where Brother Bart described being buried:

*A grave had been dug, lined with sail cloth, roofed with logs too heavy for me to shift. Resting on the top of it was a human skull, below it two crossed bones... I lay very still, listening to my breathing.*

*Pictures came: Mia in the meadow. I felt her body, her love, and how I cried... My breathing slowed. I listened to it, completely empty now of thought or prayer or plans or hope. Peaceful at last in my grave.*

Then:

*Hauled up out of the earth after I know not how long, naked and pale as a grub... I was inducted through an elaborate ceremony involving swords and incantations into the pirates' secret society.*

*"Goodness and love lie beyond religions," the advisor told me, "you find them in your own heart. That was the real teaching of Our Lord Jesus Christ."*

And:

*I then spent several weeks cooking for an endless stream of silent men on the island. They were working in shifts... Some were soaked to the skin when they came to eat, others covered in dirt.*

Looking for something, and leaving something that required a lot of burying. There was just enough time to make another list:

| Symbol | Meaning | Oak Island |
|---|---|---|
| 1. Triangle | way to divinity, creation pyramid | stones shaped like a sextant |
| 2. Skull, crossbones, coffin | mortality Chamber of Reflection The Baphomet/ Sophia/ Wisdom | headstone |
| 3. Cross | innocence, life four directions linked: an action line, a mental line | granite boulders at Joudrey's Cove |
| 4. Hourglass | time running out | pirates' flag |
| 5. Seeing eye | Eye of Horus, created out of perfect love… | |

Vanessa's pen paused. The seeing eye, five thousand-year old symbol of love's creativity, printed on every American dollar bill, sewn into great-Uncle Seamus' Freemason's apron... and the pirates were Freemasons, and the Templars, their forerunners, had known architecture and engineering... the seeing eye... Vanessa scanned her list, sketched a quick map of Oak Island, put in all the spots where clues had been found.

The doorbell rang. Vanessa stared from list to map. What if the Oak Island cross was the four directions, and the place where the lines intersected, the headstone, was where the creative power saw into the roots of life... the skull with the cross bones beneath it? And what if she extended the lines of the cross? The doorbell went on ringing, twice, three times. Whoever was there had no intention of giving up.

"God damn it!" Doorbells, phones, faxes, television: the fishermen's widows had not had to contend with any of that. *"Silencio!"* Mother Superior's roar had threatened to quash life itself in her Altamira classroom. And in the ensuing dusty minutes, disturbed only by the ticking clock, a cry from the marketplace, squealing brakes down the block, ideas could take shape and ripen, dreams, knowledge, passions could blossom—

"What?" Vanessa flung open the door.

Sanger's bodyguard/driver held a bouquet of roses, carnations, iris, lilies, hyacinth, baby's breath in one hand, in the other a gold coloured gift bag. Vanessa took them and closed the door.

In the bag was a flat lingerie box done up with a burgundy bow. There was a card attached: 'To replace the sea soaked set. I'll pick you up at seven tonight. We'll celebrate my new island purchase, then maybe play some chess. Teach.'

"Fuck you, Ed." She was about to fling the bag aside but something else was weighing it down. Vanessa tossed the lingerie box onto the coffee table, reached in again. And knew before she laid eyes on it, from the weight and feel of the ancient leather, that she was holding Brother Bartolomeo's diary.

"Oh!" Forgetting all the prohibitions about the contact of skin with ancient materials, she held the diary against her as if it were a kidnapped child returned, opened it, riffled the pages, made sure it was all there, unharmed. "Oh thank You God or Sophia or whoever You are, thank You thank You thank You!" She sank onto the couch.

So Sanger had taken the diary. Had detailed someone to watch Brigit while he entertained Vanessa, waiting for the chance to come into her home, to steal from her. And was returning it now. To gain the trust she had asked for? Trying, by admitting the theft, to negate it, reduce it to the status of 'borrowing'? Because she had jumped overboard, risked her life rather than be with him? He had not had time to have it translated. So what was he telling her?

There was no time now to think or to sit with the dictionaries, do a proper translation of the rest of Brother Bart's story, but she knew the rhythms of his voice now and the cadences he favoured. For now she could puzzle her way through what had happened to him.

In spite of the danger, Brother Bart's curiosity about the pirates' work on the island was not to be denied:

*I need to know what is being done with Mai's people's treasures. Are they melting down those stunning golden panels, turning them into gold bars, easier to bury? Men will die before I will allow this. What other path is open to me? The loss of love leaves a man a shell, empty, hollow. I could, I suppose, turn back to You, Father, devote every waking hour to prayer, but You made both the beauty of the connection between Mia and me and the destruction that killed her. You are beyond this simple monk's ability to know, not to be reasoned with, reckoned with, pleaded to, trusted. I think now that Captain St. Clere's advisor is right, there is so much more to worship than the dogma out of which my paltry life has been chiseled.*

*So I spend my free time walking and watching, sauntering along the shorelines in the evenings after the last dish is dried, and up any number of paths as if to gather herbs and blossoms for my salads, twigs for our soups. It is not difficult to circumvent the sentries and why, I wonder, do some of the men return from their shifts wet and others do not? I watch from the undergrowth as the men measure and dig and move stones under the watchful eyes of Captains St. Clere and DuMoulin. If anyone ever does catch me I will look Captain St. Clere in the eye:*

"Rings of love must not become the stuff of barter or a pirate's conceit," I will tell him. "If there is a God whom you love, you will return my rings to me." That I may be buried with them. What else have I to care about now?

Though I must confess sometimes I do fear a little. That is why late at night in the supply tent on the island, where I sleep beside the stove, or in the early dawn hours I write to You in this diary. I may not know You after these forty years, God, but I have grown fond of this conversation even though any form of communication is strictly forbidden here. If anyone finds this diary I will be hanged the way two men were just this morning, all of us forced to watch, because they had been caught with—

Vanessa struggled with the next words, skipped ahead:

... In the meantime however, having watched and thought and made a few calculations of my own, at least I can console myself that the light of Your sun will always reach my Mia's people's treasure once a day, just as it always used to.

The light of Your sun? Vanessa squeezed her eyes shut, then rechecked the words: *'sol:'* sun; *'tesoro:'* treasure; *'una vez al dia:'* one time a day: *'...the light of Your sun will always reach my Mia's people's treasure once a day.'*

The same sun that was sending a shaft of light down through the clouds above Mahone Bay now could show them where the treasure was? She put down the diary, rubbed her eyes. How could that be? Was it in a limestone cavern like the underwater cave the treasure hunter had found under Borehole 10X, where they had taken the video picture of the human hand...

A limestone cavern above the water line.

Why not? They had been found in this area, where the tides had swirled up over millions of years. Sometimes the ground above them was thin as an eggshell. Like Sophie's Cave-In Pit.

But if the treasure was close enough to the surface for the sun to shine on it every day, why hadn't one of the dozens of treasure hunters who had been tearing Oak Island to shreds during the last two hundred years found it?

Mademoiselle should see this. Vanessa jumped up, knocking the lingerie box from the coffee table onto the floor. Absently she pulled off the ribbon. Inside, a cream silk underwire brassiere, the kind that sculpts the breasts, with lace across the top of the cups, and matching panties lay on a bed of baby blue tissue. Vanessa closed the box, embarrassed. Opened it again — who was watching? — passed the silk between her fingers, looked at his card again: '...my new island?'

Had he bought Mlle. Durocher's property? How could he have? And if he had bought the rest of the island, how could he not know about her lot? Vanessa looked at the telephone.

No, it was past noon, too late for that. She would see Mlle. Durocher at the causeway.

Nerve endings signal each other much faster than thought. Vanessa could not have told you why, after she pulled off her jeans to change, she also shed her underpants and bra, then ran back into the living room, pulled on the silk panties, hooked on the new brassiere. The gold doubloon was lying on the coffee table. She hung it around her neck, then found a tank top. Her khaki cargo shorts had pockets deep enough for her list, the map she had made of the Oak Island discoveries, a pencil.

## XVI

Traffic on the coastal road was blocked. Vanessa's thumb beat the steering wheel as cars and trucks came to a halt ahead and behind her. A little way down the highway a column of black smoke billowed into the sunshine. Windows of the stores, bungalows, businesses were gaping wounds, the glass blown out by an explosion. Sirens had been signaling the arrival of the fire brigade for the last several kilometres. There was no way to get through or turn back. Vanessa pulled onto the shoulder and got out.

A stench of burning oil seasoned with something putrid-sweet clutched at the back of her throat. Her eyes smarted. An ambulance was parked at the gas station but the paramedics were not hurrying. By the time Vanessa arrived the fire fighters were dousing the spiky black ruins of the building. The gas pumps were stumps. Angled across the tarmac, its nose smack up against one of them, was a dripping black car chassis. Near it what had been a pickup truck was a charred skeleton of steaming steel.

A fat man in green overalls was holding a bandana against his nose and mouth. He shook his head at Vanessa.

"I was standin' at the diesel pump fillin' my truck when she comes cruisin' round the bend, a big Olds', white, and it looked like the car was drivin' itself, the driver was that little. Then this car pulls out to pass her but there's a truck comin' the other way, see? So she swerves right to make room but," his voice shook, "she musta lost it when her wheel hit the gravel 'cause she kept on comin' right into the station, right at me and the look on her face—" His big body was trembling.

"I tell you, I near pissed my pants. She come sailin' in not two inches from my bumper and I'm yellin' and runnin' for my life, round behind the building 'cause I could see she was gonna hit the pumps. She tried to brake and I seen her face all panicky, hands wrenching the wheel, but then whoosh!" He looked away, then back at Vanessa. "There was a man in the passenger seat. Roasted alive, the both of them."

Heat rose like a nightmare from the pavement, rippled the air.

It must be some other white Olds. People keep them forever—

No. Mademoiselle and Robert had been driving to meet her and Brigit at the Oak Island causeway. Mademoiselle's happy laughter: 'Robert got down on one knee…' And 'I have bought a lot—'

"Where's the car that passed her?"

"Didn't stop. Bastard." The man stuffed the bandana into his pocket but he was in no hurry. To leave would mean resuming his normal life, to have to go on as if the roots that kept him upright had not been shaken loose.

"What colour was it?"

"Um…" The man scratched his upper lip. "Couldn't say for sure. I was pumping my gas, see, and it happened so fast… Blue maybe?" He watched with sympathy as the young woman beside him turned, shoulders heaving, to lose her breakfast at the edge of the parking lot.

An arm came around her shoulders.

"I was coming to get you," said Brigit, "I heard the explosion all the way down at the causeway."

Litter on the ground at Vanessa's feet, gum wrappers, bits of fly-away newspaper, crushed pop cans, skittered in a squalling breeze that, full of the cloying odour of burning flesh, must surely be the smell of hell. She looked at Brigit.

"If she hadn't been coming to meet us—" Vanessa's body began to shudder.

"Easy, Van."

"Blackbeard wrote me a note this morning. He said—" She could not shape the words.

There was a coffee shop down the road. But inside voices were vying, rumbling, whispered details rising and falling: who had been where when the explosion happened, how much it would cost to fix the front windows, when the hell was the government going to stop letting old folks drive, how many more could have died. Vanessa looked at the people — overalls, greasy baseball caps, bottle-yellow perms, waitresses delivering plates loaded with eggs, bacon, homefries, patrolling with the bottomless coffee pot as if the evil that had produced this 'accident' was nothing more than grist for the morning's conversation.

Brigit got up.

"We'll walk." Outside the relentless sun still shone. Clouds scudding east across a blue sky were already sweeping away the oily black smudges at the top of the column of smoke.

"He must not even have asked her to sell," said Vanessa. "He knew she was friends with us, Brig. If I hadn't got involved with him... You both warned me—"

"Stop." They held each other. The traffic would not unsnarl for hours. Turning away, they walked down the shoulder of the coastal highway. When finally she could speak about it, Vanessa told Brigit about Sanger's presents.

"He returned the diary?"

"Yes."

He must have planned this, giving even as he was in the act of taking: the diary in return for Mademoiselle's life. The smell of Hell followed them down the road.

Δ Δ Δ

A highway sign pointed to the right, inland:

'New Ross 25 kms.'

"That sign used to annoy Mademoiselle Durocher every time she saw it," said Vanessa. "Remember her talking about New Ross, where they found earthworks of what may have been a Templar castle? But: 'If you were a Knight Templar landing in Nova Scotia in the 1300's,' she always used to say, 'why would you build your castle twenty-five kilometres inland? Why not close to the bay, where your ships were?'"

Vanessa turned left on impulse, down a side road away from the highway and the stench of smoke.

"I was going to tell her about the new clue I found in the diary." Vanessa told Brigit about *the light of Your sun will always reach Mia's people's treasure once a day.*

"The light of the sun? So it's close to the surface."

It was hard to care.

The road wound down to a large bay. The land on the far side of it, to their left, rose into a bluff. Cottages dotted the shore.

"This is Chester Basin, where I jumped overboard." Vanessa pointed to the bluff. "That's where the pirates must have buried Brother Bart."

A little peninsula jutted out of the coastline in front of them, a tiny cove curving around on the near side of it. The tide was out, the smell of seaweed drifting across the water from the scrap of beach where a large cone-shaped granite boulder sat just above the water line.

Up in the trees to their right someone had built a house. Wrought iron gates, wedged open, had not been moved in years. Brigit slipped through them then scrambled down to the sea, out of sight of the house. She was running her hand over the stone when Vanessa joined her.

"How weird that it should have been placed here."

Vanessa just stood there. When the tide came in it would cover everything except this rock, but now Brigit slithered around the seaweed and mossy stones to find another granite boulder further around the point. A third one sat alone at the seaward edge of the water. From this side it looked conical, but actually it was long, an animal squatting, waiting to pounce.

Vanessa turned back. Oak Island, treasure, the meaning of clues so obscure no one could decipher them, in the end why did any of it matter? In the schemes of life and treasures and death only death had any staying power.

A small cemetery up a little hill on the inland side of the road overlooked Chester Basin. An ancient oak tree stood watch by the gate. Brigit climbed the steps. Vanessa, following, found her bending over the most prominent tombstone.

"It says: 'Joudrey.'" Behind it another, older stone was black with lichen, the chiseled letters partially erased by the weather. Brigit rubbed it with the palm of her hand.

"Look:

Henry P. Sellers
Born 1838 Died 1912 74yrs.

Wife
Sophia Sellers
Born 1844 Died 1931 87 yrs."

"Sophie Sellers was the daughter of Anthony Graves."

"The guy who never cared about the Oak Island treasure but paid for his groceries with gold doubloons?"

"Right."

Brigit gazed at the tombstone.

"And whose daughter is buried right across the road from cone shaped boulders like those of the Oak Island cross, in the very same bay where you and Mlle. Durocher imagined a 14th Century knight would build his castle, and where Brother Bart was initiated into the French pirates' secret society four hundred years ago." She looked around. "Would this be a good place to honour Mademoiselle?"

"Honour her? How?"

Brigit chose a spot beside the Sellers' tombstone, facing the sea, and patted the ground beside her. Vanessa sank onto the grass. Brigit crossed her legs, closed her eyes, put her hands on her knees, palms facing up, fingers touching. Vanessa sat watching, numb. What did this morning peace have to do with exploding glass and burning bodies just half an hour away?

"Close your eyes." Brigit waited until she did so.

"Dear Mlle. Durocher..."

So skinny in her fake silk blouse with the make-up on the collar, always so happy when Vanessa came through the library door.

"We want to thank you for being a wonderful friend to Vanessa and..."

Her pale blue eyes lit with humour, mischief, intelligence, annoyance behind her glasses: *'Ah chérie,* the history we read is only the part the conqueror wants us to know.' Her new sheepish happiness with Robert—

"We hope that you did not suffer—"

Her burnt, blackened bones—

Vanessa's body began to shudder. Brigit took her hand.

"Let it come, Van."

Solar plexus, chest, neck, body an earthquake now, shattering the cemetery peace, sucking in the gathering wind, the trees, the water, the clouds. Until all that was left was a scoured, tinny emptiness. And the sound of Brigit's voice, struggling not to break.

"May peace and happiness be with you and Robert now, Mademoiselle. May Vanessa treasure always all that you have given her. And may we both take up and carry your marvelous courage."

The breeze played across the grass, hushed through the oak tree's new green leaves. A gull shrieked. A squirrel chucked.

Vanessa stood up. The sea, the little peninsula, Chester Basin bluff still looked the same but now she caught a sense — no more than a whiff, gone almost as soon as it arrived — that something inside herself, something beyond 'good' or 'bad' or any words, something movable, changeable but hard, non-negotiable, that had been there all along but pushed away as unacceptable, was coming alive. She looked out to sea.

"Will you come with me down the coast to Oak Island? It's not that far and we'll be the last people Blackbeard will expect. I want to find the spot where the light of the sun shines every day. For Mademoiselle."

## XVII

Sanger's limousine was parked just this side of the chain across the causeway. The bodyguard/driver was reading the sports section of the newspaper.

"Harvey?"

He looked up in surprise.

"Is Edward over there?"

"That's right, miss."

"Well don't call over," Vanessa moved towards the chain. "Let me surprise him."

"I don't think that would be wise, miss. Mr. Sanger does not like to be disturbed while he's doing business."

"Oh." Vanessa looked at her shoes, lost in thought apparently, then back to the driver/bodyguard. "And what about you, Harvey, I bet you don't like to be disturbed either when you're doing business for him, going into people's houses to swipe things, hiring spies, taking care of all the messy details."

"I beg your pardon, miss?" The driver's face was blank.

Vanessa stepped over the chain.

"Don't look back." Vanessa did not break stride. "If Gorpo makes the call and they come out of the treasure hunter's bungalow, leave it to me." She did not know what she would do, only that the new force coming awake within her felt powerful as a tidal wave. If she could harness and control it...

No one appeared.

"They must be touring the sites."

The road wound around behind the dilapidated museum to run down the centre of the island to its eastern end where the diggings were. The wind picked up the sound of engines, scattered it among the trees bending and whispering above their heads.

"We better get off the road," said Brigit. "Come on." She seemed to know her way. "There's something I want to show you at South Cove — they won't be able to hear us in the woods."

South Cove: the place where treasure hunters had found the second intake tunnel, where just offshore the government oceanographers had found a hole in the floor of the sea. Vanessa gazed out over the tumble of rocks at the sea, but—

What did she think she was doing? Mlle. Durocher was dead. Beside that, what did anything matter? Her father and Gran were right, Oak Island was dangerous, a place of greed, a hoax—

'Oh? How then do you explain...' Mademoiselle's faded blue eyes snapped at her. 'How many times must I tell you, Vanessa, think it through...' And 'We will make sense of these symbols...'

Brigit must have been reading her feelings.

"There's evil here, Van."

Vanessa nodded.

"But like my Maharishi used to say, evil will always be here. Our job is not to let it cloud our minds, to keep ourselves pure." She put a hand on Vanessa's arm. "For Mademoiselle's sake."

"Right."

The mainland was no more than several hundred yards across the water from them. Vanessa told Brigit what Sanger had said about the rising sea level.

Brigit explained erosion:

Erosion = change = new growth in a changed landscape.

Behind them the wind brought the sound of an engine coughing, from the direction of the treasure shaft.

"Natural erosion takes millennia, but any disturbance of a shoreline speeds it up." Brigit looked at Vanessa. "Just like human behaviour, don't you see? Greed, the need to have more and more, dams up the natural flow of people's energies, twists their motives, causing all kinds of destruction."

Like Mlle. D.'s death.

"That's why those who knew this always hid their meanings in symbols, to protect against the erosion of human values. And that's why greed has been forever condemned to roam above the ground on Oak Island, every one of its shafts and dams flooded, caved in."

"Like Seth." Vanessa told Brigit the story of Isis and Osiris. Seth, unregulated violence, destruction: Sanger murdering to get his way. How quickly it spread, contaminating everyone it touched. Unless it was harnessed.

Vanessa scanned the surface of the sea beyond the rocks, looking out to where the undersea hole was supposed to be.

"So it's a matter of uneroding."

"Right. All we have to do is reconstruct the way it was, then see how the symbols fit together."

Vanessa dug into the pocket of her shorts, came up with the map.

"I'm thinking maybe the lines of the cross show the fault line where the limestone on the island ends. There could have been caves as well as sinkholes—"

"What about the treasure shaft, was it a sinkhole?"

"No, the sides of it were clay," said Vanessa.

"Even though it was on the limestone end of the island." Brigit looked over her shoulder. The engine across the island was running now, and there was a clanging sound. "What do you think they're doing?"

"I don't know. Not chasing us, anyway." Vanessa told Brigit about her visit to the library in Halifax. "The Templar knight who came here was called St. Clair, which stemmed from the French St. Clere—"

"Cool!"

"And we know the Knights worshipped an older wisdom represented by a severed head—"

"Called Sophia. Wait," said Brigit, "Sophie Sellers! I wonder if her father, Anthony Graves, knew this stuff."

Vanessa had taken out her list.

"So what if the cross they found here has nothing to do with religion. What if it has its ancient meaning as a symbol of life?"

Vanessa took a pencil out of the pocket of her shorts. Brigit watched as she drew a straight line, extending the right arm of the cross diagonally across the island, past the edge of the swamp, through the opening of the flood tunnel drains here, where they were standing, at South Cove, into the ocean between Oak Island and the Mahone Bay shore, past the underwater hole. Mlle. Durocher had told them it was surrounded by piles of stones.

"North-south," said Vanessa, "isn't that the action line?"

They looked at each other.

"And there's been erosion," breathed Brigit.

"And the rising sea level. Sanger said it would have gone up a few feet—"

"So the hole could have been above ground?"

"It's pretty far out, if this drawing is to scale. But there's been a lot of work in this cove—"

"And it's on the shore side of the island, across from the mainland, so the water was probably quite shallow to begin with. So what if Henry Sinclair walked the treasure into the underground hole? But then why mark the place with piles of stones?"

They looked at the sea that knew so much. If only the water rippling could speak. Behind them, across the island, the motor ground on. And now there was the sound of another engine, a vehicle. The road looped around the eastern end of the island a few metres behind them. Vanessa and Brigit looked at each other.

"If he finds us..." said Brigit. "Who knows we're here?"

"Only his driver."

"So what do you want to do?"

"Kill him."

"No. Better to nail this sucker. Now, for Mlle. Durocher."

"And Brother Bart."

"And Mia."

Vanessa looked out at the water, heard it chuckling at the stony shoreline.

"The hole that's in the sea now was just above the water level. What if the natives told Henry St. Clair that it would lead him into an underground cavern?"

"Too obvious. If the natives knew about it, it wasn't safe enough for treasure."

Vanessa nodded.

"What if the hole was between the high and low tide levels?"

"So the underground cavern was full of water."

"Right: a perfect hiding place if you could seal your treasure in watertight containers—"

"Or could find a sinkhole leading up from the underground cavern to above the water level—"

"Which would have been much lower way back then."

"But how would they breathe in there?" Brigit wondered.

A new idea birthed itself. Vanessa smiled at it.

"Through a system of hidden air tunnels."

"Air tunnels! Of course! What everyone's been thinking were flood tunnels could have been above the water level then—!"

"Their exits carefully hidden—"

"And none of the men who dug them would have had any idea what they were for. Henry would have marked the sinkholes' rough locations on the surface, then dug the tunnels towards them."

"And as a Templar he would have had the engineering knowledge to do that."

"Sure. Think of the pyramids in Egypt. Mademoiselle was right: basic engineering is hardly new."

"So Henry and his close friend and fellow Knight James Gunn could have crawled along the air tunnels to the sinkholes—"

"Maybe built wooden bridges across them—"

"Or tunneled up into the clay above them."

"They could also have tunneled off in any other direction without ever disturbing the surface. They could have swum the treasure in then up through the sinkholes, or they could have dragged it through the tunnels, whichever way would be less obvious, because the key must have been to keep the utmost secrecy."

"They also could have split the treasure, then hidden it in separate places, and then left markers only Knights would understand. That would explain the Cave-In Pit, except nothing was found in the Cave-In Pit—"

"Nothing that we know of." Vanessa kept running her eyes over the bush behind them and down the shoreline to the treasure hunter's bungalow. Nothing moved. Behind them the vehicle engine was silent. The other one went on growling. Vanessa went back to her list.

*"Where the light of Your sun will always reach.* The seeing eye is the key, Brig."

"Wait, what about the coconut fibres they found at the end of the tunnels?" said Brigit. "They were dated much later. As are the oak beams in the treasure shaft. And Graves found Spanish doubloons. So, either we're wrong or someone else was here too."

"Brother Bart's Captain St. Clere."

"So Brother Bart's pirates brought the coconut fibre and built the treasure shaft. That fits the carbon dating. But if St. Clere knew about Oak Island, maybe even the tunnels, why did he dig the treasure shaft?" Brigit wondered.

"By then the hole and the stone piles and maybe the tunnels were under water."

"And what did he find? What did Henry Sinclair hide, the Templar gold, the archives of their learning, the severed head?"

"Brother Bart's Captain St. Clere found whatever it was, and left Brother Bart's treasure buried here."

Brigit nodded, thinking.

"Wait, if the cross is a sign of life, and the skull, symbol of mortality, is also a severed head, the Baphomet, symbol of Sophia, Wisdom, let's say the headstone is the skull that lies on the coffin, symbol of the Chamber of Reflection. Remember the picture?"

"And below it on the coffin are the crossed bones..." Vanessa looked at her, "also a symbol of mortality. They found a boulder partway down the stem of the cross. Could that have marked the crossed bones?"

"The head — Wisdom — and the crossbones — Death — and between them on the cross' east-west line, the mental line —"

"The seeing eye, the Chamber of Reflection into which an aspirant must go in order to learn to see!" This thinking together, rolling the thoughts one into the next, into unexplored territory, was a roller coaster ride on which the knowing just happened because they were on the right track. Vanessa could feel it. She thought suddenly of a pre-eminent symbol of both Templars and Freemasons: "Look at this." She drew four dots, centered three more above them, then two, then one:

```
        •
      •   •
    •   •   •
  •   •   •   •
```

"The tetraktys." said Brigit.

"Now watch." Vanessa connected the outside dots to form the triangle. It pointed up. Then she added a dot to each end of the second line down, turning it into a line of four dots. She put a third dot under the baseline of four dots, and then connected the new dots to make a second intersecting triangle pointing down. The two triangles became a star:

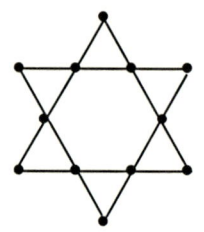

"The Star of David," said Brigit.

"Also known as Solomon's Seal, symbol of the perfect harmony a human can achieve," said Vanessa. "The upturned triangle stands for spiritual, the down-turned one for physical energies—"

"And the richness is in the stillness at the centre, at the union point of body and soul!"

"Of Isis and Osiris... Did you know that Solomon's Seal is also the name of a wildflower?" said Vanessa. "Gran has some in her garden."

"So maybe the headstone, symbol of both Sophia and the skull, is the centre of the line that goes out to make the top two points of the star, and the cone-shaped boulder they found partway down the stem of the cross is the place where the line for the bottom two points of the star goes out."

They looked at the star.

"And the Chamber of Reflection, where the initiate learns to see the perfect connection between body and soul, would lie at the centre of the star," Vanessa pointed at the central dot, "halfway between the two."

"The still centre, completely unmarked in any way." They looked at each other.

It was brilliant. They turned back onto the path into the island's interior.

"What about the swamp though, Van? Only the eastern end of the island is limestone."

"In Henry Sinclair's time, six hundred years ago, when the sea level was low, maybe there was no swamp."

"But when the sea level rose the water came up from underground—"

"Through sinkholes. There could be limestone underground—"

"But if that's right, why didn't the swamp fill again after the treasure hunter drained it?"

"Maybe all the digging and blasting blocked off the tunnels and sinkholes."

"Another thing," Brigit took the map out of Vanessa's hand, "what about the dimensions of the cross? They don't look right for a Solomon's Seal—"

"That could be because we don't have all the markings. All kinds of cut stones and markers have been found but no one's been able to make any sense of them."

"And," Brigit was still gazing at the map, "now I'm thinking, maybe the tunnels form a labyrinth, Van. You know like the one at Chartres Cathedral?"

"Which was built by the Templars."

"They built a labyrinth into the floor, it's a circuitous path — it looks a bit like a brain — leading to guess where? The centre of self, the home of love. So that too would put the treasure at the centre—"

"Where the seeing eye of the *sun will always reach it once a day —*"

"In a cavern roofed with stones, something that lets the light in when the sun reaches a certain height. I know where we can get an axe, Van. The centre point may be covered by grass now, but under it there'll be an opening."

"Imagine if the treasure's right there!"

"If it's not, it's sure to be close."

The grasses bent on the wind, caressing their ankles, tree limbs swayed out of their way as they ran, stealthy as deer, back through the woods to the place where they had left the road.

The pickup truck must have been just a few metres away, the whine of its engine snatched by the wind until it came around a curve in the road. Brigit leapt into the underbrush.

Vanessa did not think, did not decide to stay there, standing in the middle of the road. Passion, rage, freedom, truth make their own choices, and the truths here were that Vanessa had loved Mlle. Durocher and the old librarian had challenged Edward Sanger.

The truck stopped. Sanger stepped out of the passenger side. He was carrying an axe. The burgundy golf shirt and khaki slacks he was wearing looked immaculate even in the dust. Sweat popped out on Vanessa's skin, trickled down her sides. Her face felt hot.

"Vanessa, doll! There you are." He looked around. "Where's your friend?"

So Gorpo had called. Sanger was very close now. One arm came around her, strong, hard, warm. She smelled his impatience. He would put her in his truck, find Brigit, take them both off the island. Vanessa looked at Sanger's axe.

"What are you going to do with that?"

But, steering her towards the pickup truck, he was not listening.

"Ed, wait." She turned away, out of the view of the truck's driver.

"My friend Mlle. Durocher is dead." She tried to watch him — to divine whether he was a murderer as well as a thief — but the fact spoken aloud threatened to crumble her power. What if she started to cry? Sanger would put an arm around her, take her back—

"I know, I heard," he said. "Tragic." As if it were a news item, nothing to do with him.

Vanessa's fingers found the doubloon around her neck.

"Brigit has gone back to the car but I wanted to—your deal can wait a few more minutes, can't it?"

Give Brigit a chance... 'I know where we can get an axe—'

Vanessa pulled Sanger off the road, slipped his hand up under her tank top, watched as his face registered pleasure. But he was also checking his knowledge inventory of her, calculating—

She moved closer.

"I just wanted to say thanks," chewy, plasticine words, "for returning the diary."

He gave her the easy amused look she had first encountered at their Stewart Hall dinner:

"You're welcome." And then, opening her mouth with his lips, he pushed in his tongue, filling her as if her forgiveness was a given — he tasted of oranges and spearmint — then left her to walk back to the truck, to speak to the driver. The engine revved, the wheels spitting stones. Overhead the pines creaked and sighed in the wind.

He came back, put down the axe to lift the tank top over her head.

"Oh my." Leaning down, he kissed her nipples through the silk, leaving a wet circle. The power inside Vanessa turned to rage. She struggled to cage it.

"I just have this one chore, doll." He picked up the axe. "Then we'll go on home."

"What chore? Why don't we just—"

But he was pulling her with him now, down through the trees.

"There's a clearing down here. Remember that tent I saw from the boat?"

It was light green, and there was a stove. Beside it several early tomatoes had been set out to ripen in the sun. A paperback book about Oak Island lay on a stump. Was it Mlle. Durocher's?

Sanger leaned the axe against the stump and held back the flap, smiling:

"Go on inside."

Let him take her here, then leave her, his seed spilling out between her thighs while he used his axe to demolish all traces of Mlle. Durocher's ownership? Then took her back to Stewart Hall, another treasure possessed, to dress, to feed, to have sex with. Vanessa backed away. Down through the brush, at the beach, she saw a sail boat: her own Dancer, pulled up above the tide line!

Who except Brigit could have sailed it here? While she was out cruising with Sanger. Was that why she knew where to find an axe?

Sanger's hand fastened on her arm. Vanessa shook it off, ran down to the boat. The sails lay in an untidy heap in the cockpit. The wind snatched at Vanessa's hair, raised goosebumps on her bare stomach.

"Come on!" she called. "Let's go for a sail."

Brigit, are you watching? She would take Sanger right off the island, do whatever was necessary to give Brigit time to find the Chamber access point—

Sanger did not move. She came back to him, sidling close to kiss his neck.

"Come on, Ed. There are seat cushions stored in the bow. We'll be more comfortable—"

He shook his head, held her against him.

"Please, Ed."

"Come home with me, darlin'." He nuzzled her hair, both his hands running up her sides, down her back, closing on her rump as he bent to suck at her neck.

"No." She twisted out of his grasp and danced away. His expression sharpened.

"What is this?"

But where rage is the propeller caution does not stand a chance. Vanessa struck a model's pose: tall, arms akimbo, breasts jutting.

"I just don't want to go back to that stuffy hotel, Ed. I went out yachting with you. Now it's your turn to do it my way." She began to push Dancer down the beach and once again it was as if the Vanessa she had always been was watching this new one whose mind seemed to have untethered itself now from reason's tiller, to be riding free. He crunched across the beach and she saw him thinking: a crazy lady? Or—

"Come on, help me push."

Waves were running in on the wind, breaking against the back of the boat. She saw him calculating risks versus return. She unzipped her shorts, let them drop onto the pebbles and spread her arms, felt the wind stroking her back as she stood before him wearing nothing but the cream silk brassiere and panties he had chosen for her, and the doubloon.

"Do you still not get it, Ed? I tried to tell you the other night, I need to be with someone who's willing to play a little, to fly with me!" All her senses were quivering now, beyond the reach of terror, of risk, of her own will. She heard herself laugh. "It's okay, I've been sailing all my life... and we don't have to go far." Just far enough to give Brigit enough time.

Sanger was a land man, used to taking his stance, to running his patterns on terra firma, but now he kicked off his loafers, peeled off his socks, rolled up his pant legs. One last shove and they were both aboard. Vanessa uncleated the jib sail and bundled it into the storage hold in the bow. There was too much wind for it. Then, taking the tiller, she pulled up the mainsail.

"Sit up there." She pointed ahead of her on the other side of the cockpit. "It'll help keep us flat while we tack out."

He was out of his element but adapting does not take a winner long. He hung onto the jib stay, his feet braced against the top of the centreboard and leaned out, swaying into the swells, turning his face into the wind. The bow, sliding down one wave, into the side of the next, drenched him with spray, pasted his hair to his head. Sea water dripped off his chin.

What, she wondered, was she thinking of? The wind out here was too strong for a small boat. Oak Island was receding fast. Soon they would be out on the open bay.

"Prepare to come about!" She had to shout.

"What's that?"

"It means duck, watch that the boom doesn't hit you when it comes across." She changed their tack. Ten minutes, fifteen, that was all she could buy out here. "Coming about again. Once we get out a little way, we can run back in. It'll be a nice smooth ride."

When Oak Island was barely distinguishable from the mainland behind it, she set their course back towards where she thought the beach was, let the mainsail out all the way, cleated the line and lashed the tiller as both waves and wind pushed the boat. The cockpit floor was flat now. Sanger let go of the jib stay.

"You said there were cushions?"

"There, in the bow hold."

And now, watching Sanger reach for them, Vanessa understood that never before had she been truly alone, beyond the barriers of safety, the confines of choice, out past civility's border where the self counts for nothing, cares for nothing, is nothing.

He pulled her down onto the cushions, the wind ruffling his hair as he undid the brassiere's front clasp, took one of her nipples into his mouth.

"Here?"

"Come on girl, you keep telling me you want it."

And then she was lying beneath him as he unzipped his pants, yanked her silk panties down, breaking the elastic, so that his fingers could explore, while down at the far end of their bodies she glimpsed one of his feet braced against the centre board: white, stubby, more than forty years old, toes curled over the coping, tendons taut. And now, as his free hand moved up to her breasts, his grey hair flopping into her eyes, his face suspended between her and the full white sail and the sky, she watched his elegance slide away. He tipped her head back, plunged his tongue into her mouth again and she was no longer Athena, a goddess, graceful, ethereal, elusive. Now he was pushing her legs apart, shifting onto his knees between them and in his eyes nothing else existed. He nudged her thighs wider—

But there, suddenly, beyond his head was the Oak Island treeline. Too close!

She twisted under him.

"No doll—"

"Watch out, Ed!" She reached up behind her head, managed to work the tiller line free, pulled the tiller hard over. "Prepare to jibe!"

"What?" Sanger's head came up. He did not know about jibing.

Dancer's metal boom, swinging across, struck his left temple.

A sickening crack. Blue accusation sliding away as his body lifted, then dropped over the gunnel. Dragging, head down, the dead weight of him worked with the boat's momentum to bring them around, up into the wind. The boat stopped. His body slid into the water. Bobbed there, face down.

"Ed!" She reached for him, grabbed the back of his shirt, tried to pull him back into the boat but he was too heavy, limp as a sack of stones. She jumped into the water — they were only a few metres from the campsite by the shore — and turned him face up. "Ed!"

Seawater washed the nasty purple lump swelling above his left ear. His face was a bluish grey, dead colour, his eyes closed.

"Wake up, Ed!"

She towed him into the beach, then pulled him by the arms, stones slicing the bottoms of her feet, sticking to his wet shirt as she dragged him out of the water. He was so heavy, must be two hundred pounds. The tide lapped at his feet. She felt for a pulse. Found none. Opened his mouth, cleared the airway, breathed into him.

Nothing.

Pressed the heel of her hand into his chest, breathed again—

"Help!"

The wind tossed the sound.

"Brigit! Help!"

There was no reply.

She pressed and breathed, stones digging into her knees, the wind so cold against her wet nakedness, her thoughts swirling.

Please don't let him be dead—

Though why the hell not—

"Come on, you bastard!"

I haven't killed him? Dear God—

"Help!"

But there was no one, apparently, to hear.

Sanger blinked.

"Ed!" Thank God. But then the hairs on the back of Vanessa's neck stood up. There was no life in his eyes. His hand, clammy as a dead man's, came up, tightened around her wrist, pulled her closer. She leaned towards him, thought he wanted to speak. His free hand fastened onto one of her breasts, twisted it. The pain made her cry out. She tried to pull away, but—

"No one," the voice was a whisper, colourless, rattling, the rest of the words unintelligible. Sanger twisted his hand again.

Pain shut out vision thought breath. Then suddenly his grip loosened. Confusion seeped into his eyes. Fear peeked out. Vanessa used the instant to pry herself free, started to back away up the beach towards the road while out on the water her skipperless boat drifted.

Sanger struggled to his feet, staggered towards her.

She saw his axe leaning against the stump beside the tent, picked it up.

Sanger took another step, his head thrust forward, bull-like, bellowing.

She raised the axe. And knew without a shadow of a doubt that she was capable of killing, that should he lunge toward her, she would not hesitate to bring the axe down, split open the top of his head.

He stopped, his head swaying from side to side as if he did not know where he was. Vanessa dropped the axe and ran. Up the beach into the underbrush, branches scratching her arms, chest, back, stomach, tugging at her hair, slowing her. Her legs were stiff with cold, her skin covered with goosebumps. Some inner sense of direction took her to the road that ran down the centre of the island. She could turn right, running towards the treasure hunters and help. But she did not hesitate, went straight ahead, across the road and into the undergrowth to the lowland place where the headstone was. She could hear Sanger stumbling along behind her, crashing against trees, snapping branches, cursing.

Think, Vanessa. She found her direction, then counted paces from the headstone, dodging bushes, keeping as straight as she could, towards what should be the large cone-shaped granite boulder partway down the stem of the cross. Found it. Came back half the number of paces to a place where a little patch of grass was long and soft, shiny in the sun.

"Brigit?" She whispered.

Nothing. Beyond the trees she could see Sanger, turning his head this way, then that, a grizzly bear picking up the scent.

Beside the grass, flowers — a couple of lady's slippers, the long stem and arching green leaves of the Solomon's seal — grew around a jumble of small orange and black lichen-covered rocks.

And look, here was a hole, just large enough for a body to slide through, where two stones had been moved out of the way! The edges had been hacked out to make it larger. An axe that must be Mlle. Durocher's lay in the grass.

Sanger had spotted her, was lumbering this way. Only one choice presented itself.

## XVIII

THE HOLE DESCENDED ON AN ANGLE. Stone scraped Vanessa's skin, cold earth stuck to her bottom as she slid down it into a horizontal tunnel large enough to stand in. The floor was gravel, man-made.

"Brigit?" The tunnel walls bounced the name back to her. "Brigit!"

No answer. The only sound came from Vanessa's own breathing.

This must be the Chamber of Reflection. Brigit must have come down here. So where was she? Where was the treasure?

Further down the tunnel there was a glow, flickering light from a side room. Vanessa moved toward it, felt the warmth of fire.

Silhouetted against the light stood a presence clothed in a floor-length hooded black cloak.

Not *La Vieja*, the Old Woman? This person was tall, erect, yet familiar somehow, the way a dream can be, though Vanessa could not see her face. There was no goat carcass, no sweet cloying smell of blood and decay.

"Who are you?" She took a step towards the figure. There was no time for fear. "And why are you hiding inside that hideous hood?"

A gnarled hand reached up, pushed back the black wool. "It can get cold down here."

*La Vieja* in Altamira had been terrifying, a figure of death. This creature's face was a sallow map of wrinkles. The dark eyes were of no specific colour, older than time, remorseless and luminous, containing a world beyond the reach of human compassion anger greed, where a person was as likely to be ripped limb from limb as she was to be cared for. A concrete material person, or a nonsense, a figment of Vanessa's fear? She came closer to the fire. The Old Woman picked up a log, fed it to the flames.

"Go back."

"Where's Brigit?"

"She was not ready." The voice was emotionless. "Neither are you."

Do not think. Do not speak or wonder what has happened, what it means. Vanessa knelt, holding her hands out to the heat. Stay still, balanced, focused.

There was, in this underground room, a sense of sitting in the lap of eternity, a place with no past, no future, just this fire and the Old Woman and Vanessa's certainty that to keep the vision she must not question or doubt—

The Old Woman stared at her, unblinking.

Vanessa forced herself to meet the gaze, to look directly into centuries of birth beauty blood destruction distilled into the dark pools of the eyes until finally the ancient shoulders arched into a shrug.

"Go on then, if you will. But if you do, remember three things." She ticked them off on her bony fingers: "One, the rules that run the surface world do not apply down here. Two, from here there is no turning back. And three, what's down here must stay down here." She turned back to the fire.

Far away and above, Vanessa heard a thud: axe against earth.

"Excuse me—?"

But the Old Woman was no longer listening.

Vanessa stood to let the fire heat her nakedness. When she was warmed through she returned to the tunnel, felt her way along its wall into total darkness. Brigit must have come this way.

Except, "She was not ready."

Behind Vanessa, at the end of the tunnel, pebbles trickled down through the hole, and now there was a body sliding.

"Brigit?"

Someone landed, grunted.

Sanger! The firelight in the side room went out.

Vanessa took a step away into the darkness. Another step.

Into thin air.

She dropped straight as a stone, air whistling past her eyes, her stomach lifting. Down and down, breath gone, until the bottoms of her feet smacked against water that swallowed her, cold as death. She kicked against it, beat her arms, broke the surface.

The tunnel must be at least ten feet above her.

"Hey!"

Oh dear Mother of God.

"Help!" The water's cold fingered her bare stomach, her breasts, the small of her back: "Ed, help me!" Her cry echoed off stone walls.

*"Vieja!"* The word rang up, out, around the world. But—

'Brigit was not ready,' the Old Woman had said, and 'Neither are you.'

Vanessa was breathing hard, precious life energy leaking out. She lay back in the water. Her skull ached in the caress of its cold.

"Ed? Help!" Her stomach, legs, feet were nearly numb already, her eyelids wooden. She would close them just for a moment.

"No, Vanessa."

A female voice. Whose?

Not Mademoiselle's, she's dead. But this is the place of the dead—

"Are you ever going to learn, Vanessa?" The voice was exasperated, the way Mlle. Durocher became whenever Vanessa allowed herself to become mired in confusion, failed to see the point. "Remember what the Old Woman said."

"What?" she cried. "What did she say?"

"There is no going back."

No way back. Think it through, Vanessa. No way back: did that mean there was a way forward? Vanessa felt the sides of the sinkhole: rock polished smooth by the swirling grind of glacial stone and water, no foot purchases, no handholds. No sign of Sanger above. Had he passed out, or was he watching her? The only way to go anywhere was to dive down into the blackness.

To dive or to die here, within the next few moments. The air smelled of minerals. To dive was to die, surely? But where was the choice?

Don't think about it. Vanessa looked up one last time, filled her lungs, once, twice, then ducked down under the water, kicking down, down, legs stiff with cold, keeping one hand on the wall of the sinkhole, deeper, her body cutting through water colder surely than any human could stand, down, down into a complete absence of light, every kick such labour now—

Don't stop. Kick. Keep going—

The water above her suddenly became turbulent. Something fell past her, large, heavy, clothed. A body. It bumped against her thigh. Bubbles from it broke against her cheeks as she swam down through the water. Her hand, sweeping blindly ahead of her, brushed against flesh — fingers reaching for her? — but then the body sank away into the blackness. Too heavy to be Brigit.

She kept on kicking, feeling her way down the sinkhole wall, muscles so stiff now, lungs crying for oxygen.

Found a break in the wall: another tunnel. She swam into it, no longer thinking or knowing that in doing so she was giving up any possibility of retracing her path, of replenishing her air supply.

But now here was another opening, in the roof of the side tunnel, a widening. She kicked upwards, lungs bursting, into black, rank, mineral laden air. Took great gulps of it.

She was too cold, the feeling gone in her hands, her feet, her thinking fuzzy but full of thanks that she was breathing again.

The darkness was absolute, a total absence of light, the perfect place in which to rest, to give in finally, to close her eyes, unless—

"Brigit?"

The sound ricocheted, became metallic. There was no response.

Was there at least was a place to sit? So as not to die in the water, not to sink down to where the sunken corpse that must be Sanger would have come to rest, not to have to be with him forever in death. She dogpaddled, looking for the wall of the cavern, then felt her way along it, found a ledge just above the water level. But now her hands, as she pulled herself up, kept knocking against objects. Not rocks. Crouched against the wall, she picked one up. It was long and smooth, the sound light as, falling out of her hand, it plopped into the water.

This one was rounder, with holes in it. And now here were more long thin ones with bumps at the ends—

Bones! Vanessa recoiled, hugged her knees. Were they human? Had other people huddled right here on this ledge, waiting, rocking, struggling not to vomit, not to lose the precious warmth, teeth beating a ghostly tattoo into a blackness unknown to life?

She was sitting in the doorway to death. Because where else was she going? 'What's down here must stay down here,' *La Vieja* had said.

How much oxygen could there be in here? Soon she would be just like these others. She reached out, felt along the ledge, found a medium sized bone, an arm maybe? She held it in front of her face, but where there is no light there is no sight. Still, with her other hand she shook the end of it—

"How do you do? My name is Vanessa. What's yours?" Her voice was a friend. "Are you a man or a woman?" Man probably, according to Oak Island's history. What woman in her right mind would come down here? A high keening sound started, hitched with sobs—

Stop it. Save your energy, Vanessa. She looked at the place where her hand holding the bone must be.

"Okay," she told the bone, "Never mind history, I'll call you Eleanor." Eleanor: her mother's middle name after Eleanor of Aquitaine, heroine of the middle ages, Christian Crusader, lover, mother of England's King Richard I, the Lion Heart. And, "There may not be anything in the books about female treasure hunters, Eleanor, but history is written by the conquerors. Only God knows what really happened." She turned the bone over in her hand.

"So, pleased to meet you, Eleanor. Just think, once you were a living breathing person like me, sitting here having thoughts. When was that, I wonder...? Well, one thing's for sure, conquerors we ain't!" Vanessa giggled and now she could see Eleanor, so thin, naked, sitting knees drawn up to her chest, skin so cold it hurt. Then went numb. Then died, energy extinguished. "Where did you come from, Eleanor? What did you think about, sitting here—?"

Thoughts, feelings, memories: her own came to her now fully coloured, textured, complete with smells, one after the other, faster, then faster still, colliding one into the next—

Stop it.

"Is that you, Eleanor?"

Breathe. As long as you breathe you are alive.

Oh, okay. Breathing: in....

Out: The treasure was probably down under the water at the bottom of this cavern with Sanger, his body draped over the lost chests: the first man to find the treasure, the winner! She shouldn't laugh but the sound was a mountain brook bubbling over sun-splashed stones, a few silver-backed fish hiding among the pink granite, white quartz... In...

Out: She could make anything real in this blackness. Think it and there it was in living colour:

Henry Sinclair. Brigit was right, he was small, barely five feet with his armour on, but so were the men in his retinue. Look at the fervour in his eyes.

Captain St. Clere was slim, stronger looking, also cultured, his eyes piercing, as ruthless as Sanger's. Hawk's eyes, Mlle. Durocher had called them. Vanessa shuddered.

Brother Bart in his brown monk's robe, tall, gangly, his middle-aged face open in wonder at the honey-coloured girl holding his hand, smiling her invitation, helping him now to lift the rough robe... And now, just a few months later his body bent, staggering across the Altamira beach, kneeling to kiss the sand. Vanessa could feel the hot summer air, hear the sea breaking behind him in the moonlight—

Altamira. The smells of the sun and sea and sand, of fish up on the dock where venders were shouting out the day's catch; *el mercado*, where everyone congregated to gossip and laugh and haggle on a Saturday morning; the dust caught in the convent chapel's coloured sunbeams as Mother Superior rasped her way through the morning prayer, the feel of Vanessa's navy wool tunic against bare legs on a chilly winter afternoon; the sweet greasiness of *churros;* all the colours and smells of Altamira life calling to her in a language that sang as she, Carlita, Paco and Adrian roamed the beaches and hillsides of the Spain she had loved. And then lost.

But look, here came her parents, walking toward her across the beach.

"Dad?"

He seemed to glance her way, the sun reflecting off the lenses of his glasses.

"Dad listen, there doesn't seem to be any Right Choice, any one right way—"

He just kept walking, continuing his conversation with her mother.

But now here was Brigit. Thank God. Except that she was pushing her way through the Canary Island tomato plants, standing speechless for a moment at the edge of the deserted beach before running down through the hot sand, shedding her clothes and sandals and pack to splash through the waves—

"Hello Van." Charlie. Smiling, and now here were scents: of the sun on the Canary Island sea, of the roses he had given her on the first anniversary of their meeting, of his favourite aftershave. She breathed in his every detail — the line of his whiskery jaw as he lay asleep in the early morning, the way his eyelashes curled, the curve of his earlobe, the brush of his lips on her breasts in the surf — until these pictures too faded. Disappeared.

∆ ∆ ∆

True silence is devoid of feeling thought instinct. Need and fear find no holds here.

∆ ∆ ∆

This light — golden, glorious — must be coming from inside her because her eyes were closed.

To have the thought was to lose the light. The sound of her breathing returned, and with it, through the numbness of this cold, a feeling:

Love, for her fingers, her toes, for life even here in the darkness.

Soon the tide would rise.

"Right, Eleanor?"

She would turn into Eleanor because there was no turning back, and maybe that would be all right...

There was, however, oxygen in here. From where? Vanessa looked up. The Templar, Henry Sinclair, would have dug upward once he was inside the tunnels, right Brigit? Upward to reach above the water line at high tide.

Vanessa forced her muscles into movement, stood up, face against the cold cavern wall, and ran one hand up the rock, using the other to steady herself as she inched along the ledge, trying to avoid Eleanor and the others.

Found a horizontal iron bar, each of its ends sunk into the rock, a rung. There was a second one above it: a ladder! Vanessa tugged. The ancient iron held.

The cold had turned her body to wood but somehow she pulled herself up the rungs into the ceiling, into a tunnel up, or a sinkhole like the one she had fallen into. She began to climb.

Test each step. God only knew how old the rungs were. Rust crumbled under her fingers. Her hands and feet, gripping, were clumsy, barely able to feel as she climbed higher into the shaft in the cavern ceiling, but the cold and the blackness held no fear even as she wondered how high she was, how far it was to the bottom now, whether Eleanor had fallen.

A trickle of new air cooled her face. Vanessa reached out, felt the walls. If whoever had buried the treasure had tunneled upwards, were there also side tunnels? She climbed higher, tried again. Found the opening. Digging her fingers into the earth, she wiggled into it, flat on her stomach, until she could inch ahead, beetle-like. The tunnel, no more than three feet high, went on and on. She was crawling through the inside of the earth and it did occur to her that no one in the world had any idea where she was, that if the earth in this ancient digging collapsed and she died, no one would ever find her. But the thought was inconsequential, disconnected from feeling or other thoughts, and now the tunnel was widening. The roof became higher, and now here was a thin, diffuse, bluish reflection of light. Vanessa got up onto her hands and knees, scurrying forward until she could come to her feet.

A ray of daylight came in through a hole high in the ceiling. Around it hair-like roots dangled. Vanessa stared. Directly ahead of her, on the other side of the cavern, the sunlight was illuminating three panels of worked gold.

A vision.

A dream.

A chamber in Heaven. In front of the lit panels six metal chests had been stored side by side.

Vanessa closed her eyes, opened them again. Dared finally to cross the room, to run her hands over the golden panels.

She was not dreaming. See the sun, and the people, and the animals? This was Brother Bart's temple gold! She moved closer, Brother Bart's wonder flooding into her now at the perfection of the figures, each one rendered in detail, right down to the bird's feathers, the salamander's toes, the kindness in the faces of people no bigger than any of the other animals.

The images — animals, insects, birds, people — were a chronicle of the universe unfolding, of a people's history. Any people's history because wasn't it true that in the end, whatever the race, century, geography, all humans have grown from the same source, love. The beauty of this golden monument to every living being brought tears. Vanessa wiped them away with hands covered in mud.

There had been no need to lock the treasure chests. Their lids creaked as she heaved them open. One held ingots, another plates, goblets, jugs made of gold and silver inlaid with jewels that winked red, green, blue, amber in the first light they had seen in centuries. She lifted out a silver chalice. Was this the one Brother Bart and Mia had drunk from?

Inside a third chest were necklaces, bracelets, rings, headpieces. Vanessa let them dribble through her fingers, felt their heaviness: a fortune in four hundred-year-old gold. Here was the gold chest plate the chief must have worn. Vanessa picked up a bracelet inlaid with rubies and through the intricacy of the designs worked into the gold felt the love, palpable as her own heartbeat, with which it had been wrought.

Oh Brigit, if you could see this—

And look, here was a gold ring molded into the shape of a butterfly, its wings a mosaic of red amber green blue! Had the cook who had pocketed it been one of those hanged? Vanessa laid the ring in the palm of her hand, felt Mia and Brother Bart and, smiling, sat down in the puddle of sunshine. Its warmth came into her feet, legs, arms as she slid the ring onto her wedding finger, turned it this way and that. Cried.

The face of the sun at the top of one of the gold sheets looked down at her through the ray of light, immutable. Across from it the moon also watched. She would lie down just for a moment to rest...

"Vanessa?" Charlie's voice was a whisper, a movement of air, a wish. And look, he was kneeling over her, so wet and filthy. She dared to reach out—

Were they both dead? Was that why he was here?

He felt real. She pulled him down into the sunlight.

"I couldn't find you and I was so scared," His face was smeared with tears too.

"Ssshhh." There was no need to cry when you were dead. And his arms around her felt so right. She could feel his breath on her hair and reaching up, she felt his face, his muddy whiskers, his silly grin. She kissed him. Kissed him again because in this death place he felt very much alive. Taking off the butterfly ring, she put it into Charlie's hand. He slipped it back onto her ring finger just as Brother Bart had done for Mia and together they watched it pick up the sunlight. Then, in the sacredness of this temple, naked and muddy, Vanessa and Charlie left the world of cold and death and secret codes. Came without thinking trying wanting into the place where love lives, where there was no 'he should' and 'she didn't,' no 'if only,' where there was only the miracle of touching feeling being, of wanting to open body heart and soul, where riding the waves that dissolve time space separateness, and receiving the joy of his thrust into the centre of herself, Vanessa touched with Charlie the golden energy that powers the universe.

The Old Woman was right. The rules of the outside world did not apply down here.

# XIX

Edward 'Teach' Sanger is dead. The police know I had something to do with it. Because I am Vanessa. The story you have been reading is mine.

I don't know how long I spent in the Oak Island treasure room before the shaft of sunlight shifted away from the hole in the cavern roof, returning the room to shadow, bringing me the realization that I was alone. A puddle of sea water started to seep in through the tunnel, spreading across the floor as the water came up from below, the way it always does on Oak Island: silent, cold, terrifying.

By the time I had taken all the ingots out of one of the treasure chests and then heaved the empty chest up onto the top of one of the other ones, the water was knee high. Then all I could do was wait, teetering on the top chest, while the tide sweeping in through the tunnel now, so cold, roiled higher and higher until I could float up to grasp the roots dangling out of the ceiling, hang from them to pull the dirt and stones above out of the way.

I won't say anything about the hole I finally pulled myself out of, except that it was hidden completely by the underbrush. I tamped down the earth, pushed the stones and brush back into place and was moving away through the bushes when three police officers, accompanied by Brigit and Sanger's driver, found me. I noticed the butterfly ring still on my finger.

"What's down here stays down here," *La Vieja* had said.

But how could I go back, and wouldn't it be all right, I asked her silently, to keep this one connection to Brother Bart and Mia? The butterfly, symbol of wisdom, token of love?

There was no reply and now one of the officers was covering me with blankets, listening to my story about Sanger's and my boat ride, Sanger's injury and his pursuit of me into the tunnel on the stem of the cross.

I showed them where it was and the police went down, shone flashlights into the sinkhole:

"You say you and Edward Sanger both fell in?"

"Yes, but he was already badly injured by the boat boom."

"How did you get out?"

"Um," I grinned a little stupidly, knowing only that this was a truth I would not tell. The rules of the outside world did not apply. "I'm sorry, I can't say. I think I kind of went out of my mind after Edward sank."

The detective in charge did not believe me, kept harping about the time lag, where I was found. He took in my nakedness, my hair matted with mud, the look in my eye probably. He would send a diver down the sinkhole, he said. Only Brigit noticed my ring.

A police psychologist came from Halifax. She said our brains are closets full of jumbled ideas. Writing out the whole story might help me to sort them. So that's what I've been doing, sorting the bones of fact, clothing the skeleton of a truth that may be too big, too complex for my little closet to contain.

One thing I find difficult is what happened to Brigit. Venturing down the hole, she had encountered only darkness, had recognized how foolhardy it would have been to proceed alone without a light:

"I was so excited though because now we had the spot. It was just a matter of waiting for you. But by the time I got down to the shore you and Sanger were way out in the bay, so I thought: okay, I'll use the time to go get a light—I'll string Gorpo some line—but before I got to the causeway you were running back in so I doubled back. And then I couldn't find either of you. It was clear you had gone down the hole though. I called and called and I was so scared! That's why I finally went for help."

Why, I wonder, did *La Vieja* decide that Brigit was not ready? She is so beautiful, so free of inhibition, so quick to love, to laugh. She's the one who taught me to see. I look out at the clouds sailing across a blue summer sky. Brigit is right, this universe is a great mix of energies in which the perfect white light that is the core of life guarantees no more than each instant's creation. Passion lives outside happy/sad, good/bad. A geyser of energy, passion happens to us. And when the passion is love our choices make our fortunes. The people both Brigit and Brother Bart loved lost their lives. Brigit is still hurting, hiding in her woods, 'not ready.' We have begun to talk a little about this, about my father's belief that whether we know it or not we are making a choice, to grow or to die a little, in every moment.

∆ ∆ ∆

I was lying in the hot tub under the full moon, thinking of Charlie and me making love in the treasure room, and wishing... How real that had been to me, as achingly real as any moment I can recollect in my life, a golden moment as powerful as Mia's people's treasure panels. Brigit was inside booking her flight home. And watching the moon rise cold as a coin in a cloudless sky, I was trying to distract myself, contemplating the relationship between the words *'luna'* and 'lunatic', when footsteps sounded on the deck stairs.

Seeing me in the tub, Charlie stopped. I could find no words. His hair lifting in the breeze, he looked indescribably beautiful.

If all life is energy, then the tsunami wave of my grief on Mlle. Durocher's death must have reached him in Toronto, fracturing his concentration, demolishing his equilibrium. He had bought a case of twenty-four beers, had snapped open one after another as he and Pete put the finishing touches on 'Tunnel Warrior' until:

"You wanna get a bite to eat?" Pete had asked. It was late. Outside their studio Queen Street bar signs were flashing yellow, green, red. Reggae music was pumping out of a loudspeaker down the block.

Charlie had shaken his head.

"Thanks man. I think I'll take a walk."

Kids were bunched on street corners, a few cars still cruising, stopping to let leather jacketed men and their high heeled companions scurry across the street as Charlie raised his jacket collar and, hands in his pockets, turned south into the teeth of the night chill. Light from the street lamps pooled yellow on the pavements of side alleys where cars were parked nose to rear below darkened curtains, where a couple sat kissing on the stoop while a group of skaters jeered:

"Hey mister, got a dime?" Eyes appraising his clothing: "Or a C note?"

Heel toe, heel toe: after a while all he heard was the rhythm of his loafers on the pavement, their echo off the concrete walls of the darkened buildings. He should have been afraid. Dark concrete under a sky that is never really black, city life is an endless game of choices: Left? Right? Straight ahead? Muggers, gangs, accidents, fires, there were no caches of gold, no power packs to give him an extra life.

Heel toe, heel toe: his mind showing a series of snapshots now, of dancing at the Bamboo Club, me flopping into his lap at the end of the song, laughing; of my arm cranking back, releasing Flamenco Dancer.

Heel toe, heel toe: how, he wondered, had he landed in this grey lightless maze? How to reach me from there? How to get up tomorrow? Ethiopian grocery stores, storefront dentist, lawyer, African aromatherapy centre, palm reader. The upstairs apartments were dark, pastel curtains open to take in the night cool, a radio playing a single mournful horn.

Heel toe, heel toe: farther and farther from our high rise condo, and now there was no one, not even a car, just Charlie and the concrete and the lights at the crosswalk — yellow, red, green, little man walking: GO.

Where? He stopped. Why go anywhere? He would sit down, here against the wall. He was too tired to try any more paths, to reach the next level, then the next, and the next. Better maybe to stop, to rest.

"Hey bud." A prod in the side. Shiny black boots, blue pant legs, a cop car at the curb. Another prod, painful—

"Okay, okay." Charlie struggled to his feet.

"You want to spend the night downtown?"

"No officer." Charlie pushed away from the wall. "Sorry I... guess I fell asleep."

The policeman must have seen that this was not a junkie or a drunk.

"You want a ride? I can take you as far as the subway."

"Ah..." A taxi turned into the empty street, its overhead light on. Charlie watched it approach, then suddenly it was as if he was above the empty street, looking down on the traffic light painting the tarmac yellow red green, on the parked police car, the baffled cop and the crazy man huddled on the pavement one minute, then leaping up to flag down the taxi, to fly away, straight as an arrow, out of the twisted canyons of his mind.

"Where to?" The driver's accent was African.

"The airport."

Δ Δ Δ

Most of Chester came to Mlle. Durocher's funeral. Then Brigit, Charlie and I took her ashes to Oak Island. The old librarian had no family so the will named me her beneficiary.

I found the hole above the treasure room, behind the underbrush, where I had climbed out. Brigit knelt, closed her eyes, but nothing came.

"Never mind," I told her, "next time we'll bring a rope. Wait'll you see those awesome gold panels and all that jewelry! Maybe *La Vieja* won't mind if we keep just a little—"

"And who knows what else is down there? How many other tunnels there might there be? If the Templar Henry Sinclair used Oak Island and the pirate St. Clere knew about him, who else did?"

"Francis Bacon?"

There might be a next time because the Oak Island lot, along with everything else Mlle. Durocher owned, belongs to me now.

But no. How easy it is to be carried away. Treasure, even the word births greed. I looked down at Mia's ring and knew that what's down there must stay down there, for now.

We poured some of Mlle. Durocher's ashes into the hole. The rest we scattered on the beach beside the new lot she had bought and as the tiny grey particles whirled up into the wind, I swear I heard her laugh.

Back home in the evening, Charlie poured scotches out on the deck. I lit the candles. He raised his glass:

"To Mlle. Durocher, a little old lady who was a Colossus among humans."

At night I still dream of her, hold her soft bird-boned hand and wake up weeping, thinking that ideas about choices and fortunes and growing and dying are nothing more than the mind's way of trying to tidy away the fact that Mlle. Durocher died because Sanger wanted the lot she owned. He did not kill her outright, but isn't that always the way with ambition, with evil? She had sensed danger in the man, had known that Sanger was Seth, the force of wild, destructive ambition, ungovernable. And still she had challenged him, had stood up for love.

A new thought arrives: the detective is right, I am the reason Edward Sanger is dead. I took him out into the wind. But maybe it was the same energy that has rained on Oak Island treasure hunters again and again, flooding their digs, sending giant waves to smash their dams, that gusted behind Dancer's boom that afternoon.

Δ Δ Δ

The evening air on the deck grows chillier. A few wisps of cloud move lazily across the sky. Brigit, Mlle. Durocher and Edward 'Teach' Sanger are gone. Brother Bart's testament has been housed finally under glass in the Halifax museum. But now here is Charlie, sitting beside me in the candlelight on Gran's deck. The new moon is a sliver above the horizon.

"Don't you have to get back?"

Charlie shrugs.

Pete can launch 'Tunnel Warrior,' eat and drink at the galas, do the interviews, take the orders. Charlie will not leave until I am ready.

The police say I am free to go. The diver found that the silt at the bottom of the sinkhole, once disturbed, was too thick to see much, but they did find Edward Sanger's body. After my testimony at the inquest the police pathologist said that blood vessels behind the shattered bone in Edward Sanger's temple would have been leaking since the moment he was hit. And murder is not usually committed with the boom of a sixteen-foot sailboat.

Yesterday morning a publisher called: he had read both my magazine article "Treasure Island North" and the newspaper stories about Edward Sanger's death. Would I write a book about what had happened to me on Oak Island? It could establish me both as an expert in Spanish treasure history and as a writer.

Last night we stayed up late talking, planning. Charlie will go on designing computer games. It is what he loves. I will turn my story and the translation of Brother Bart's diary into a book. We will sell the condominium overlooking Lake Ontario. Ours must be a wilder, freer landscape, closer to the ground, where the sun shines and the moon comes and goes, and that which dances in their lights has been born out of the silent centre where time is the servant, not the master.

Still I can not help wondering how, in the concrete maze of city life where sun and moon shine mostly through windows, Charlie and I will manage not to lose our gold again. But then my robe falls open and Charlie's hand on my stomach feels so gentle. I reach for him, crying a little, not only out of sadness, but because with his touch I know that there never was anything wrong with who we are together. In Brother Bart's and Mia's era the taking and killing were visible, gruesome and gory. Charlie and I had allowed these same energies to thrive unseen, to take over and make barren our little world. But now:

"I'm thinking, with your publishing contract and my 'Tunnel Warrior' prospectus, we could buy your uncle's share of this house." Charlie's hair sticks up in spikes as he runs his hand through it, thinking, creating. "And if there's anything left over we could travel." His eyebrows arch. "Maybe find ourselves an abandoned Spanish beach?"

I bury myself in his kiss.

Beyond the deck summer is ripening into autumn. The Solomon's seals in Gran's garden are puckering, withering, dying. Clouds race on a cold wind that, over on Oak Island, will be sending great grey waves up to pound the shoreline, laughing through the trees in the brutal way it always does in the fall.

## XX

**M**y book and Brother Bart's will end on the same page:

*You know the rest, Father. The last thing we did on that little island was remove every sign that we had been there. My stove was taken apart. Captain St. Clere had us pry up an enormous boulder. We deepened the hole and buried the stove, then pushed the rock back before sailing for France.*

*A Spanish flota in the Azores, the galleons sitting like mother ducks surrounded by a flock of smaller faster chicks, was irresistible as we were no longer fully loaded. Captain St. Clere gave the order to attack but I saw nothing. Once we had left the calmness of our bay in the New World, the fever had struck me a third time. All I could do was lie in my hammock mumbling to You as our ship rocked and shook and crashed under the fire of the cannons. The reek of cordite and gunpowder and human sweat set me to retching until finally, in the midst of all that chaos, I lost consciousness. When I awoke the world had returned to calm. We had captured one of the Spanish ships. The rest had taken flight.*

*Once the treasure had been transferred to the holds of our two ships, Captain DuMoulin summoned me to his cabin.*

*"Here," he handed me three bags of gold, "your share." The captured galleon, a termite palace, was of no use to the pirates. They were releasing it. I was to go with it back to Spain.*

*But what use was money to me now? I was little more than a useless bag of bones.*

*"Take it, brother," DuMoulin pressed the bags into my hands. "And know also that where it lies, your treasure is safe."*

*As You know, Father, just before they reached Saint-Malo, St. Clere and DuMoulin were set upon by British frigates and killed in a battle that sank both L'Amitié and L'Espérance. The news was all over the Spanish coast by the time we arrived.*

*We had to wait off Altamira while the rest of the flota was unloaded. Our ship's crew would likely be hanged for the loss of our cargo but, if the comandante believed I was a passenger monk he might spare me, unless he found my three bags of gold.*

*I was on deck in the wee hours, trying to cool my fever in the night air, when some men rowed out from the shore in a dinghy. I could see ripples of the phosphorescence left by their oars. These men were my Altamira brothers, with whom I had kicked the football, wrestled in the dust. They were heading for this ship because we were anchored farthest from shore. Silly fools, couldn't they see how high we were riding?*

*What is it, I wonder, that makes a loveless, hopeless old man refuse to die? I tied the bags of gold and this diary wrapped in its oilskin around my waist inside my breeches and slid down a rope into the water. Then, mustering the remains of my strength, I swam toward the dinghy.*

*They hauled me aboard. I warned them to turn back, and when at last I fell to my knees in the Altamira sand, up where the beach meets the cliff wall, I prayed, thanking You and, while no one was looking, burying my three bags. Then, as I stumbled after the men into the cavern that opens onto that beach, an arm closed around my neck. A knife point pricked my chin.*

*"No, no," I cried, "there is no need to kill me, I will be dead soon enough, but listen!" I drew them a map of the little island in the New World. Why not? Everyone needs hope.*

*There was a certain sad pleasure in giving one of the bags of gold to Jose's Maria with his love. The other two will look after my sister in whose bedroom I now lie, a jug of wine by my side as I write.*

*I know this is the end, Father. All I ask, as I lie here, is that Mia's people's gold, my beautiful sun ring and Mia's jeweled butterfly, symbols of the only love beyond understanding I have ever known, if these treasures ever leave their hiding place, please may they stay out of the clutches of pirates and kings. For I have to tell You, Father, that as the fever steals what little energy I have left, so that even raising my arm to dip the quill is difficult, I would still give all that I am, no matter the damnation that awaits me, to have my Mia back for just one moment of the love we knew in that mountain glade.*

*And struggling now to form the words, as my eyelids begin to droop, I smile, for in the final moment there is no defense required. There is only the afternoon sunlight slanting in between the curtains, and these wings, light as a butterfly's, shining gold, hovering, waiting.*

*Satis verborum, Laus Deo*

## Acknowledgements

*Thanks to the many people whose information, memories, stories, books and internet articles helped me research this book; thanks also to Lea Harper, Julie Johnston, Betsy Struthers, Florence Treadwell, and to editors Catherine Marjoribanks and Janie Yoon; special thanks to Hilary Boyd, Sarah Collins, Patricia Stone, and Georgia Dent and Paul Cohen at Epigraph. Most of all, thanks to my family, especially to Grant without whom this book would not exist.*

*J.B.*